I0587056

DRIVEN BY PASSION

GAMBLE RACING
BOOK 2

RENÉE DAHLIA

DRIVEN BY PASSION

RENÉE DAHLIA

*Engine fires, sabotage, and two
friends falling in love....*

Engineer Victor Tsui needs to figure out why his race cars keep failing. Being Gamble Racing's Chief Engineer is his dream job and he's built a fast car. But there is something wrong with his design and he needs to understand how to fix it before next season.

Hot headed driver Lucien Grenville has nowhere to go over the winter break, so when his friend Victor expresses frustration at the recent run of engine failures, he decides to hang out and offer support.

Things get awkward when Lucien gets an intense urge to kiss Victor, and they need to decide if this is going to remain a friendship or become something more.

ABOUT THE AUTHOR

An avid reader, Renée Dahlia writes contemporary and historical queer romance. Renée is a bisexual cis woman who is fascinated by people and loves to explore human relationships, with a side of humour, through her writing. Renée has a degree in physics and mathematics, using this to write data-based magazine articles for the horse racing industry. Her love of horses often shines through in her fiction, and she loves a good intrigue and to escape the real world in the pages of a book. When she isn't reading or writing, Renée spends her time with her four children, usually watching them play cricket.

FOREWORD

Welcome to DRIVEN BY PASSION, the second book in the Gamble Racing series.

If you love gay sports romance with a friends to lovers theme, family, workplace tension, and a little mystery thrown in, Driven by Passion is the book for you. This series contains a few mystery plots that continue between each book; however, I have tried to make each book a stand-alone read.

Please note this book contains toxic parenting, suicide ideation, car crashes, and assault.

This book is written in Australian English and some spelling and phrases may be unfamiliar to American readers. If you are keen to keep up to date on new releases and, more importantly, sales, I recommend you sign up to my newsletter at reneedahlia.com or follow me on social media.

I hope you enjoy reading this book!

Renée

facebook.com/reneedahliawriter

twitter.com/dekabat

instagram.com/reneedahlia_author

bookbub.com/authors/renee-dahlia

patreon.com/reneedahlia

CHAPTER 1

Gamble Racing's Series E driver Lucien Grenville had never seen his friend so frustrated. For the past few hours, Victor Tsui had paced back and forth across the engineering workshop floor, muttering, and occasionally stopping to stare at the two deconstructed S1 cars carefully arranged on the floor. Lucien wasn't sure how their friendship worked, unless it was a case of opposites attract. Victor was a data focused mechanical engineer—diligent and careful—while Lucien was a risk taker, a hot-headed driver, or at least he had been back when they'd met. Now he drove with more control, thanks to the efforts of the Gamble Racing sports psychologist, and he was getting results, finishing third on the Series E driver's championship this season. Two seasons in Series One—the pinnacle of motorsport—at the back of the grid had almost killed his love of being a racing driver, and being sent to the electric cars had helped him find the thrill of competition again. His teammate, Lord Alexander Islington, had finished in fifth. It was always satisfying to beat his teammate.

"Maybe you should take a break?" Lucien had known Victor for several years. Back when he'd been a Series Three driver for a different team, Victor had been the assistant engineer there, and they'd become unlikely friends. When Lucien had gained a Series One drive with Gamble Racing, moving away from Victor's team, they'd stayed in touch, even though they'd been working for different teams. Now Victor has been promoted to Gamble Racing's Chief S1 Engineer—responsible for the design of the team's S1 cars —their friendship had grown in a comfortable place, as they spent time together in the workshop, or during the summer break. The Series E season was much shorter than the S1 season, so Lucien had been hanging around Victor since September because he'd been the third driver, the backup, for the second half of the S1 season. Being the backup driver meant all the work and none of the racing.

"It makes no sense. It's almost like the three engine fires all started near the exhaust systems." Victor tugged at his thick black hair and scowled at the engine pieces.

"Take a break. Come for a walk with me." Lucien knew better than to say anything about the engine problems. Victor was the expert.

"What good will that do?"

Lucien shrugged. "Sometimes it helps to get away from the puzzle for a while." He spent a lot of time walking and he found it helpful for sorting out his myriad of problems.

"Fuck. Okay. At this point, I'll take any suggestion. If you want me to hang upside and cluck like a chicken, I'd do it if it would get me a clue to solving this fucking mess."

"Come." Lucien had a couple of hours before his meeting with Socrates and the rest of the SE team to discuss the upcoming season. Series E was different to S1 in that the batteries were all the same between teams, although teams were able to design their own power train and other parts. A lot of the racing came down to driver skill and race strategy only, making it much better for him as a driver to prove his talent, than when he'd been in S1 in the world's slowest car designed by Victor's predecessor, Reginald Whitehall. Lucien grabbed two Gamble Racing branded jackets off the hook near the back of the engineering workshop and passed one to Victor. December in England was bloody freezing.

"Where are we going?"

"Let's walk the test track." Gamble Racing's headquarters were part of Socrates' large estate—Pewett Downs—once owned by a Duke who'd gone bankrupt. Socrates had built his own racing track that threaded through the woods behind the engineering workshop, and he gave all his team drivers the freedom to take any of his car collection for a spin whenever they wanted. Today, Lucien would walk the track beside Victor to see if walking helped shake out any new ideas. They walked through the practice pit garage and out onto the track.

"Bloody hell, it's cold today." Victor frowned. "This better work."

Lucien nodded. He didn't have any answers. "Walk, then talk me through the problem from the beginning."

"Are you sure?"

"I asked you."

"Okay." Victor strode down the track towards the

starting line and Lucien deliberately positioned himself on pole position. They walked in silence for a while.

"This is pointless." Victor stopped in the middle of the track just under the start/finish line and glared at Lucien. Between the way Victor's dark brown eyes crinkled at the edges and the way he stood with his hands on his hips, drawing Lucien's attention to the way his puffy jacket pulled tight across his shoulders, Lucien's chest filled with an odd flutter. He dismissed it. It must just be the cold air, messing with his mind a little.

"It's not. We've barely started." The test track was 3,802m long.

"I have too much to do. Why am I walking?"

Lucien winked. "Technically you aren't walking. Now start walking and tell me the whole problem."

Victor's glare deepened but he started walking again.

"I mean it. From the very beginning."

"From pre-season testing?" Victor's frown disappeared for a second.

"Yes." Lucien wasn't that keen to rehash the whole season, but if it might help Victor, he'd listen.

"Remember when we were in S3 together?"

Lucien nodded. "Must we go over this? When I said start at the beginning, I didn't mean when we met."

"People told me that drivers were intense." Victor chuckled, shaking his head. "Intense! They had no idea. You were the walking version of toxic masculinity. A twenty-year-old ball of rage."

"Yes." Lucien sighed; that's why he didn't want to talk about his time in S3. He'd been awful, just horrible. An abused, traumatised, angry man-child who couldn't cope with the pressure of the job.

"It's always puzzled me." Thankfully Victor stared ahead, not at Lucien, allowing him space to squeeze his eyes shut for a second to fight back the rush of heat behind them. "How could you be the life of the party away from the track, but put that helmet on, and you'd push that car so hard, it was like you didn't care if you died."

Lucien shrugged. "I'm a driver. I still don't care if I die. Winning matters more." He'd spent his life training to be first, training to be fast, and pushing to the absolute limit. Sometimes beyond. Back then, always beyond, because he was often so upset, so angry, that he did want to die. A bad crash could be the chance to take away all the pain from all the things his father said. His therapist had a term for it, suicide ideation, which made it sound super bad, and he'd fought against the idea for a while before learning to deal with it.

"Something happened. I've always wondered about it." Victor had a knack of getting right to the heart of things. Damned perspective of him.

"I thought we were going to chat about your puzzle, not mine." Lucien shoved Victor lightly on the shoulder. This was his friend, someone who'd stood by him when no one else had, who'd been there when Lucien hadn't known he'd needed a friend.

"You told me to start at the beginning. What happened?" Victor referred to the middle of Lucien's third S3 season when his focus had shifted. When he'd gotten his first real tattoo, the one he loved, not the silly one on his thigh that listed all his podiums since he'd won his first karting championship as a teenager. Lucien felt that rush of blood to his head and breathed out. He wasn't that guy anymore, so he grinned instead.

"Are you asking me why I stopped being a complete fuckwit?"

"Yes. It was so obvious. Suddenly, you stopped having a death wish and you started driving like a proper driver. You went from being reckless to being deliberate, strategic, and you started winning."

All those things were true. "My father died. I'm not sad and I don't want your pity." His father had crashed his car, driving far too fast on an ordinary road in the rain. Thankfully hadn't hit anyone else in his ridiculous quest to prove that he was a better driver than he really was. A cliched end for a mid-field IndyCar driver who history had forgotten years before he died.

"Pity?"

"Never mind." Lucien bent over and brushed his fingers across the tarmac as they walked into the second turn. "The team made me go to grief counselling." He held his breath. Victor was his friend, he wouldn't judge him, and besides this reluctance to mention it was part of his own issues around what being a tough guy was all about. He stood up. "I kept going to therapy even when I moved to Gamble Racing. Personal therapy, I mean, not just the team's sport psychologist. It's been helpful."

"Good for you. If more people went to therapy, the world would be a kinder place."

"Would it, though?"

"I'd like to think so." Victor sounded sincere. "But then, my mother is a therapist, so I'm probably biased." It made sense; Victor had the innate confidence and peace that belonged to someone who'd grown up in a loving home without any bullshit.

"Mostly likely." Lucien's head spun with a bunch of questions, none of which were relevant to helping Victor solve the engine failure puzzle. "Now you've solved the puzzle of me. I was an asshole, my father died, the team helped me become a better driver, and hopefully a better person. Let's return to your problem."

"Hold on a second. There's one thing I don't understand."

Lucien mock-glared at Victor. "I'm not a data point." They walked across the apex of turn two, past the tyre barrier that protected the track from the natural siltstone cliff that lined the edge of the track. Socrates' husband Mike had a collection of fossils he'd found in the cliff-face, but Lucien only thought of it as a place he needed to avoid while driving the track.

"Ha." Victor didn't smile at Lucien's poor attempt at a joke. The track followed alongside the cliff, curving into two high speed turns; three and four, before they would reach Socrates' indulgence. "If the toxic anger stopped when your father died, and therefore it came from him, there's one thing I don't get."

"Okay, fine. I'll ask. What?" Lucien knew what Victor was going to ask; it was the thing everyone was curious about.

"You were always out, and some might say you were aggressively gay."

Aggressive. Yes. Lucien laughed so hard that he couldn't

breathe. "I was ... am ... absolutely ... aggressively gay. Fuck. Only you could articulate it so well."

"How does that work?" Victor and his puzzles! It must be the influence of his mother, always wanting to know how things—and people—worked and understand why.

"This one bugged my therapist too. She couldn't understand how my father could instil so many toxic angry behaviours in me, often encouraging me to be an asshole in the goal of beating every other driver, yet accept my sexuality without issue." Lucien hadn't cared to think about it. It was a relief to be able to be himself—loud and free—and have all the sex with all the people in nightclubs around the world. The ideal rich fuckboy lifestyle. In reality, it was simply more toxic behaviour from him as he selfishly used people for pleasure. Oh, for sure, they got pleasure in return and the chance to say they'd been with someone famous. No one, not even him, got any emotional joy from the encounters. It was unlikely that he'd ever get that—love—given all his issues. He didn't know the first thing about love.

"It's more common to wrap all those angry man issues up with a good dose of homophobia."

"How did this walk become all about me?"

"Well. I'm curious."

Lucien shook his head. "Apparently so."

All of a sudden, Victor clapped him on the back. "Drivers! You can't help it. You just cut me off even when we are walking."

"I'm walking the racing line. You are meandering in my way. Five second penalty for you." Lucien glanced over his shoulder at Victor, who was frowning. He jogged to the apex of the fourth turn and turned around to face Victor.

"You want to know how I could be openly gay and also a toxic asshole?" As if those things could be unpacked so easily...

"Yes."

"Growing up it was just me and my father. Kurt Grenville. He'd been a mid-field Indycar driver, obsessed with winning and not quite managing it. My mother, Suzy Smith, was a champion badminton player, so yes, with the addition of her fast reflexes, I was purpose bred to be a race car driver." His mother had won a bronze at the Olympics for England; and his father had moved to England with the excuse to be closer to her family when he really only wanted Lucien to be closer to the S1 training programs. His mother had soon seen through Kurt's bullshit and had run off with another man, abandoning her toddler son to the whims of her shitty ex. Lucien had never seen her again, and when he heard she'd died, when he was just ten years old, he hadn't known what to feel. How dare she?

"That explains the aggression on the track, but not—"

"My father said he didn't care who I fucked as long it helped me win. It was always about winning. He pushed me to always go faster, drive the car beyond its limits, take the space, the racing line, get the win at any price."

Victor nodded with a solemn expression. "That explains a lot."

"He always said it was better to DNF trying to win than to lose."

"That literally makes no sense. It's always better to get points than to get none."

Lucien purposefully rolled his eyes. "I know that now. When he died, I didn't have his constant stream of pushy words anymore. I didn't have to balance what the team was telling me and wanted from me with the things he said. Suddenly all I had to do was listen to the team. They sent me to therapy, and they coached me. I stopped crashing and I became a better, more strategic driver."

"It worked. Your improvement in that second half of the S3 season was staggering. No driver had ever improved to that extent. It was no surprise to anyone that you got an offer from Gamble Racing and an S1 drive."

"The irony, right?" It'd taken Lucien a while to find this amusing, but now, looking back, Lucien would always find this hilarious.

"What?"

"The only thing my father ever wanted was for me to drive S1. For him, it was the ultimate proof that he had bred a competitive driver. He moved from America to England to pursue that for me. If I could make S1, then it meant his mediocre talent in an Indycar didn't matter, because he'd achieved his own dream through my success. The irony is that it took him dying and a lot of therapy for me to be capable of achieving S1. His training, his bullshit, held me back from his goal." And it had allowed Lucien to figure out his own goals, away from the need to be an S1 driver. It allowed him to walk away from S1 because it wasn't his dream and find success on the Series E circuit.

Victor walked past him, heading into the small tunnel, and Lucien jogged to catch up. "I think I'm looking at these engine failures the wrong way."

"Yeah?"

"I keep thinking it's something I did wrong, but how can it be?"

"If it's an engine issue, surely that's the manufacturer's problem." Like many teams, Gamble Racing bought their engine from one of the big manufacturers.

"Yes and no. Obviously I've run all the data with them."

"And?"

"They couldn't find anything either. That engine is in four of the ten teams and no one else had any issues." Victor's breath curled in the breeze, little trails of fog swirling around him. "I made some mods to the engine throughout the season."

"You think it's the mods you did?"

"What else could it be? No one else had any problems with the same engine."

Lucien agreed. They walked into the braking zone before turns five and six; part of the wildest part of this track. Apparently when Socrates had built the track, there was a soft patch of ground at the end of the cliff, presumably from where all the water ran off and collected. So Socrates, being who he was, had built a tight circular turn that led to a ramp that took the track over itself, then up onto the cliff. They'd put a gravel trap at the end of turn five for driver safety.

"The first half of the season was good. Our goal was to be a solid mid-field team and get points. The car had some drivability issues but—"

"It was quick." Lucien wished he'd been able to drive it. It wouldn't have suited his late-braking style because it was too twitchy, but just to be able to go that fast on the limit would be... well, like flying.

"Ondrej picked up points in the first race of the season. We met the goal almost immediately."

"I never doubted you. Back in the day, you were the brains of our S3 team."

Victor nodded once. "Thank you. I was surprised to get the call from Mike Patel though."

"Not from Socrates? I always assumed he head-hunted you." Gamble Racing's owner, Socrates Drayton had retired from S1 after his big crash in the 1990s, and together with his husband, Mike Patel, they'd built Gamble Racing. He'd built a diverse team and now with the lead S1 driver, Ondrej, coming out, Gamble Racing had both himself and Ondrej as the only two openly queer drivers in the Series leagues. There were others—statistically there had to be—and it was good to see the majority of fans accepting both himself and Ondrej. Most fans only cared about the racing; almost none of the driver's personal lives were ever discussed by fans. His fan boost stats certainly showed that fans thought he was worth voting for.

"No, his loyalty was to Reginald. They'd been an engineer/driver team for so many decades, and Socrates is an incredibly loyal person."

"Are you saying that the team went around Socrates to get rid of Reginald and his slow cars to get you?" Lucien had always assumed it'd been above board, because Socrates had been the one to suggest he move from S1 to SE. When his S1 contract ended, he'd leaped at the chance to get away from his father's dream and build something for himself, so taking on Socrates' offer had been perfect for him.

"No. Socrates made the final decision. I was his choice, eventually."

"What does that mean?" Lucien pulled his jacket tighter around his chest as they rounded turn six and started the rise, up the ramp bridge to the top of the cliff. At this point, the cliff was only three metres high although the ramp had a sharp elevation that went over the lower part of the track. This whole section of the test track was so perfectly Socrates; outrageous and clever and unique. It also helped test cars for tracks like Spa, COTA, and Monaco that had sharp elevations changes.

"Paulo Sanchez came with a huge sponsorship deal, and those types of deals always come with conditions. One condition was that Socrates sack Reginald and get new chief engineer. I'm not sure how my name ended up on that list; the rumour is that I was the fifth choice."

"Fifth is ten points."

Victor snorted a laugh. "Midfield engineer for a midfield team."

"Stop that. You are going to win a constructor's championship one day."

"I hope so."

Lucien nudged his friend with his elbow. "Think about it. You had virtually no time to design a car for the new season, and you produced one that was fast enough to take the team from dead last into the mid-field."

"True."

"You like to win as much as I do." Lucien said. It was a statement he'd often said to Victor.

"Of course. I didn't become a race car engineer for the travel or the long stressful hours. I want the challenge of winning."

"How competitive of you." Lucien teased, loving the

way Victor tried to underplay his achievements, and yet how his eyes glowed with pride in himself.

"Says you."

"Takes one to know one."

Victor threw his head back and laughed. "Are we children now?"

"Yes. Giant man children who can't control themselves."

"Or figure out why the fuck my engines kept blowing up."

Lucien nodded. "That's why we are walking. So perhaps stop asking me all these pesky questions about me and talk about your damned petrol engines."

"Don't tell me. Now you finished third on the Series E championship, you are a convert?"

"Electric vehicles are the future." Lucien walked wider on the track, setting himself up for the next turn. From the top of the cliff, the track lost elevation quickly, following along the ridge of the cliff down into the very tight turn nine at the end of the cliff. The braking in this section was tricky.

CHAPTER 2

Victor had always envied the way Lucien was so secure in his identity as a gay man. Obviously, Lucien would never give someone like Victor a second glance; Victor was nothing like the exuberant party boys that Lucien favoured. He'd seen Lucien's social media, and the stream of beautiful, very fit, men on there. He was content to be Lucien's friend and hopefully grab some of that self-confidence in his bisexual identity for himself.

"How can electric vehicles be the future when your sport doesn't allow innovation?" Victor teased.

"An excellent question. And one that's not completely true; only the batteries are the same across every car. And the battery technology has improved every year, with almost a 20% increase in power and durability in the last three seasons." Lucien paced down the hill, staring at the next turn, as if he were visualising how to drive it.

"Well?"

"I can see what you are doing." Lucien glanced over his shoulder. When they'd first met, it was obvious that Lucien needed a friend, someone to keep him from going completely off the rails. To hear Lucien's story wasn't a surprise. His father had always been hovering around the garage back in S3, an ignorant bully of a man with an ugly expression on a face that ought to be handsome but was marred by his sneer. The week when he'd died had been a strange one. Victor remembered the relief at not having him around pitlane anymore, nothing more. It was logical that Lucien had improved so quickly after that. Why hadn't Victor ever tied those two events together? He ought to have noticed.

"Whatever do you mean?"

"Stop stalling. We came out here to walk and to solve your engine puzzle."

"What do you want to know? Your season was finished by the time we started having issues. You were with the team for most of those shitty days."

"Start at the beginning. Pretend I know nothing. Better yet, let me drive the car around this track." The way Lucien's face lit up was everything as he stopped in the middle of the track, turning to face Victor. "It's last season's car now. The no-practice rules don't apply anymore."

It wasn't the silliest idea. "You just want a taste of how fast it was."

"Yes." Lucien's grin reminded Victor of the way his nephew's face looked on Christmas morning.

"No. It's not safe to send you out on this track in a car with an unreliable engine."

Lucien raised one eyebrow. "Come on. It'll be fun."

"Do you actually want to help me with this puzzle, or do you just want to drive fast?"

"Both." Every driver on the various racing series had one thing in common. Beautiful intense eyes, and Lucien was no different. Medium brown coloured with flecks of amber, it was the way Lucien focused his gaze on something that differentiated him from non-drivers. He looked at Victor—at everyone—as if he was the only person in the world; the same way he looked over at a racetrack, with a brilliant intensity as he absorbed all the information at speed.

"I'll see what I can do." Victor began to plan how to get enough mechanics together to put one of last season's cars back together, just for Lucien to drive in the guise of testing what had gone wrong.

"Until then, talk to me. Stop avoiding the issue."

"I'm not avoiding it."

Lucien leaped towards Victor and grabbed his shoulders. Warmth rushed down Victor's spine and he reminded himself that Lucien didn't mean anything by it. It was friendship, nothing else.

"Are you sure about that?"

"No. Of course I'm avoiding it. I've been obsessing over this problem for months already. What use can more talking do?"

Lucien shrugged one shoulder. "Talking to my therapist has helped me a ton. Why not talk to a friend about a problem?" The casual way he spoke about therapy would make Victor's Ma smile. It was so unexpected for who Lucien had been when they'd first met, and yes, Victor had talked to his mum about Lucien back then. She'd reminded him that people had their own journeys, they made their own choices, and Lucien would need to decide for himself if he wanted to heal himself. She'd love to see the changes in him now.

"It's very technical."

"Are you saying that I'm just a driver and I wouldn't know enough?" Lucien released Victor and resumed walking.

"No. It's just..." Victor clicked his tongue. "Is it arrogant to say that if I can't figure this out, then no one can?"

"Yes." Lucien laughed. "But also ... true. Look, I didn't ask you here for a walk so I could solve this problem. I know you can do it. You just need a change of scene and to talk through the issues. Tell me about it and you'll solve it yourself."

"Fine."

"You built a fast car. Then what happened."

"At Austin, Ondrej's exhaust began to smoke at lap ten."

"So early in the race?"

"Yes. We couldn't find anything on the data, and he drove the car slowly back to pitlane. When he arrived, there was still nothing on the engine data and then it just stopped smoking. We checked everything. He wanted to continue and there was no reason not to, so we sent him back out in last place."

"Hard work from there."

Victor shrugged. "Jaxxon wanted to have a crack. He said you never know what will happen in racing."

"It's true, which is why Jaxxon is a brilliant race engineer. And?"

"Ondrej drove well enough and finished in sixteenth.

We examined the whole car and aside from some smoke damage in the exhaust itself, we found nothing."

"Maybe some debris got in there and caught fire, then burned itself out?"

Victor breathed out, his breath smoking in the cold air. "If it was just that one time, then yeah, I'd agree with you."

"Was that the race that Paulo DNF'd as well? What happened?"

"You weren't there?" Victor was so caught up in the drama that he'd forgotten which races Lucien attended as the number three driver for the team. With Series E finishing in August, surely Lucien had been the back-up driver?

"No. Alex did Austin, Mexico, and Brazil because his wife has family in that part of the world."

"Right. Of course. Paulo's brakes caught fire on lap five and we retired the car."

"So earlier than Ondrej's problem?"

"Yes. But that's not related because we figured that one out. One of the mechanics had installed them incorrectly with the wrong type of casing. It melted and caused the issue."

Lucien lengthened his stride and Victor pushed himself to keep up. Damned drivers were so fit. "Just a shitty coincidence, then?"

"Definitely not the same engine issue that we had again and again."

"Didn't Ondrej DNF in Mexico?"

Victor growled. "Unrelated. He had a puncture caused by a shard of carbon fibre. We figured he must've run it over on the track. Just bad luck."

"That's a lot of bad luck in two races."

"I know." Victor ground his teeth together. "Look, I've already tortured myself over this. I can't figure how a brake issue, caused by a mechanic, and a random puncture have anything to do with the engine failures."

"You are the expert." Lucien's easy phrasing didn't help when Victor felt like anything but an expert right now.

Victor rubbed his hands together. "This is pointless. It's fucking cold and it's not helping."

"Come on. We are half-way around the track, heading into turn nine. You've got to be careful going into this one because of the downhill elevation change; it's almost like Eu Rouge in reverse without the s-bend."

"So nothing like Eu Rouge then. Aren't you supposed to be an expert?" Victor enjoyed teasing Lucien, whose smile was so much nicer than his scowl.

"I'll show you one day. We could take Socrates' 1982 Le Mans car for a spin."

"Sure." One of the perks of this job was getting driven around by the world's best drivers in amazing cars. Victor had access to drive them all too; Socrates let anyone in the team take any of his car collection for a ride on the test track; but Victor would never drive as fast or as competently as a proper driver. "Why have you never done that before?"

"Offered to take you for a spin?"

"Yeah?"

"We've been busy. This is literally our first winter break together since we both joined Gamble Racing." Lucien had been here a lot longer than Victor. Lucien's two seasons in S1 for Gamble Racing had happened while

Victor was still in his old job at their old team; dreaming of an S1 gig.

"How have you been busy? Your season ends in August." Victor knew the answer, but teased Lucien anyway. He loved seeing the way Lucien reacted, then forced himself to stop reacting. The control he showed was like nothing Victor had seen, and it really highlighted how he could be so successful as a driver. Before, back in S3, Lucien hadn't had that control and without it, he was never going to go any further up the driving ranks.

"I suppose you think you are funny or something. I was the third driver for most of the races, which meant I still had to train and be ready in case something happened. Being on constant standby is a different sort of stress..."

"To driving?"

"Yes. Obviously, I'd come off a good season at Series E—"

"Third." Victor's obvious comment disappeared into the woods lining the track. The dense trees muffled the sound of any car as they sped along the test track. Due to the lack of access caused by the woods, the track was wider than a normal track, allowing other cars to quickly get to the scene of an accident if a test driver crashed. Solar powered cameras were mounted regularly along the track, so the entire 3.8km could be monitored from inside the engineering workshop.

Lucien jogged ahead and stopped in the middle of the track. "You've done it again."

"What?"

"Turned the discussion into being about me, instead of your problem. I'm wondering if you even want to solve this thing..." Lucien winked, then turned around and kept walking along the straight towards the chicane of turns ten and eleven.

"Damn you. Yes. I want to solve this. Why the fuck are my cars failing?"

Lucien glanced over his shoulder. "Then walk and talk." He waved his arm and Victor quickened his stride to catch up. The casual way Lucien assumed Victor would figure this out reinforced their unlikely friendship.

"If I don't figure this out..." Victor paused. Could he voice his greatest concern? "Well, you know what this sport is like."

"Has there been any hint that Gamble Racing might sack you?"

"No."

Lucien sighed. "You'd be the last to know if they were, so ignore my question. What is the risk?"

"Of being sacked? Look at the evidence. I'm young. Too young for a chief engineer. My car is fast but hard to drive. We've had far too many problems this season."

"Define too many." Lucien, somehow, knew the right question to ask.

"The team... My cars had eight DNFs this season. That's 17% of the opportunity to race. That's one every six starts and far too many missed points. By any measure, it's not good enough." Victor knew all the numbers and none of them were good. Lucien nodded but didn't say anything. Good. Victor didn't need a platitude; he knew how much of a disaster this was and no amount of pretty words would help.

"The season before, there were only three DNFs. Seven percent of all race starts. That's where it should be."

"Two of those were mine." Lucien gave Victor that sly over the shoulder glance again. On anyone else, Victor might have assumed Lucien was flirting, but it was nothing like that. Lucien was like that with everyone. It wasn't personal, no matter how much Victor might want it to be. Lucian laughed, a soft chuckle that floated past Victor's skin like the steam from a laksa on a cold day. "Although, honestly, I don't think you should use my last season in S1 as any sort of benchmark. Ondrej only scored one solitary point. My best finish was thirteenth. It was a shitshow in a slow car."

"Socrates is loyal. He didn't sack you after you had no points in a season. He gave you a better opportunity." Victor automatically boosted Lucien, pulling him away from any negativity.

Lucien thumped Victor on the shoulder. "Can you listen to yourself? What makes you so special that you think Socrates would sack you, when he literally doesn't sack anyone?"

"He sacked Reginald."

"Only under severe duress, after how many seasons of terrible cars and finishing near the back of the pack. You've said it yourself. Socrates is loyal. He trusts that you'll solve this engine problem."

"I suppose he does."

"He does. Now you need to trust yourself."

Victor had heard that phrase his whole life. The joy of having mother who worked as a therapist; and unlike the stereotype that a therapist was so busy fixing everyone else that she couldn't run her own family, Victor's Ma was the best mother. She encouraged him to follow his dream. He probably should call her. It'd been a couple of weeks.

"This is my favourite part of the test track." Lucien stood on the outside of turn eleven, his hands on his hips as he stared down the long curving straight.

"It's the fastest part."

"Yes." Lucien turned towards Victor, whose stomach sank as the joy on Lucien's face disappeared. "Victor, what is the matter? Why are you frowning?"

CHAPTER 3

Lucien hadn't expected to have to cajole Victor to get him to talk about his engine problems. The engine failures had consumed Victor since they'd happened. It ought to be easy to get him to talk about it; and now Victor was frowning? Obviously Lucien had missed something crucial, and he didn't think it was as simple as Victor worrying that he'd be sacked if he didn't figure out why their cars kept catching fire. If that was it, wouldn't Victor talk more?

"I'm fine."

"Stop lying." Lucien was bored with this game. "What are you not telling me? You are evading this discussion. Why?"

Victor shoved his hands into his pockets, his shoulders slumped. "Trust myself? That's what you said."

"Yes." Lucien was struck by the urge to hug Victor, to comfort him. He shook his head to clear away something so silly. Lucien knew nothing about comforting people; it was a harsh world and only the tough survived, or so his father had always said. After a couple of long breaths, Lucien was able to boost Victor, not tear himself down for not being friendly enough. "I know this puzzle is frustrating, but you are the literal expert. You designed these cars. You took the engine from the manufacturer, fit it to your design, and made it better. Faster. You should trust yourself."

"But what if I can't solve this?" Victor's voice had lost all tone and he bowed his head, as if it were too hard to keep holding it up.

"What are you talking about? You can solve this. It's just a few engine fires."

"Just."

"Yeah." Lucien wanted to shake his friend. How could he be so harsh on himself? "What is really going on?"

"Fuck. You sound like my mother." Victor sighed. "I'm sorry. That's a good thing. She's great. It's just—"

"Just what?" Lucien was missing something crucial here.

"What if I fail?" Victor pressed his hands to his face, covering his eyes. "I never fail. This one has me stumped and I don't think I'll cope if I actually fail."

Lucien blinked. "Are you fucking kidding me? Are you avoiding talking to me about these engines because you are self-sabotaging?"

Victor's nostrils widened and he gasped. "Fuck."

"You are?"

"Yes. Maybe. No. What if this makes no sense because it's not a failure? What if it's not something I did wrong? What if it is ... sabotage?" Victor's dark brown eyes flashed, and Lucien could see his brain working. The lacklustre stance disappeared, and Victor began to pace down the

DRS zoned curved straight. With a slight banking towards the outside of the track, this was the quickest part of the test circuit and Victor was certainly walking quicker than he'd moved today. Not that the two things were related, it was just a little ironic to see Victor move faster into the speed trap.

"How?" Lucien jogged after Victor, who was walking with renewed energy, his arms swinging at his sides as he rushed towards the engineering workshop. Could it be so simple as someone trying to upset Gamble Racing? They had done much better this season than in the last few seasons, making it into the midfield and therefore earning more prizemoney as constructors than in previous years.

"Brazil. Ondrej finished P3. Paulo's car had engine failure. It was our fourth problem in three races. Then we travelled to Abu Dhabi and both cars caught fire. What a way to end the season."

"I was there. What a fucking day."

"Yeah." Victor stood on the outside of the curve, far from the racing line, with his hands on his head. The dark winter shadows of the woods behind him reflected the grim atmospheric expression on Victor's face. "Is this too convenient? Sabotage? What am I thinking?"

Lucien tried to keep his expression blank, but yeah, those were good questions to be asking. The security around S1 teams and their cars was pretty tight. "Keep walking. Let it percolate for a while." He didn't know much about life or how to be a decent person, but he knew that walking helped him sort out the mess in his head. If it worked for him, hopefully it would also work for Victor. They walked in silence all the way down the long straight towards turn twelve and the technical part of the track.

"I'm going to cut through the old part of the track and head back into the workshop." Victor didn't wait for Lucien's answer, not that it mattered because taking Victor out of the shed and making him walk had helped. This annoying niggle in his own chest as Victor marched away shouldn't matter. He was hardly being abandoned by Victor because this wasn't about him. Lucien just wanted to help a friend solve a puzzle that had been evading him. A handsome friend whose legs and ass looked great as he power-walked back to the engineering shop.

Lucien rubbed his temples. It'd obviously been too long since he'd had sex if he was noticing how amazing Victor looked. Shit. He didn't even know if Victor was queer. Normally, Lucien would've guessed in favour because Socrates collected queer people, recruiting them into his racing teams. Whether this was purposeful, or merely because Socrates could see past people's backgrounds to value their achievements, it was hard to tell. It didn't really matter. Being at Gamble Racing felt like the home Lucien had never had. It was a place where everyone accepted him exactly as he was, anger management issues and everything else, and put their efforts into helping him grow and become a better person. It was truly magical; especially for a boy like himself who'd never had a loving family. He'd had a father who'd grudgingly accepted that his son was gay because nothing except winning races mattered, and that meant his acceptance was conditional on his success.

Lucien glanced at his watch. He still had another forty

minutes before he was due at the big house to meet with his team.

He didn't have many solutions to his lack of family, and it didn't matter. He was still young—twenty-five—he didn't need to settle down and think about having his own family yet. Ha. Lucien kicked the tyre barrier at the edge of the track. What the fuck did he know about how to be part of a family? All he knew was car racing, and he was damned good at it. He walked back up the track, the wrong way, until he reached the section heading into turn twelve. From here, he stood quietly, assessing the track to find the best driving line even though he'd driven this track hundreds of times. Turns twelve and thirteen were designed to replicate Variante Villeneuve at Imola; hold the outside line through twelve to maintain speed, then turn in late for thirteen, leaving half a car width of space to the exit barrier. From there, come in wide to fourteen, taking the apex late and touching the exit kerb towards turn fifteen. Late brake and turn sharply to follow the outside barrier until the turning point for the second apex of the double apexed turn sixteen to take the kerb heavily on the exit. Carry the exit speed into the chicane of seventeen and eighteen, braking to avoid the sausage kerb on the apex of seventeen and cover the apex of eighteen to make as much room as possible for a good exit, and a quick slingshot onto the home straight. Push hard down the straight, heading wide on the right side of the track to set up for turn one and the next lap.

Lucien automatically held his hands up, on a fake wheel, practicing each turn as he ran through it. This technical part of the test track was well designed, allowing for drivers to really test the cornering and downforce of a car under pressure, as well as how quickly the car responded coming out of a slow tricky segment into the flat-out speed of the long home straight. Lucien vaulted the tyre barriers that formed the edge of turn fourteen and headed directly across the old part of the track, avoiding walking the technical section. He wanted to check in with Victor once more before his own meeting.

The noise of several excited people greeted Lucien as he walked in from the pit garage practice area. Victor had gathered all of the engineering and mechanic staff that were currently in the building, and they all stood around the deconstructed cars, talking in loud voices.

"Stop." Victor raised his hand. He'd taken off the large team jacket and stood there in his shirt with his sleeves rolled up, exposing his forearms. "One at a time with your theories." Had Victor always had such lovely forearms and hands? Lucien felt a tug, pulling him towards Victor. Nothing real or tangible, just a weird feeling that he wanted to be beside him as he weathered this storm of over-enthusiastic puzzle solving. Was that the second or third time today that he'd had a weird, almost chemical attraction around Victor? It couldn't be lust. Lucien had enough experience to know physical chemistry when he encountered it, and this wasn't that. It was something more elemental, like attraction but different. Lust but not. It was on the tip of his tongue, except it wasn't, because this wasn't what lust usually felt like to him, it wasn't the flashy chemistry that promised immediate pleasure. He dismissed it all as situational, nothing to stress about. As far as physical inputs went, this wasn't one he needed to worry about. It didn't impact on him as a driver, so it was likely irrelevant, just a niggle caused by seeing Victor in his element, commanding a group of enthusiastic engineers.

"Do you have an idea, Lucien?"

"Me?" Lucien had tuned out the noise and now everyone stared at him. "With regards to the engine fires?" He needed to buy himself some time, since he'd spent the last God-knows how long, thinking about families and the driving line on the test track and other things that weren't going to help Victor resolve this puzzle. At all. The burgeoning obsession with how sexy Victor was really wasn't going to be any use right now.

"Yes."

"You guys are the experts. I'm just a driver."

"Okay. Driver's perspective. Ondrej and Paulo aren't here. You are."

Lucien chuckled. "Therefore, I'll do? Even though I'm only an E driver." He winked at Victor whose cheeks pinked.

"You have S1 experience. Your opinion is useful."

Lucien didn't need the reminder that he wasn't the top dog anymore. He didn't even want to be in S1, and yet he couldn't get rid of that irritating voice that said S1 was the pinnacle of motorsport. The only achievement worthwhile aiming for.

He breathed in. "Fine. Play me the radio recordings for each engine failure, and I'll give you the driver's perspective."

Skye, one of the tech people, tapped on their laptop. "Give me a second. I'll pull them up. They aren't the best quality, though."

Lucien leaned in closer to Skye. "You didn't get the remastered versions from that TV show?"

Skye glanced at him. "No. This season doesn't air until March. This one is Ondrej at Austin." Skye pushed a button and the recording played.

"We have smoke. Box for retirement, Ondrej."

"What the fuck?"

"Box, box. I'm sorry." Jaxxon's concern was apparent to all, even through the crackle of the recording.

"That's all there is," Skye said.

"We couldn't find anything in the pit, then the smoke faded, and Ondrej wanted to keep going, so we sent him out again," Victor said.

Lucien nodded. "Play the next one."

"Okay. This is Paulo at Brazil."

"We have smoke, Paulo." Paulo's race engineer, Monica, said.

"How? There's no loss of power."

"Please pull the car over and power down."

"Ahhhh. Fuck." The recording didn't have anything for a while until Monica spoke again.

"We have fire now, Paulo. Pull over quickly and power down."

"Fucking fuck."

"I don't think we need to listen to Paulo's frustration. Let's listen to Paulo in Abu Dhabi," Victor said. Skye pressed some buttons and Monica's voice came through the laptop speakers.

"I'm sorry, Paulo. We have fire. Please pull over and get out of the car."

"Fuck. Again?"

"Yes. If you can get near a marshal, that'd be good. Get out quickly."

"Okay. But what the fuck?"

"Agreed. Paulo. Stop the car."

Lucien had one question. "Can I hear Ondrej's radio calls too?"

Skye nodded. "Here you are."

"Fuck." Ondrej swore first this time. What had he felt?

"Fire. Pull over and turn off the engine." Jaxxon sounded frustrated.

"What the fuck, man?"

"Fire. Stop the car."

"Fuck. What a shit way to end the season."

Lucien pinched his nose. Until the last recording, Lucien had wondered how the drivers had no notice of anything going wrong, no loss of power, nothing. In the last one, Ondrej had maybe noticed something, but with all the other problems before, perhaps he'd been paying more attention, waiting for it.

"Well?" Victor asked.

"One thing stands out. In every single case, except the last one, none of the drivers had any loss of power before the fire. They didn't notice the fire. How is that possible? It makes no sense that in all those situations, the driver knew nothing, felt nothing, saw nothing on the wheel." His perspective didn't add anything. No wonder Victor wanted to pull his hair out, because this made no sense.

"We had no warning on our data either."

"How? How did no one have any notice? How do you have an engine fire with no loss of power?" Lucien understood the racing data well enough; speed into corners and that sort of thing, but the technical mechanics data was a bit beyond his mathematical abilities.

"That's a very good question. We had nothing on our data either. It's very odd."

"Don't you have sensors everywhere?"

Victor ran his hands through his hair. It shouldn't look as interesting as it did. "Not everywhere. Skye, Georgie, Isambard; where don't we have sensors on the car?" Victor asked.

"Skye, can you pull up a schematic?" Isambard asked. Everyone huddled around Skye's laptop, squeezing in close to each other to get a good view. Lucien drifted to the back of the group. This next part of the discussion was beyond his capabilities.

"Hey Victor. I have a meeting with Socrates. Fill me in on what you find later, yeah?" Lucien had said his part, now the mechanics and engineers could take over and use their actual expertise to find the problem. He rested his hand between Victor's shoulder blades to say goodbye and warmth flowed up his arm in the most disconcerting way. Odd. Victor glanced over his shoulder.

"Yeah. Thanks for this. We needed your perceptive." The way Victor held Lucien's gaze was … nice. He yanked his arm away and nodded quickly before fleeing the building and this new confusion.

CHAPTER 4

Victor rubbed his eyes. Since Lucien's comment about sensors, he'd spent four days in the workshop with his team, barely sleeping, as they ran tests on every part of the car that didn't have a sensor. The most obvious theory was that the fire had started in the exhaust, but he didn't want to miss anything. And the little niggle that it was sabotage wouldn't go away either. Surely not. Sabotage was just a convenient excuse because he couldn't find the actual problem.

"Please tell me you brought coffee?" Victor blinked at the hazy view of Lucien.

"I think you need sleep more than you need coffee."

"I have to figure this out."

"You do realise that it doesn't have to be done today. Sleep, Victor."

"I can't."

Lucien rested his hands on Victor's shoulders, and Victor could just about let himself fall against his chest and snooze. He blinked rapidly instead. The idea of sleep sounded so good, he could succumb to it and never mind the engine issues. No. Snap out of it. He had to solve this. He couldn't fail.

"Are you wearing the same clothes?" Lucien asked.

"Um..."

"You are. Have you even been home in the last couple of days?"

"No." Victor had been sleeping on the couch in his office and ignoring his staff who kept telling him to go home. He couldn't. There wasn't much time until the new season. He'd spent most of the year designing next year's car, so it was still on schedule, yet he would never be happy with it until he'd resolved this problem. What if the same issue also plagued the new car?

"Come with me." Lucien picked Victor up and slung him over his shoulder. He fucking just picked him up. All the breath squeezed out of his lungs.

"Put me down." This was ridiculous, even by Lucien's standards.

"No."

"How are you doing this? I'm heavier than you." Victor was around the same height as Lucien. Lucien was lean, fit, an athlete, while Victor was broader across the shoulders. He used to be plumper too, but he hadn't really been eating since Abu Dhabi and the disastrous race there. The floor looked weird from this angle.

"My trainer gets me to help Xenia move feed sacks for strength training."

"I'm a bit bigger than a feed sack." His guess might be wrong. Victor knew nothing about horses. Socrates' niece Xenia ran a racing stable on the other side of the estate, and the most Victor understood was that the horses looked pretty in the paddocks.

"Yes you are." Lucien wasn't even puffing as he marched across the engineering workshop floor carrying Victor.

"Fuck, I hope no one sees this." He twisted his head to try and check the room. Awkward.

"Hush. Just relax."

"What are you going ... doing ... where?" Victor couldn't make his mouth make sense. His face was far too close to Lucien's torso, and he could see muscles moving through the fine cotton of Lucien's t-shirt. The dark lines of Lucien's tattoo were a shadow underneath the fabric. His own stomach was pressed against Lucien's sharp shoulder and strong neck.

"Victor. You are so tired that you can't talk. I'm going to put you in bed."

"I can walk myself." He needed to stop touching Lucien or stop Lucien from holding him. Bed. No, he couldn't be this close to Lucien—pressed right against his body—and be thinking about bed. He really needed some distance from Lucien and his offer of a bed. Lucien didn't mean anything by this; he was just being a friend by ensuring Victor got some much-needed sleep. God, he was so tired. He could just shut his eyes and let Lucien carry him to ... anywhere, really. It was probably good that this wasn't very comfortable. It took all his remaining strength to keep his head held away from Lucien's body, as far from Lucien's waist—and groin—as possible. His whole spine and neck ached with tension.

When they'd first met, Victor had had a massive crush

on Lucien. Everyone had. Lucien was so vibrant, so full of life—and angry energy—and yes, he was utterly handsome. The ultimate young driver with a stunning face; perfect for marketing. Curly brown hair, flopping around his face, and his golden brown eyes, sharp nose and jaw. Each element combined into a face that was more handsome than anyone ought to sport, and when he left his face unshaven with just the right amount of stubble, well, it was more than Victor could deal with.

From those days back in S3, the tiny snippets when Lucien was kind to him were seared into Victor's memory, tiny moments when Lucien had let himself be free from the ugly focus of what Victor now understood was Lucien's father's push to win at all costs. Whenever Lucien was temporarily free from his father's bullshit, he surprised Victor by listening to him attentively. Victor had suppressed his crush once it was obvious that Lucien had a type, and it wasn't the workaholic engineer with dreams of S1. Victor would never be the happy-go-lucky party boy that Lucien favoured. Only in his dreams could something different happen, so he'd given up on hope and focused on being the friend that Lucien obviously needed. He closed his eyes and let the world go dark.

There was only a thin t-shirt—Lucien's—and his own work shirt between his skin and Lucien's skin. Heat flickered around him and he swallowed.

"Okay. Walk." Lucien hefted Victor off his shoulder and placed him gently on his feet. Victor swayed a little as he opened his eyes. He wanted to stay leaning against Lucien's lean, strong frame. His wish almost came true as

Lucien helped him into a cosy jacket, then pushed open the door.

"It's dark." And cold. The December chill slammed into his cheeks, waking him up with a sudden blast. He'd lost track of time in the workshop. If it was night, what day was it? He rubbed his arms.

"Yes. Socrates is concerned that you aren't looking after yourself. He sent me to get you."

Every warm happy feeling fled as the chilly reality slapped Victor in the face. Lucien wasn't interested in him; of course not, he was just being kind because their boss said he should be. Damn, Victor was so tired that he hadn't been able to control the old flare of attraction from his ancient crush. He shivered.

"Come on. Let's get you into the big house and tucked up warm in bed."

"Fuck. Are you going to feed me soup too?" Victor had to push Lucien away. This kind version of Lucien was too much. He'd always known—from the day he'd first met Lucien—that if Lucien ever dealt with his anger and showed people how kind he was under the sudden bursts of rage, well ... Victor had always known he'd fall so hard for him, and it would be messy. For him. Lucien could never know.

"No. Don't be absurd." Lucien grabbed Victor's hand and pulled him along, forcing him to make his exhausted body move. It wasn't a nice romantic gesture. It was a brutal non-negotiable force. Victor was essentially being dragged into bed and forced to rest. If he had anything left in the tank, he would've asked Lucien ... something. He couldn't even form a question.

"One foot after another. Keep going, or I'll have to pick you up again." If only Lucien knew that wasn't really a threat.

"Gah." Victor needed coffee or a kick up the ass. He didn't need to be lead like a bloody horse to a bed and be tucked in like a baby that couldn't look after himself. Hell. He trudged along, unable to summon the energy to get mad at Lucien for upsetting his work. They entered one of the back doors of Socrates' mansion, and Victor let himself be led all the way up some narrow stairs, then through a tiny door that opened out into a grand hallway.

"What was that?"

"The old servant's staircases. This house is riddled with them, and it's much faster than going up the main stairs."

"How?"

"How do I know about them?" Lucien pushed open a random door in the hallway and pulled Victor into a room. A bedroom. With a giant bed in it. Victor kicked off his shoes and bolted towards the bed, half-stumbling over his heavy feet. He needed sleep so badly. Seeing the bed took all the fight out of him. The bed was like a bloody oasis, sitting there in the room, welcoming his shattered body and offering respite. He fell onto the bed and crawled towards the pillows, hugging one of them tight.

"Hell, Victor. At least take off your grubby clothes."

Victor probably should do that. Yeah. His head was so heavy and the pillow so soft.

"Fine." Lucien's annoyed tone was the last thing he heard before he fell asleep.

Lucien jumped off the podium, champagne bottle in hand, and popped the top. Champagne sprayed everywhere, landing on Victor's neat team uniform, soaking him. Holy shit. Lucien had won the race and Victor stood nearby on the winning constructor's podium. Both cars on the podium and himself standing up there to take the constructors trophy for the race on behalf of Gamble Racing. He'd done this a few times in his career now, but never with Lucien. His Lucien. It was the stuff of dreams and his whole body felt alight with the thrill of it. He stood under the shower of champagne and stuck his tongue out. Champagne dripped into his mouth, a heady taste. Winning always felt good. This one, this win was one for the ages, the best win among many wins. The one he'd remember forever.

"Congratulations." Lucien's giant grin made him even more handsome than usual. Victor laughed and Lucien poured champagne all over his face. The dry alcoholic taste over-whelmed him. This whole situation was breath-taking, like he'd never be this alive or awake ever again. Adrenalin pumped, emotions spilled into fat tears hidden by the spray of alcohol, he wanted to scream and shout. Nothing came out except excited woots. He grabbed Lucien around the waist and pulled him towards him. Lucien stepped closer, bending his head for a kiss, and Victor slid one hand up to cup the back of Lucien's head. They kissed. A kiss to celebrate Lucien's win. A full-mouthed, I love you and I don't care who sees, kind of kiss. Victor's head spun and his body was on fire in the very best, burning for more. He held Lucien as tight as he could, wanting to revel in the way he tasted. A winner, who tasted like champagne and glory and Lucien. Always Lucien.

"Wake up." The real Lucien's voice broke the dream kiss and Victor growled under his breath, not wanting to let go of the dream. "I think you were having a dream or something. You were making weird noises."

Hopefully not sex noises. How embarrassing. He jerked away, with his face and ears burning hot, and not the good sort of hot.

"Why are you in my bedroom?"

"Technically you are in my bedroom."

Victor wasn't awake enough for this. First Lucien interrupted a perfectly wonderful dream, and now he was being his usual pain in the ass.

"Ergh, whatever." He buried his head under the pillow, willing himself back to sleep, and back into that kiss. Damn it, he could almost taste it. It'd seemed so real. He sighed. He'd better wake up properly and face reality; a reality where Lucien wasn't going to kiss him in front of millions of adoring fans. A reality where Lucien would never kiss him, and he'd have to learn to be content with just being his friend. It was enough to make him want to sigh again.

"Hell. Two sighs. I didn't pick you for a slow waker. I thought you'd be one of those leap out of bed, ready to smash out another successful day, annoying types of people."

"Uh huh." Victor wanted to stay in this warm bed much longer.

"Besides, it's nearly midday. Aren't you hungry?"

Victor threw off the pillow and sat up. "What the hell? Midday." His stomach growled. Shit, he was hungry.

Lucien sat cross-legged in the middle of the bed, just out of reach. "You've slept for nearly fourteen hours. I guess that Socrates was right when he told me to get you into bed."

"I'm sure that's what he meant." Their boss was notorious for teasing people.

"No. He was genuinely worried about your health. The fact that he also got a euphemism out of it would have been a perfect bonus. You know what he's like."

Victor's brain slowly started to function. "What did you mean about it technically being your bedroom? Don't you live in Monaco?"

Lucien shook his head. "Yes. Technically for tax reasons, I live in Monaco. I also have a room here."

"Are you saying that you don't live anywhere?"

"It's a bit early to be asking me about this, isn't it?"

Victor pulled the blanket up to cover his chest, but it didn't budge because Lucien was sitting on it. He shivered, not sure if he wanted Lucien to see his naked body. "Early? You just told me it was midday. I don't understand. None of the other drivers have a permanent room here." Victor needed to talk about something else, something that wasn't the question he actually wanted to ask—had Lucien undressed him last night when he'd put him in bed? How much had he seen? And most importantly, did he like what he saw? Fuck. He needed coffee.

"It doesn't mean anything. Socrates offered."

"Why?"

Lucien frowned. "I'd rather talk about your tattoo. How long have you had that?"

Victor pressed his hand over his left chest muscle, over the tattoo of his car. "I got it in Australia."

"Before or after the first race of the season."

"After. To commemorate my first design in its first race." He shouldn't be embarrassed about being proud of his achievements. It was just the way Lucien stared at his bare skin that was ... confusing.

Lucien grinned. "That's awesome. Let me see."

"Only if you tell me why you live here with Socrates, while pretending to live in Monaco."

"Fine." Lucien rubbed his temples. "Socrates offered because I don't have any family and he wanted me to have a base, a found family I suppose, if and when I ever needed one. Everyone else has a family of their own."

"And since your father died, you have no one?" Victor couldn't imagine it. His parents and sisters were so proud of him, and while he lived alone, travelling with the team for most of the year, he could still call them or visit whenever he needed. "Like, no one?"

"It's not that big a deal. Socrates and Mike, well they offered and it's ..." Lucien shrugged. "Nice, I guess, to have a place to stay when I want to hang out with people. I'm sure Socrates would do the same for anyone in his team if they needed."

Victor had his own house in the village down the road, just like many people in the Gamble Racing team. Syresthorpe used to be part of the Pewett Downs estate— with some of the buildings owned by the estate, although Victor owned his house—originally part of the huge property Socrates' grandfather had purchased from a bankrupt Duke around fifty years ago. It was a good setup as everyone's families were all in the same community, supporting each other when the team was on the road for the season. The mechanics were evenly split between those who were young and wanted to work every race because they wanted to travel, and those with families who worked every second race to split their time between work and family. S1's global racing schedule meant a lot of time away from home. He loved it, the travel, the intensity, the continual push for improvement and success.

"And there were no other beds available?" Victor didn't understand how or why he'd slept in Lucien's room. "What about you? Where did you sleep?"

"There are plenty of guest rooms."

"So why put me in your bed? Why not a guest room?"

Lucien rolled his eyes. "Victor, you were so exhausted that you could hardly walk. I wasn't going to make you wait while the staff made up a bedroom for you. My bed was the easiest option and the fastest way to get you to sleep."

It had the added bonus of smelling faintly of Lucien. No wonder Victor had slept so well and dreamed of kissing Lucien. Shit. So much for suppressing his old crush.

"I'm hungry."

"Why don't you have a shower? I'll get something from the kitchen for you."

Victor growled. "You have an answer for everything, don't you?"

"Do you need more sleep? You aren't usually this surly."

He wasn't. Just caught off-balance in a situation that reminded him of everything he couldn't have. Why did his body have to fixate on someone so far out of his league? Curses.

"I'm probably just hangry." He made an excuse to try and get Lucien away from him. He wasn't awake enough to deal with Lucien and the impact he had on him. It wasn't usually this difficult.

"There's a clean towel in the ensuite, and you can wear some of my clothes. We are about the same size." Lucien pointed to a door. "Did you know that Socrates' grandfather had the whole building remodelled? He took out every second bedroom, split them in half, and created ensuites for each room to totally modernise the whole place."

"He must've been loaded." Victor knew the stories. Socrates' grandfather had made his money in liquid packing, apparently there was good money to be made from putting milk and juice and whatever into containers.

"And we all get to benefit."

Victor nodded. Without Socrates, Gamble Racing wouldn't exist. The former dual World Champion had created his own S1 team after an accident that had left him with concussion and inconsistently blurry vision, and he couldn't drive competitively anymore. Victor's stomach grumbled again, and Lucien laughed.

"Let me organise something for you to eat."

"And coffee."

Lucien nodded. "I wouldn't dare forget." He bounced out of the room, much more awake and alive than Victor felt, leaving Victor alone. Time for a shower, and then he'd have the pleasure and pain of wearing some of Lucien's clothes. This was the most inconvenient time for his old crush to surface.

CHAPTER 5

Lucien paced down the hallway towards the servant's staircase that would take him to the kitchen. He'd made a tactical error by heading down to dinner last night after helping Victor go to sleep. But after undressing his friend and tucking him into bed, he'd needed to lose himself in chit chat with people, so he didn't think about the sprawl of Victor's body on his bed. After chatting at dinner, he'd left it too late to get one of the staff to make up a guest room, so he'd planned to simply sleep on the lounge chair in his room instead, but from the moment he'd walked back into his bedroom, there'd been no other option but to join Victor in bed. Ultimately, that was his second—and biggest—mistake. His friend cuddled a pillow, snoring softly. Lucien had stripped down to his boxers and slid under the covers. He'd left space between them—close but not touching—and lain there listening to Victor's breathing. In and out with that little flutter of sound telling Lucien that Victor was still alive, until eventually Lucien slept too.

And now he was taking this mistake even further by getting food for Victor. Like a good boyfriend. He shook his head hard. See, tactical error. The problem was that Lucien had latched onto Victor as someone who'd supported him when he couldn't support himself, and that was problematic, wasn't it? It was typical that he couldn't just be friends with someone without wrecking it somehow. He couldn't do life without falling back into toxic old habits.

He jogged down the narrow stairs and pushed open the door to the kitchen.

"Lucien. How's Victor?" Socrates stood in the kitchen with the chef, Angie, with a bottle of wine open between them. Angie had a notepad with some scribbles on it.

"Good. He just woke and he's having a shower. I said I'd get some food for him."

"Angie, can you make something for Victor?"

Lucien shook his head. "Don't bother. You guys are obviously busy. I'll just make him a sandwich." He opened the fridge. Angie bumped him on the shoulder.

"I'll do it. It's literally my job."

"Okay." Lucien stepped out of the way. He hovered vaguely out of the way as Angie pulled out a bunch of things and made a sandwich worthy of a fine dining restaurant.

"I take it things are going well with you two?" Socrates asked.

"What do you mean?"

"You and Victor."

"We are just friends." Lucien couldn't ignore the smug

expression on Socrates' face. "Don't play matchmaker. It doesn't ... It's not like that."

"Okay." Socrates drew the word out, like he didn't believe Lucien. The rise of heat up Lucien's neck and the beginnings of a roar in his ears meant he needed to get out of here before he lashed out. "Thanks for the sandwich." He grabbed the plate from Angie, uncaring if she'd finished or not, and bolted out of the kitchen. Every footstep jarred. He wasn't the angry young man with no control anymore. He wasn't going to let Socrates' little jibes affect him. No. Just because Socrates poked at that niggle inside him, the one that said Socrates was right and Lucien had made a tactical error in sleeping next to Victor, that he wished he and Victor could be more than friends. No. This wasn't a road he could go down. He was too angry, too toxic, and knew nothing about love to be someone's partner. God. Imagine. He couldn't hold someone's heart in his hands. The responsibility of being able to wreck someone—and be wrecked in return—was too much. He couldn't do that to anyone, let alone a friend like Victor. It was just one more thing his father had ruined for him. Lucien had to fix himself before he was capable—worthy—of loving someone.

By the time, he'd arrived back outside his bedroom with the damned sandwich, his temper had eased enough that he wasn't going to dump the whole fucking thing on the table from a great height. Unlearning anger sucked. It took so long to learn new, calmer, habits, and it was too easy to get trapped by the addictive rush of blood in his veins when difficult things happened.

He opened the door, breathing in deep and letting the

air ease out of his lungs. Control. He didn't have to be like this. His father had taught him how to be angry, he could teach himself not to be. He breathed out again. Slow, steady, breaths. If only it were that simple.

"One sandwich, just for you." Lucien put the plate on the small side table, then made the mistake of looking up. Victor's hair was still damp from the shower, and it was all damp against his temples, and ... He gulped. He needed to get control of himself and this impossible burgeoning lust before he inevitably screwed up their friendship.

"Did you make that? It looks incredible."

"No. Angie, Socrates' chef, made it. My cooking is much more pedestrian than this."

Victor tilted his head. "I don't believe it. You are good at everything you do."

"Ha. No." Lucien could drive a car fast. He didn't have any other useful skills, like how to be a decent person or control his rage; although he was getting better at that thanks to years of therapy and practice. But he wasn't 'good' at it. "I'm mediocre at most things."

"Allow me to disagree."

"I forgot your coffee." Lucien couldn't even manage to get what his friend needed.

"An unforgivable crime."

"I know." Lucien bowed his head for a second.

"It's fine. I'll grab one in the shed when I get back to work." Victor picked up the sandwich and took a bite. The flash of pleasure in his eyes was too much and Lucien walked over the window. He needed to look anywhere else.

"Oh my god. This is incredible." Victor wasn't helping.

"You have to try some. This is literally the greatest sandwich I've ever had."

"No thanks." Lucien's voice cracked. "I'm not hungry. It's for you." He was already ruining this friendship by thinking that Victor's happy eating voice sounded like Lucien imagined his sex voice might sound; all rough and throaty and filled with pleasure. Fuck.

"Just one bite. Try it." Victor rested his hand on Lucien's shoulder, and he jumped away from the touch.

"No thanks."

"What's the matter? Did I do something wrong?"

Lucien forced himself to turn and look at Victor. "No. You did nothing."

"Then why are you acting so weird?" Victor ate more of the sandwich, his gaze piercing Lucien.

"Fine. Socrates is trying to matchmake us."

Victor clamped his hand over his mouth. He blinked rapidly and chewed for a moment. "Shit. Sorry. I nearly spat the world's best chicken sandwich all over you. What?"

"Socrates is trying to matchmake us."

"I heard you. I just … I'm not your type."

Lucien couldn't make sense of what that might mean.

"Stop staring at me like that," Victor said, and Lucien made himself look out the window. "We both know it's true. You like your men sexy and extroverted and going to parties together. I'm not that."

"I—" Lucien didn't know where to start. He spun around to face Victor again. "Is that what you think?"

"That I'm not your type? Yeah. We've been friends for a while now, Lucien. I've seen … well—" Victor dragged his hand through his damp hair.

"But if you were my type, you'd be okay with Socrates setting us up?" Lucien felt like he was driving on three wheels, off-balance and missing something crucial.

"But I'm not, so it's not relevant."

"Not according to Socrates." Lucien wanted to kick something, so he pressed his toes hard against the floor. "He's so meddlesome."

"Who? Socrates?"

"Yes. Who else?"

"I don't know. This is weird, right. Why would he—" Victor shook his head again. "It makes no sense."

"He's probably bored. It's the winter break, nothing is happening. I'm gay. You're—" Lucien wasn't actually sure.

"Bisexual."

"See? Socrates is just playing with us because he's got nothing else to occupy his mind."

Victor growled. "That's not even true. We need to figure out why our engines keep catching fire. You'd think he'd care more about that than anything else." The passion in Victor's voice sent a flash of heat down Lucien's spine. Oh no. He was in so much trouble.

"He has you to solve that for him."

Victor frowned. "Do you think he has that much faith in me?"

"Yes." It was absolutely the truth.

"I'd best get back to it then." Victor finished the sandwich, then grabbed his shoes from beside the bedroom door. "Thanks for the clothes."

"They are team gear. It's literally no problem." Lucien's shirt was slightly too tight for Victor, pulling across his back as he bent over to tie his shoelaces in a way that Lucien really shouldn't notice. He really needed to go out and get laid before he did something inadvisable, like kiss Victor. Jesus, Socrates and his nonsense needed to fuck all the way off before it ruined a good friendship. Luckily Victor left before Lucien could react. He breathed in deep, trying to settle the way his heart thumped irregularly. Perhaps he'd take one of Socrates' cars for a spin around the test track. Driving fast always helped when nothing else would.

———

"What the hell is he doing?" Victor stared at the screen in the workshop showing the test track. Someone was driving on the test track in this weather. It could only be two people—Socrates or Lucien—and both of them ought to know better. They were the only two people currently on the estate who had the skill to drive like that. Water sprayed out behind the blue sports car and the speed sensors on track flashed up on the screen, clocking the car at over 180mph.

"Doesn't the Ferrari FXX-K have a top speed of just over 200mph?" Skye asked. They were frowning at the screen too.

"It's too wet to be driving that fast today. Who is it?" Victor's gut told him the answer—Lucien—but he needed it confirmed. For safety reasons, no one was allowed to drive on the test track unless they'd filled in an electronic form that notified the security system, and even then, they couldn't open the barrier gate onto the track until someone was watching.

Skye tapped on a nearby laptop. "The log says that it's

Lucien."

"Who gave him permission?" Victor growled. It was raining and cold. The track was probably slippery as hell. He'd been distracted by his own problems the other day when they'd walked together and hadn't thought to check the track surface, but with the woods nearby, surely there was moss or whatever at this time of year. The car flew along the track, ducking under the tunnel, around the three-sixty, and up over the ramp to the top of the small cliff.

"The logs say it Amari approved his access." Skye looked up. "Relax boss. Lucien is a good driver. He knows what he's doing."

Victor nodded. The car entered the long back straight and Victor counted the seconds until the braking zone into the technical section. With every corner, the car hugged the road, and Victor slowly eased out the breath he'd been holding. Skye was right. Lucien knew what he was doing. The car didn't understeer under braking, flying through the corners smoothly without the slightest hint of lack of grip on the wet track. Not even a twitch of the backend.

"Keep an eye on him. I'm going down there." Victor rushed across the workshop floor and through the pit garage until he climbed the barrier at the edge of the track. The blue Ferrari tore past him, covering him in a fine spray of freezing cold water.

"Fuck." Now he had to wait just over a minute while Lucien did another lap. Or not. He grabbed his phone and sent Skye a text.

Victor: Could you flash the yellow flags for me?
Skye: You want him to stop?

Victor: It's very wet and slippery down here.
Skye: Sure thing, boss. Safety first.

Lucien was approaching the technical section again when the solar powered screens flashed yellow on Skye's command. Thankfully Lucien slowed up and took the technical section at a much safer speed—safer for the conditions and for Victor's heart—and soon enough, the car pulled into the pitlane and parked next to Victor. He tapped on the window. Lucien turned off the car and jumped out.

"Is there a problem?" Lucien walked around the car and pulled off his helmet. At least he'd been wearing one. "You are all wet. What happened?"

"You happened. I came down here to stop you killing yourself and you sped right past, spraying me in water." And then he'd stood in the rain holding his breath as Lucien careered around the track. Victor's wet hair dripped into his eyes and he shoved it back, shaking water off his hand.

Lucien frowned. "What are you talking about?"

"It's not safe today. Why are you out driving?"

Lucien rolled his eyes. "Just letting off some steam."

"Can you try and care about yourself?" Victor's heart thudded so hard against his breastbone that it hurt.

"What?"

"Look at the weather, Lucien."

Lucien frowned. "It's December in England, Victor. What other weather are you expecting?"

"It's not safe."

"This car has wets on, that's why I picked it for today. I need the practice in these conditions too." Lucien made it all sound so reasonable.

"Are you blowing off steam or are you practicing?" Victor didn't like the way Lucien was so dismissive of his own safety. The risks were unacceptable.

"Both. Whichever. Why do you care?"

Victor shook his head and walked away. "Someone has to care about you," he muttered. Fucking hell. All it took was one night with Lucien caring for him and now he was yearning for something he couldn't have.

"Come back." Lucien yelled out. "I promised you a ride."

Victor shook his head again and kept walking. A few seconds later, a warm arm was slung over his shoulder.

"Come on. It'll be fun."

"Lucien."

"Please."

Victor couldn't do this. He couldn't be friends with Lucien when he flirted like this as if it meant nothing. "I have work to do."

"Oh. You are no fun."

"Correct. Put the damn car away, Lucien." He brushed off Lucien's arm and walked faster back to his workshop and the infernal puzzle that he needed to solve. Some things were important than a joy ride in the rain around a test track in a Ferrari. As tempting as that was, Victor had a job to do. When he knew the answer and had a solution, then, maybe then, he'd let Lucien reward him for a task well done. He shivered and cleared his throat. Reward him with a ride in a fast car, not reward him with ... kisses. Victor waited until he was alone, then leaned his forehead against the pit garage wall for a moment, eyes closed, and waited for the rush of need to dissipate.

CHAPTER 6

After ten days away, sunning himself in the Maldives, Lucien didn't feel any better. Being scolded by Victor for driving in the rain had been the impetus for getting away from everything; Victor, Socrates, work ... himself. But it hadn't helped. There were too many happy families, too many couples draped over each other, and he was the lonely single man reading S1 memes on his phone in the bar. A few women tried to pick him up but sadly no men. He could've done with a good holiday fuck or two. Talk about self-sabotage, he should've gone to Ibiza, not to a place filled with people in relationships, hanging out with their families, smiling at each other as if no one else in the world existed. Blergh. No amount of warm sunshine, gorgeous water, or random thrill-seeking had made him feel any better. What good was it to spend the days diving old wrecks, or paragliding off cliffs, or exploring on a jetski, if there was no one to share it with afterwards? Previously he'd spent his summer and winter breaks chasing adrenalin rushes, climbing live volcanoes, bungy jumping in New Zealand, the cliff walk on Mount Huashan in China, or snowmobiling in Canada. It used to be enough.

Now he stood in the grand entranceway at Socrates' manor house filled with regret. The place had been decorated for Christmas and looked amazing, if people were into that sort of thing. Had he ever had a good Christmas day? He couldn't remember. Perhaps he should've gone to his apartment in Monaco instead and spent the day alone, slowly pretending to get drunk. It would've been less depressing than being here with people who treated him like part of their happy family. He didn't deserve it. He didn't know how to behave in this situation, or what he was supposed to do.

"Did you get a tan?" Socrates pulled him into a hug with a thump on the back.

"Sure." Lucien always had such a mixed reaction to being hugged by Socrates. It was the hug he should've had from his own father and never got, and he couldn't imagine what it would be like to have grown up with someone so affectionate as a father figure. He wanted to stay forever and get all the comfort he'd missed out on, and he wanted to spurn it, push it away, because he didn't need it.

"And now you are back in time for Christmas." Socrates stepped back, assessing him.

"Yeah."

"Come on, where is your enthusiasm?"

He shrugged. "It's not really my thing."

"What? Christmas?"

"Yeah."

Socrates grimaced. "I get it. We really only started doing

it here for Xenia, whose mother was Russian Orthodox, and then it became a habit to celebrate all the festivals from her heritage; Diwali, Holi, Easter. It's fun and I rather like the gift giving parts." Socrates' niece Xenia was probably twenty years older than Lucien, and Socrates still treated her with the type of Christmas joy Lucien could've only dreamed about as a child.

Lucien smiled. He needed to get over himself; what a self-indulgent prat he was being by naysaying Socrates' efforts. "Sounds fun."

"You are welcome to stay. As always."

"Thanks. I'm not sure what my plans are."

Socrates winked. "You could go home with Victor. His family always do a big get together."

"Do you know everything about everyone?"

"Yes." Socrates' simple answer was the connection Lucien needed. He clapped Socrates on the shoulder and laughed. Socrates was such a magnetic person; his love for life was only outweighed by his love for his husband, Mike. It was an honour to be granted even a fraction of that sense of family by his boss.

"Thanks. I'll let you know my plans when I've figured them out." He walked past Socrates and up the grand staircase to his room, where he dumped his suitcase. What now? He needed to do something with this restlessness. He wanted to know how Victor was getting on with his puzzle. Yeah, just that, nothing else. He flopped on the bed, staring up at the ornate plaster ceiling. If only life and people were as simple as driving a car. It'd been months since he raced. After his own season finished in August, he'd driven in a few rally races, and he'd been the third driver for the S1 team, spending time in their pitlane just in case Ondrej or Paulo couldn't drive. It'd been good discipline, waiting, fucking waiting, and then more waiting, until he was going to explode with it. He couldn't just mope about here. He jumped up. With a couple of deep breaths, he jogged on the spot, before shaking out his hands. He was being a baby and he needed to stop avoiding Victor. *Stop being a fucking pussy, Lucien.*

Fuck. Having his father's voice echo in his head was the last thing he needed. He stripped off his jeans and threw on some running shorts. A good long run should get rid of all these bloody competing voices. No one would be out on the grass gallops at this time of day—late in the afternoon—so he'd go over to the racehorse side of the farm where no one would see him and just run until his brain stopped circling with all of this crap.

———

Victor wasn't any closer to solving this puzzle and he really needed to focus on next season. In three days, it would be Christmas—his self-imposed deadline—and he still hadn't replied to his mother's email about Christmas dinner. He thumped the desk with his fist. Sitting here alone was a waste of time. Everyone else had left for the week and he had ... well, no decent progress except a bunch of data proving that he had nothing new. Victor had gone around and around in circles, like a kid on one of those old spinning things in a playground. This puzzle had the same dizzy hopelessness, just being flung around, clinging on tight, hoping not to fall off and scrap his knees on the grass. Decision made, he pulled out his phone, dialled, and leaned back in his chair.

"Ma."

"Victor. It's so good to hear from you. When are you coming home?"

"Tomorrow." He informed her of his decision. "Tomorrow."

"Brilliant."

"Are you working too hard?"

"Ma!" Victor choked on a laugh, then sighed. "Yes. You know I am."

"Come home. Have a break and let me look after you."

"I'm not your baby boy anymore." He was nearly thirty.

"You'll always be my baby."

"Ma." Victor protested but not very much. "I'm lucky to have you as my mother."

She chuckled. "You certainly know how to give me an early Christmas present. I can't wait to see you tomorrow."

"Tomorrow, Ma. See you then." He hung up, then stood up and tucked his phone into his pocket. He'd better go home and pack. It was a long drive to Dochgarroch; he'd need to get an early start.

An hour later, after checking the workshop was locked up and secured for the next few days, he got in his car to drive down the road to Syresthorpe. He flicked on his headlights as he drove down the driveway. A shadow startled him, and he slammed on the brakes just in case an animal had gotten loose from one of the paddocks. There was a thump on his window. He twisted around.

"Lucien?" Victor opened the window of his car.

"Fuck me, Victor. You nearly ran me over." Lucien opened the car door and slid into the passenger seat.

"Sorry."

"I'm kidding." Lucien's cheeky grin settled the squirm in his stomach. "Really."

"What were you doing out so late? I thought you'd gone on holiday?" Victor had too many questions and he struggled not to fire them out in the same rapid fire as his heart was racing.

"Yes. I had a few days away in the sun. I'm back now. I was outside because I'd gone for a run."

"A run?"

"Victor. The first race of the new season is in a month."

Victor was glad he was still stopped in the middle of the driveway. He rubbed his eyes. "No. I still have three months." Next year's car was almost ready to go—he'd spent nearly a year designing and refining it—but this engine drama needed resolution in case it impacted on the new design. Obviously. He really needed a few days with his family to get out of his own head. It just went around and around and around without solution.

"Yeah, you do. Series E's first race is at the end of January. S1 doesn't start till the end of March. You have time. I don't."

"Right. Of course." Regardless of the details, Victor had run out of time; he needed to get the new car ready for pre-season testing.

"Would you mind giving me a lift back to the big house? It's cold outside and now I've finished running, I don't want to cool down too much."

Victor nodded and turned the car around. Lucien

fiddled with the heater and a blast of warm air filled the car with the scent of Lucien's sweat. It shouldn't smell so enticing.

"Come home with me."

"Excuse me?"

Victor swallowed. How could his throat be dry and wet at the same time? "Um, come home with me for Christmas? My parents won't mind an extra person."

"Sure. I'm not doing anything else."

"Seriously?"

"Yes."

"I'm leaving tomorrow morning. Early. Shall I pick you up?"

Lucien shoved Victor on the shoulder. "Are you driving?"

"Yes."

"In this?"

"Of course." Victor gulped. "What is wrong with my car?"

"Nothing. It's just ... boring. I'll pick you up at seven. I'll drive and you can direct me."

Victor laughed to cover the rush of heat at Lucien's command. "Come at six." He pulled up at the front of Socrates' house, and Lucien jumped out.

"I can do six in the morning, sure. How many days should I pack for?"

"Four nights." Victor couldn't stay too long. He had so much work to do.

"See you in the morning. Bright and early!" Lucien closed the door of Victor's car and walked away. Victor put his boring car into drive and went home with a wide grin on his face. This was likely ill-advised, but he didn't care anymore. His phone beeped with a message which he ignored until he pulled into the driveway of his home in Syresthorpe.

Lucien: How far are we going?

Victor: Why?

Lucien: I want to select an appropriate car.

Victor: From Socrates' collection?

Lucien: Yes. I don't own a car.

Victor called and Lucien answered with a 'what'? "You don't own a car. But—"

"I'm a race car driver. I know. I know. The thing is, though, I don't need a car. When I'm in Monaco I use cabs and when I'm here I borrow one from Socrates, and when I'm anywhere else, I'm working or I use ride shares or whatever."

"That makes sense. Um, we are headed up to Dochgarroch Locks. I'll see you in the morning."

"Sure. Is six too early?"

"It's fine, as long as you let me go to sleep now."

Lucien chuckled, the sound warm against Victor's ear. "I do know how grumpy you get when you haven't had enough sleep."

Victor rolled his eyes. "Good night, Lucien." He hung up before he could say something far too intimate. The reminder of waking up Lucien's bed was going to haunt him all night.

CHAPTER 7

ictor stood under the shower with the water slightly too hot. He hadn't slept well, not with the spectre of spending a whole day in a car with Lucien, followed with seeing all his family again. God, he missed his family. His older sister, Collette, had married a Scotsman named Gordon McKay, and they ran the inn at Dochgarroch Locks that had been in Victor's mother's family forever. Their son, Rory, was an eight-year-old terror. The paintings by his great-great-times however many-grandmother still hung in pride of place in the main dining area. Victor's favourite was the portrait she'd done of the canal engineer David Mattson in 1812 when the locks were still under construction. And his younger sister, Nicole, had finally settled down to start a degree in law after a five-year gap year. He was so proud of her for taking the time to work out what she wanted.

He turned off the water, dried himself, and was just pulling on pants when there was a loud knock at the door.

Victor glanced at his phone for the time. Lucien was ten minutes early.

"Give me a second." He muttered, threw on a shirt, then walked out of his bedroom, down the hall and opened the door. Lucien stood on his porch under the yellow glow of the artificial light wearing a green linen shirt that made the amber streaks in his brown eyes more apparent than usual. Paired with jeans and a casual puffer jacket, Lucien made the ordinary appear extraordinary. Hell, Victor was in so much trouble.

"Good morning."

"Come in. Do you want a coffee or something?"

"No. There's one in the car for you. Grab your stuff. We have a long drive ahead of us."

Victor nodded. "Yes, we do." He went inside and grabbed the small suitcase he'd packed the night before, then locked his front door. It was too dark to see which car Lucien had borrowed for their road trip. "Which car?"

"The 1957 Merc 300SL Gullwing."

"Seriously? Socrates let you take that out?" Victor peered into the dusky street and saw the silver glinting under the streetlight. The car was Victor's favourite in Socrates' collection; sleek, sexy, iconic, with the gullwing doors that opened upwards, rising like, well ... gull wings, above the car. It was worth something like a million pounds; in original Mercedes silver with red leather interiors.

"Yes. It's the privilege of being one of his S1 drivers; past or present. We can take any of his collection whenever we want. And this one is the best for a long road trip, it hugs the road, is a smooth ride, and has comfortable seats."

"I guess you are driving then." Victor knew he was allowed to drive some of the collection on the test track, but the idea of taking a car like the 300SL on a road trip was beyond his comprehension. And Socrates just said it was cool because Lucien had ... well, Lucien was one of the world's best drivers. If anyone could care properly for a rare car, it was him.

Lucien laughed. "Fucking nine hours, Victor. I looked it up. Your family home is a bloody long way away. No, we will share the driving."

Victor pressed his hand against his chest. "Socrates said I could drive the 300SL?"

"Yes. You can drive a manual transmission, yeah?"

"Of course." Victor couldn't believe it. He loved this car so much. Sometimes he visited it during his lunch break and just stared at it.

"Good. Just because I drive for my job, doesn't mean I'm going to chauffeur you for nine bloody long hours." Lucien winked and Victor's shoulders relaxed. "We will change every two hours."

With the boot of the sports car filled with the fuel tank and the spare tyre, Victor placed his suitcase inside one of the two custom built storage cases that sat behind the seats. A box was tucked on the floor on the passenger side of the two-seater. "What's in the box?"

"Christmas presents for your family."

"You didn't have to do that."

"Socrates did it. It's just merch, so it's not super special." Lucien jumped in the driver's seat and Victor climbed into the passenger side with his legs pressed against the cardboard box. The car roared to life with the turn of the key, and Lucien pulled out onto the small village road.

"You'll have to do directions. This car is too old for Bluetooth or maps or whatever."

"Take the M1 and then the M6 to Glasgow. That's the first five hours."

Lucien turned on the radio and they listened to the latest in pop music as they drove north.

"Can I adjust the air?"

"Sure. I'm not Niki Lauda. I don't need all the dials perfectly aligned." Lucien laughed quietly.

"He did? Did you ever meet him?"

"Sadly, no. He died in 2019 when I was still in the lower ranks, but I saw it on a doco once. Someone mentioned that whenever he got in a car, any car, he'd adjust all the dials until they were exactly as he wanted them before he'd start driving."

"I guess when you are a legend, people notice stuff like that."

"Are you saying we all have quirky habits?"

Victor stared at the way Lucien's hands rested on the steering wheel. He really did have lovely hands, strong fingers, and a prominent vein that led towards his forearms.

"No? You don't have any?" Lucien asked in that teasing voice that felt like flirting but couldn't possibly be.

"Did you say you brought coffee?"

Lucien waved at the two travel mugs neatly stashed in the centre consul, and Victor handed one to Lucien before taking the other one and slowly sipping. Now that they were on the motorway, the miles disappeared. Lucien drove just above the speed limit, cruising in the fast lane. This early in the morning, and two days before Christmas, the roads were surprisingly empty, although the rush of people travelling to see family would soon make it impossibly busy. He finished his coffee and put the travel mug down, then rested his head against the seat, enjoying the way the car's straight six engine growled, a much preferred noise to the tinny pop music coming through the speaker. The Merc 300SL had been the fastest production car of the late-1950s with a clever mechanical direct fuel injection to boost power. The engineering design of the car with the super-leicht chassis was a perfect piece of design. Victor hoped that one day he would design such an iconic, incredible machine.

"Victor."

"Huh." Shit, had he fallen asleep?

"We are almost at Liverpool. Time for a quick bite to eat, then it's your turn to drive."

Victor glanced at his watch. Nine am. "Hell. Did I sleep for three hours?"

"Yes."

"I'm sorry."

"Why? I picked this car because the seats are comfortable. You've been working too hard lately and you need the sleep." The casual care in Lucien's voice filled his torso with warmth, wrapping around like a damned hug.

Victor chewed the ordinary muffin as fast as possible. They'd pulled off the motorway to grab fuel for the car and a quick breakfast for both of them. Lucien leaned against the bonnet of the car, eating his muffin slowly, looking like a damned model, while Victor ate quickly. He wouldn't dare suggest eating in the car. There was no way he wanted to be the dickhead who got crumbs on the leather upholstery.

"Relax. We have all day."

"Says the guy who has already driven this car."

"You are impatient to drive?"

"Yes. Some of us might be used to driving amazing cars all the time, but I'm not. This is—" He paused. "—like a dream for me. I had posters of this car on the wall of my bedroom."

"No boy bands for you, just the gullwing?"

Victor damned near choked on his muffin. "Boy bands? You had posters of boy bands on your walls, like One Direction or some shit?"

"No." Lucien growled. "Forget it. Are you done yet?" Lucien threw the rest of his food in the bin. He stalked around the car and sat in the passenger seat. Had Victor said something wrong? He ate the rest of his muffin without tasting it, then sat in the driver's seat. Lucien handed him the keys, still warm from his jeans pocket. Victor pulled the door shut and turned the key. The engine roared to life, yet he couldn't quite enjoy it because Lucien sat beside him with a sullen expression. He gingerly drove over the kerb onto the road, then eased the car into traffic. They'd gone about ten miles and Victor had settled into the rhythm of the car when Lucien cleared his throat.

"I'm sorry."

"For?"

"Being angry at you for mentioning my childhood. I brought it up, then blamed you for laughing at me."

"Hey." Victor didn't dare take his eyes off the road. "You are allowed to have feelings, especially about your childhood. I met your father. I would guess your childhood must've been pretty traumatic."

Lucien chuckled. "I swear if I didn't know your mother was a therapist..."

"What?"

"You are allowed to have feelings." The sarcasm rolled off Lucien in heavy waves.

"Well, you are."

"Was she really annoying when you were a teenager?"

Victor glanced at Lucien. "What? No. Besides I was away at boarding school most of the time."

"You were?"

"I didn't grow up in Dochgarroch. When I was a kid, my parents both worked in Carlisle on the border, then I went to high school in Manchester."

"That explains the lack of Scottish accent."

"Och, aye." Victor grinned as Lucien laughed. "My parents retired to the family inn a few years ago, and now just do online consulting. My oldest sister, Collette, and her husband have been running the inn for a decade or so now. She started out working for our uncle Craig when she was a teenager, then trained as a chef before taking on the business when he decided to retire and travel the world." Victor didn't tell the whole story; about how Craig's husband had died and left Craig a huge trust fund that no one had known about. Had Craig known? He must have. In the nineties, they'd expanded the inn from a tiny sixteenth century two room inn into a thirty-room hotel.

"How old are your parents?" Lucien asked.

"They were older when they had us, in their late thirties, so they are nearly seventy now."

"Hold up a moment. Aren't you the same age as me? This maths isn't adding up."

"I'm nearly thirty."

"So old!"

Victor shrugged. He had always known he was almost five years older than Lucien because driver's ages were frequently discussed by the media. "Not everyone has their age splashed across the media and internet."

"I have my own wiki page and everything. Random fans update it with my results which always gives me a thrill." Lucien stretched his arms out. "Sorry for teasing you about being old. I'm twenty-five, but some days I feel fucking eighty."

"Why?"

"I don't know. I guess I've always been an adult, even when I was a kid. My father wasn't a soft person, he didn't give me much of a chance to just be a kid."

Victor glanced at Lucien for a second before focusing back on the road. The long motorway cut through the countryside in a brutal fashion, efficient, but hardly moving with the land. "Let me guess, everything was focused on getting you to S1?"

"Yes. From the time I showed promise in karts as a youngster, all we did was travel around Europe to different championship events."

"What about school?"

"I did a lot of correspondence school."

"Like remote?"

"Yeah. There's a few specialist driving schools that the richer kids went to, but we couldn't afford that."

Victor nodded. "Yes, Paulo went to the one in England. It's a good system."

"If you can afford it." Lucien tapped his fingers on the dashboard. "Everything in motorsport is expensive."

"And yet talent will get you through. There are at least three drivers among the twenty who didn't have wealthy backgrounds."

"And the other seventeen do. Money talks in this sport, and it takes an extraordinary talent to overcome the lack of it."

Victor chuckled. "Did you just humble brag?"

"Excuse me?" Lucien shifted in his seat.

"It takes an extraordinary talent to overcome the lack of money." Victor mimicked Lucien's words, adding a flirty tone.

Lucien coughed. "I suppose I did. Look, I am talented—"

"Third in the Series E championship in your rookie season."

"Rookie..." Lucien breathed out. "True. It doesn't feel like my rookie season after having two years in S1, but yeah, it was my first season in Series E."

"It's a very different driving style and strategy."

"Yeah, the torque on an E car is so different to a petrol engine, so they accelerate and decelerate in a less organic way compared to what I was used to. Ultimately, a car is a car and the basic stuff like tyre management and brake temperature and all that stuff is the same. Learning to manage the battery was a new challenge."

"It's all about having bundles of talent..." Victor teased. It was odd to drive a beautiful car and tease Lucien; surreal, really. He must be on holiday because this wasn't like his normal everyday life.

"I'm not about to pretend I'm not talented. Besides, driving is the only thing I'm good at, so I may as well own it."

"Fair enough. Before this blasted engine issue, I would've said I was a talented engineer."

Lucien growled under his breath, reminding Victor of a cheetah warning another predator away from his cubs, just like his tattoo. "You are a talented engineer. You will figure it out because you are one of the best."

"Sure. Fifth best pick for Gamble Racing." Victor wasn't sure at all, but his deadline for resolving it had passed and after these few days away with his family, he had to get next year's car ready for pre-season testing. "If I assume it's an engine manufacturing issue, then there's nothing to do done about it anyway."

"Is it?" Lucien just didn't know when to quit, did he?

CHAPTER 8

Lucien didn't believe Victor's assumption, or rather, he didn't believe that Victor believed it. If it was an issue with the engine, then all the other cars running the same engine—a third of the grid—would've had the same problems.

"You don't know when to stop, do you?" Victor didn't hold back his annoyance with a stringent tone.

"What? I thought we were talking about the engine fires."

"We are. But I don't want to. There's nothing I can do until after Christmas, and I can't solve this blasted thing, so I'd rather not talk about it."

"Sure. Okay. Want to listen to some music?" Lucien asked. He was happy to change the subject. The old radio in the car only picked up some of the channels, so he fiddled with the dials for a while until he found something innocuous. He must've dosed off because suddenly he heard the engine change down gears, and he opened his eyes to see Victor pulling into a car park.

75

"Where are we?"

"Carlisle. Want to grab something to drink?"

"Water might be good."

"Cool. I'll grab some from the corner shop here and then it's your turn to drive again."

Lucien nodded, opened the door, and stepped out to stretch his body. When an older Indian man wandered over, Lucien smiled at him.

"Oh my word, a Merc 300SL with the gullwing doors. In real life."

"She's beautiful, isn't she?" Lucien loved talking to fans, he always soaked up the joy they brought. It'd been the best thing when he was a teenager, having fans in the lower leagues—the die-hard racing fans who couldn't get enough and the ones who wanted to see the next big thing before they were big just so they could say they knew first —it was the only time people showed that he mattered. His father brushed those fans away, saying that they were a distraction, and Lucien had taken the way that had pissed him right off and made sure he always gave his fans as much time as he could. If he could give them a fraction of the joy, they gave him, it was worth every extra moment.

"I can't believe it. Please can I touch her?"

"Sure. Want me to take a photo of you beside her?" Lucien asked, loving the way the man's eyes opened wide.

"That'd be fucking amazing." He fiddled with his phone a bit, then handed it over, and Lucien took several photos of him standing next to the car. The man's goofy grin filled the screen. Lucien handed him back his phone and he checked through the photos, then looked up.

"Thanks so much. I never thought I'd see one of these in real life. What a treat."

"No problem." Lucien smiled.

"Do I know you? You look so familiar."

Lucien shook his head. "Unless you are a car racing fan, I doubt it."

The man stared at him for a second, then Lucien could literally see the moment when he figured it out. "Holy shit. Lucien Grenville."

"Yes." Lucien held out his hand and the man shook it.

"Arav Singh. I knew I recognised you. It's such a thrill to meet an S1 driver in real life."

"I drive Series E now."

"Oh, I wondered where you'd gone when they replaced you with Sanchez."

Lucien smiled. "Technically I offered to go to the E class races first. Gamble Racing partnered with a big tech firm to launch a car there and it made more sense to drive where I could win, than stick with a slow S1 car."

"Makes sense. I'll have to check it out. Man, I can't believe it. This car is a legend. In real life." Arav's sigh summed up how Lucien felt too. The 300SL was a truly iconic sex-on-wheels car.

"Thanks. It belongs to my boss, actually."

"Oh. Well, he's a lucky guy, and you are lucky to be able to drive it."

Lucien nodded politely as Victor walked out of the shop, carrying two bottles of water.

"We'd better be on our way. It was nice to meet you."

"Thank you so much for the photos."

"No problem."

Arav turned to walk off, then spun around again. "Is that Victor Tsui? Gamble Racing's engineer?"

"Yes." Everyone on the pit wall got plenty of media attention during race weekends. The coverage was quite intense with cameras everywhere, and the fans loved being able to have access to the whole team on screen. It would be even more intense once the annual streaming show that covered the season was released in a couple of months. When that happened, Victor would be famous amongst fans of the show as well as racing fans. It was fascinating how the two groups mostly crossed over, but not always.

"You guys are friends?"

"Yes. I'm going to hang with his family for Christmas."

Arav smiled. "That's super cool. Could I trouble you for one more photo? With both of you?"

"Sure. Come on, Victor. You are famous now too!" Lucien laughed at the shy expression on Victor's face. He stood between both men, pulling them together and prompted Arav to hold up his phone and take a selfie. After a few shots, Lucien laughed and stepped away.

"We need to hit the road. Enjoy your photos and if you put them on your social media, remember to tag me."

"I will. This has been one of the greatest days of my life."

"Awesome." Lucien walked around the car and slid into the driver's seat and waited until Victor joined him in the car. They both pulled their doors shut and Lucien turned the key, revving the car a little bit just for Arav whose grin split his face. Lucien waved and drove off. Once they were a couple of miles down the road, he eased out a long breath.

"Is it hard?" Victor asked.

"What?"

"Talking to fans like that."

"Nah. I love their enthusiasm. It's weird though."

"What is weird?"

"How many of them say it's the greatest day of their life? Seriously."

Victor laughed. "I don't think that reflects how boring their life is. It's probably just excitement talking, and by the time the adrenalin wears off, they'll realise it wasn't that thrilling after all."

"Hey. People are always thrilled when they meet me." Lucien winked, uncaring if Victor saw or not. It was the vibe of it, and honestly, so nice to tease someone, rather than be mad at the whole world all the time. Was this progress? He'd have to remember to ask his therapist next week in their fortnightly appointment. "Can you pass me some of that water?"

They made good progress up the motorway and Lucien was pleased to notice that Victor slept again; he'd been working too many hours in the last couple of months trying to figure out this engine issue. It was an obsession for him, and Lucien probably shouldn't have prodded him about it. Ever since his father had died, he'd racked up a long list of things he had to apologise for, and now it was automatic to feel rage, then take a deep breath, and work out what he needed to say sorry for. It was a cycle he wanted to break, to get rid of the initial burst of anger at inconsequential things. But the habits of childhood took a long time to unlearn. As his therapist said, he could forgive himself for tripping over the same damned step over and over, because each stumble wasn't as bad as the one before.

"What is it about this car? I can't believe I slept again." Victor's voice had a slight hoarseness as he woke up from his snooze. Foolishly, Lucien wanted to wake up next to Victor every day and hear the same raspy voice in his ear, with his warm breath against his neck.

"You must need it. A more important question is where are we going to eat lunch?" He had to change the subject before he let some of this spill out in a ... He squared his shoulders to avoid an ugly word vomit that would be guaranteed to cause a mess.

"I don't know."

"Aren't you a local?"

Victor scoffed. "To Scotland? Yeah, which obviously means I know every restaurant in the whole place and have recommendations for you."

"Enough of the sarcasm. We are almost in Glasgow, over half-way to your parent's home. Let's stop off and get some lunch and go for a walk or something."

"In Glasgow. In winter. I have no desire to freeze my ass off."

Lucien laughed. "That's fair." It was a nice day for a road trip. The sun was out, and the heater in the car made him forget that the outside air was crisp and cool. It'd probably freeze overnight. "Why don't you look on your phone and figure out somewhere, then direct me."

"Direct you, or give you directions to the place?"

"That depends on what you want..." Lucien immediately regretted opening his mouth. What if Victor thought he was flirting? Shit. He was flirting with Victor. This couldn't end up anywhere good; of course, he had to go and ruin a good friendship by thinking about sex. He really should've gotten laid during his break at the Maldives.

"Lucien." Victor's admonishment reinforced it. There was a long silence, an empty silence filled with regret, but Lucien couldn't figure out what to say.

"I take it we want something close to the motorway, so we aren't doing a lot of extra driving?" Victor asked.

"Sure." Lucien took the relief that came from a basic question and clung onto it. "And make it somewhere nice. Life is too short to eat boring food."

"Okay. Oh, and turn onto the M73, then the M80. There's an Italian place a few miles ahead."

"Perfect. Let's go there." Lucian could eat a pizza, or maybe some pasta. He hadn't really eaten enough today, just coffee, a muffin, and some water. His trainer, Hettie, would be annoyed at him. "Do they have parking?"

"Um." Victor flicked his thumb over his phone screen. "Yeah, looks like it."

"Okay. Direct me."

"You just love saying that, don't you?" Victor's quiet chuckle washed across Lucien's skin, distracting him from the task of driving for a second. Nothing distracted him from driving, oof, that wasn't good at all. With anyone else, he would've said something cute, like 'you know it baby', but this was Victor and he really didn't want to make their friendship awkward, so he ended up just mumbling a yeah in response. Victor read out directions off his phone map, and soon enough, they were parked outside an old pub with a sign that promised an authentic Italian restaurant.

"Let's hope it's as good as the reviews."

Lucien rolled his eyes. "Never trust internet reviews. It's

either, Five stars, so amazing, I wish I could give it ten, or one star, the worst experience of my life. No one who has a mediocre experience bothers with a review. Have you ever seen someone write, yeah, it was fine?"

Much to Lucien's pleasure, Victor laughed loudly. "Is that what people write about you on the internet?"

"Grenville drove a mediocre race today." Lucien scoffed. "I try to stay off social media after every race, just let the chat die down for a few days before I read the memes. Some of them can be hilarious."

"I do love a good S1 meme. People are so clever."

Lucien had one saved on his phone. "Did you know there's one of you?"

"Me? Why?"

"It's a photo of you on the pit wall with your hand on your forehead. People write all sorts of comments to go with it."

"They do?"

"Yeah, wanna see?"

"Maybe after we sit down. I'm hungry." Victor walked inside the front door and spoke to the person on the front desk. They followed the young woman to a table near a roaring fire. She handed them menus, then another staff person came over with some table water.

"This is lovely. What do you want?" Victor asked. Lucien read the menu and couldn't pick anything. His leg jiggled under the table. The fire was too hot, and he plucked at his collar, then removed his jacket and slung it over the empty chair next to him.

"Fuck, I don't know. Maybe a pizza or something simple."

"How about we get two pizzas and share them? Then we can get two different types."

Lucien pushed his heel against the floor to stop his leg moving. "Sure. Fine. How about you chose?" He stood up. "I'll be back soon." He walked quickly to the back of the restaurant, hunting for the toilets. He was actually a little dehydrated, not really needing to go, but he needed to move. He'd been sitting for too long, even though he'd slept during the times he wasn't driving. Road trip driving was a different type of concentration to race driving; it didn't take the same amount of energy or focus. The same restlessness that had bugged him yesterday returned, and he could hardly go for a two-hour run now, not while they were on a schedule. He locked himself in a cubicle, pissed, flushed, and then buttoned up his jeans again. After washing his hands, and with a few quick breaths, he began. He shadow-boxed the wall, running rapidly on the spot, until he was out of breath. And then just a little bit longer so his lungs burned. Good. He shook out his hands. Took a long deep breath. Okay. His brain had settled a little, enough. It had to be enough.

"Right, what did you order?" Lucien slid back into his chair as if nothing had happened. Yes, he was pretending to himself, or as his therapist liked to say, he was visualising the future he wanted and putting his goals into practice.

"I got a traditional Margherita and a Gamberi, so I hope you like garlic and prawns."

Lucien nodded. "Sounds good."

"I also got a little starter to share. Some bruschetta with tomato and oregano."

Lucien had nothing to add. His damned leg was jiggling

again, and he shoved it hard into the floor. "Tell me about your father. You don't really talk about him." Lucien needed something to distract him, anything, even a story about a father. Fuck, he must be desperate for a distraction.

"He's a good bloke. An engineer—"

"Your inspiration?" Lucien was glad he'd asked, although the similarity between them hit him like a slap in the face too. His own father was a race car driver and obsessed with his son following—improving—on his own record.

"Yes and no. He's an electrical engineer; you'd get along with him well. He thinks Series E is the future too."

Lucien winked at Victor. "He is correct."

"This is going to be such fun."

"What?"

"Listening to the two of you talk crap to each other."

Lucien paused. "Hold up. You get along with your father?"

"Yes."

"You are lucky."

"I know. And I'm sorry that you didn't have that. Every child deserves to know they are loved and cherished."

Lucien leaned forward. "You want children?" He expected a yes, but Victor shook his head slowly.

"No. My job is such long hours. I would be travelling all the time and I wouldn't be able to give a child the time and attention they need. I'm happy to spoil my nephew Rory."

"Cool." Lucien had never given it any thought. Actually, no, that was a lie. He breathed in and leaned back in his chair. He didn't believe he was capable of a relationship, let alone caring for a vulnerable child. His anger still flashed too often. Thankfully his ruminations were interrupted by the arrival of their bruschetta.

"Thank you." He smiled at the waitress. After she'd walked far enough away so she wouldn't hear him, he winked at Victor. "You know that bruschetta is just fancy toast."

"And you just drive fast." Victor grinned.

"Hey, there is more to it than that."

"Just like there is more to bruschetta than simply being fancy toast. Eat up, we still have four more hours of driving ahead of us."

Lucien ate a slice of the fancy toast. The fresh tomato and oregano was fragrant, wholesome, and enhanced by a simple olive oil and pepper dressing. "Good choice."

"Excuse me?"

"Picking this place. It's warm and the food is delicious."

Victor flushed a little with a dash of colour across his cheeks. Lucien was about to tease him when the waitress reappeared with a coffee for each of them.

"I thought it might be a good idea, given how far we still have to go."

"Thanks." Lucien's torso tightened, unexpectedly, and he knew what he had to do. "I'm going to drive the next stint."

"But it's my turn."

"I know, but this way, you get to drive the last bit, meaning you'll be the one to arrive at your parent's home. It's the glamour moment."

The flush on Victor's face deepened in colour. "Oh. That's very considerate of you."

"No problem. I'm more than just a driver, you see."

Victor grinned. "I know." Just as the air thickened and almost became weird, Victor frowned. "It'll be dark when we arrive, so it doesn't matter who is driving."

"Their house doesn't have lights?"

"Yes. We do have electricity in Scotland, you know."

Lucien loved the outrage on Victor's face. "Then text your mother. Tell her when we will arrive and to wait outside with the lights on."

"Sure. It's so simple."

"Yeah. It is. Come on, she's a beautiful car. Don't you want everyone to gush over her?"

CHAPTER 9

f Victor had been someone else, he would've said Lucien was flirting with him. Definitely flirting. But no, it couldn't be. It only felt, in the depths of his heart, that Lucien meant he would gush all over Victor, that it wasn't about the car, but about Lucien wanting to give Victor a moment to shine.

"She is a gorgeous car. My favourite one in Socrates' collection." He ignored the swell in his chest, and lower, to focus on reality.

"I know."

Victor's brain froze. All the warmth fled, leaving his body icy. "How? How do you know that?" He stared at Lucien and forced himself to shut his mouth as he tried to compose himself. The very idea that Lucien paid him enough attention to know his favourite car was a bit overwhelming. It made no sense - Lucien didn't have the time or the inclination to care that much about Victor's favourites. Or to want to gush over him. It was all nonsense; just the product of an overactive imagination.

"You do realise that the whole collection has 24-7 security cameras including heat sensors. Socrates suggested taking this car because he knows you spend time..."

It was nothing to do with Lucien, then. His breath whistled out slowly between clenched teeth. Victor had forgotten about the security cameras, and all of this came down to Socrates knowing that he came to stare at the car. It was eerie to think anyone bothered to look at the security recording when they didn't need to. They were merely back up in case a car was stolen, or whatever. "Staring at her. Yes, whenever I'm stressed, I like to go and look at the 300SL."

"Why this one?"

"Apart from the aesthetics, this car broke all the rules with a tubular light-weight frame and made it work. Its innovative design is something I admire and aspire to."

Lucien blinked. "Wow, you really love her."

"I do. I'm not afraid to admit that. She's the pinnacle of mechanical engineering design for her era, a triumph of material usage and the clever fuel injection system was so innovative at the time."

"And all wrapped in a sexy package." Lucien's grin reflected the intense love Victor had for this car.

"Yes. Some cars are wonderful because they are innovative and some are amazing because they are beautiful. The 300SL is a rare example that is both aesthetically pleasing and cleverly designed."

"And fast."

"Of course." Victor could talk enthusiastically about this car all day. "I'm a race car designer and engineer. Absolutely, my favourite car is a fast one."

Lucien winked. "Not the Lamborghini tractor for you?"

"What? No." Victor squinted at Lucien's weirdness. "Would you prefer a transit van over a sports car?"

The way Lucien grinned made Victor's stomach flip flop. "Perhaps if I needed to move a piano."

"How many times have you ever needed to ... move a piano?"

"Never. But maybe one day I will."

Victor couldn't imagine Lucien sitting still long enough to play a piano. Even when he was driving, he wasn't still. "Sure. What is your favourite car?"

"Whatever I'm winning in." Lucien winked. "That's pretty much it."

"Really?"

"Yes. You are bisexual; don't you understand?"

What? Victor didn't know what to say. After a couple of breaths, he swallowed. "Do you mean because bisexual people obviously can't make up their minds, or—"

"Jesus, Victor. Not as a slur. Just because cars are all amazing for different reasons, just as people are beautiful to you for different reasons. Why should I have a favourite?"

"One day you might have a favourite person, then you'll understand." Victor realised he was staring at his plate, and he deliberately looked up. "I'm sorry I assumed—"

Lucien waved his hand. "Stop looking at me like that."

"Like what?"

"Like you are trying to therapy me. Your expression screams that I just need to be loved by someone to make up for my awful childhood."

"Um—" Victor hadn't been thinking that at all, but the

accusation made him want to shrink away and apologise anyway. He'd been hoping, maybe, that Lucien might pick him as his favourite person, but of course that was a flight of fancy. Look at him. He could have any man in the world, why would he want a pedantic engineer? Especially one who was overly sensitive about how being bisexual meant he was erased constantly. Fuck, he probably just wanted Lucien's confidence, he was who he was without caring what others thought of it. The arrogance of being able to dismiss any negative comment about his sexuality was as incredible as the way he drove a car. Perhaps both things came from the same place of arrogant cockiness.

"I'm kidding. Where is this pizza?" Lucien glanced over his shoulder.

"I'm sure it won't be far away. Have the last piece of bruschetta if you are still hungry."

Lucien cut the last piece in half and ate the slightly smaller piece.

"You can have the rest too. I'm okay." Victor pushed the share plate closer to Lucien who nodded once and ate the rest of the bruschetta. Victor tried his best not to stare at Lucien's mouth as he ate, and when Lucien's tongue darted out to lick away a crumb at the corner of his lip, Victor forced himself to stare into his half-finished coffee. Thankfully the waitress arrived with their pizza, saving Victor from himself.

"Thank you. This smells great." Lucien smiled at the waitress.

"If there's anything else you need, just wave."

"I think we'll be fine. Thanks again." Lucien said. He

waited until the waitress had walked away before starting to eat, and Victor was struck by his good manners.

"I hope you don't take this the wrong way, but I'm really impressed by how nice you are to the staff."

Lucien squinted at him. "Why would I take that the wrong way?"

"I don't know. Is it awkward that I noticed?" Victor tried to sink into his chair. Every time he opened his mouth, he was messing up.

"Nah. Just don't go all therapist on me again…" Lucien drummed his fingers on the table. "Fine. I'm nice to people because my father wasn't. He always treated service and retail workers as if they weren't people. And early on, I decided I was going to be everything he wasn't. A fucking much better driver for a start … And also all the smaller things like being nice to people who were being paid to help me and had to do be pleasant whether I was nice or not."

"That's a fair point. There are so many jobs where people don't have the option but to put up with whatever crap someone dishes out."

"Yeah, and what kind of asshole adds to that? Most of these people aren't getting paid very much. If I can be a decent human and that makes their day a little easier, then I'm going to do it."

Victor smiled. "I think you'd have figured that out, even without your father providing an example of how not to do it."

"And I thought I said not to go all therapist's kid on me." But Lucien was smiling, and so Victor knew he was only teasing.

———

It wasn't until they were back on the road, over an hour later, when Lucien tapped his fingers on the steering wheel. "Have you heard of a thing called hindsight bias?"

"No."

"It's where you look at the past and believe that you could've made better decisions."

"Is this a therapist thing?" Victor was surprised that Lucien would start that all over again. Lucien eased the car around a slower one, changing lanes smoothly. His command over the car would always be sexy, appealing, to Victor, and he had to stare out the window away from Lucien for a couple of breaths to push away the thought.

"Yeah."

"Okay. You've said that hindsight bias is returning to past decisions. Is it like saying, if I'd changed tyres at lap 34, instead of waiting until 37, I wouldn't have had a puncture?" Victor tried to hold back the breathy interest from his voice, but damn, he was so invested in why Lucien wanted to talk about this concept.

"In simple terms, yeah. But mostly it's a kind of lie that people tell themselves, that you could've made a different, better, decision in the past. Except you couldn't have because you didn't have the information you have now, back then; you only have it in hindsight."

Victor tried to stay quiet. A little hum of encouragement slipped out. Embarrassing.

"When you were talking earlier about being kind to people, it made me realise how bloody lucky I am. In hindsight, every other driver in the lower grades, from karting all the way through to S3 had at least one parent who supported them."

"It's an expensive sport."

"Yes. I've been thinking a lot about the drivers who had crappy parents. The type who pushed too hard, who behaved as if the kid's success was their own, who could imagine sitting in a S1 pitlane as a proud parent when their kid was not even a teen. Too many of those kids stopped. A lot of them had plenty of talent, but they didn't progress. They gave in to the pressures and gave up, and I think it's because there was more pressure coming from their parents than from the sport."

"But not you?" Victor didn't understand this line of conversation. "Wasn't your father one of the ones who pushed too hard?"

"Absolutely. He was toxic as hell and taught me that I needed to be angry and to trample everyone else to win."

"So why didn't his behaviour stop you from progress-ing? From being just like all those others? Why are you unique?"

Lucien took his hands off the wheel for a second and spread his hands wide before grabbing the wheel again. "Now isn't that the eternal question?"

"Yes." Victor low-key adored this introspective side of Lucien.

"Obviously I'm special."

"Obviously." Victor chuckled, then took a breath and made sure he sounded serious. "You've overcome a pushy parent to make your own success on your own terms."

Lucien cleared his throat. "Or it could be that my father died when I was in S3, and the sudden loss of his toxic words helped me work out my own pathway. Or it could be that I'm not actually that good. I only spent two seasons in S1 with twenty points in the first season and none in the next."

Victor shoved Lucien on the shoulder. "You made it to the top. You scored points in S1. Yes, you are that good. You were hamstrung by terrible cars, especially in your final season. Don't you dare tell me you aren't that good."

"I didn't say this to fish for compliments. I know exactly how good I am. Third in the Series E drivers title in only my rookie season and that had nothing to do with the car—"

"Because the cars are all almost the same spec in SE." Victor spoke at the same time as Lucien.

"Snap." Victor laughed.

"It's good for racing but it's not great for innovation."

Victor was surprised by the insight from Lucien. "I wouldn't have thought you'd care about that."

"The racing?"

"Ha." Victor rolled his eyes.

"Oh, the innovation. Because I'm just a driver, therefore I can't have thoughts?"

"I didn't say that."

"You literally did. You said I didn't care about innovation."

Victor sighed. "Okay, fine. I did imply that. I'm sorry."

"Victor. You don't need to apologise."

"I don't?"

"No. Fuck, you can be so serious sometimes. I was kidding, mostly."

"Mostly?" Victor's rush of anxiety didn't fade much.

"I feel like we've talked about this already. Just because we still have hours to go to get to your family's home, doesn't mean we need to completely rehash the discussion on how electric vehicles are the future and if Series E is serious about being part of that future, they should allow innovation in the same way they do in S1."

"It's not really hours. I mean, it's not the Outer Hebrides."

"Right. My ass tells a different story."

"Says the driver who drives for a job. Aren't you used to sitting down?"

Lucien's burst of laughter was worth it. "Yeah, that's why my ass is so lush."

Victor's face heated. "I don't want to think about your ass."

"Why not? It's a lovely ass. Good for—"

"No." Victor was going to burst into flames.

"Are you blushing? Victor. I thought you were a good boy and here are you thinking about my ass."

"Lucien. Watch the road."

"I am. ... Unfortunately." Lucien's voice deepened and Victor turned to stare at him. Neither of them spoke for a while until the silence became stifling. Victor played with the radio until he found a song with a heavy beat that could distract him and maybe hide the way his heart was beating far too fast and too loud.

CHAPTER 10

Driving with an erection wasn't very comfortable. Lucien couldn't even dismiss this burgeoning—annoying—attraction for his friend as something as simple as not having had sex for a while. There was that, of course, but it was more than that. It was the way Victor blushed so delightfully when Lucien unsubtly mentioned his own ass. It was the way Victor apologised unnecessarily when Lucien teased him. He probably shouldn't tease him with such a serious tone but damn if it wasn't so tempting to try and make him flush again. The way colour painted his cheeks gave him the hint of what Victor would look like after he'd been thoroughly kissed. Did Lucien really want to kiss his friend? Yes. He didn't need to make this complicated. Eventually, by focusing on the way the road moved with the land now they weren't on a major motorway, Lucien's dick finally softened to a more comfortable state, but he needed a distraction.

"I can't imagine you as a kid. What did you do?"

"Normal kid stuff."

Lucien ignored the tingle that swept across the back of his neck. "Indulge me, Victor. What normal kid stuff?" He knew enough about his childhood from talking to his therapist that he'd missed out on a normal experience. Most kids weren't set up with a replica driving kit and forced to play racing games on the telly. He'd never had any downtime away from learning about being a better driver. He hadn't minded, mostly, because he didn't know any different and he was obsessed with racing. It was fine. Totally fine.

"We would come up to the inn for a few weeks every summer and stay with Uncles Craig and Zac. I loved it there."

"Hold up a second. Your uncles were gay?"

"Yes. Craig ran the inn, and the story is that Uncle Zac just turned up one day and they fell in love. Zac stayed and that was it."

"When was that?" Lucien couldn't imagine how hard it would be to be openly gay in country Scotland way back when. People had always done it, carefully living with their best friend, or whatever, but it mustn't have been simple.

"The 90s. It was the heights of the AIDS crisis and Zac's family in America weren't very supportive."

"We are so lucky now." Lucien had always been out— not with a declaration—just in the way he lived each day, and he knew it was only possible thanks to generations of queer people doing the work to make the world a safer place for him.

"We are. There's still work to do."

"Yeah." And all the gains could easily be taken away with the swipe of a bigot's pen, which was why he enjoyed himself as openly as he wanted while things were good.

"Just look at the fuss the media made when Ondrej came out this season."

Lucien rolled his eyes. "The funniest thing of all was how many people talked about him being the first openly gay S1 driver."

"Why was that funny?"

Lucien slapped Victor on the thigh. "Seriously? I'd already been doing that for two seasons before he decided to announce it."

"True." Victor buried his face in his hands. "Does everyone erase you like that?"

"Yeah, but I don't mind. I'd rather the attention was on my driving. What I do away from the track is no one's business. Honestly, who cares about the driver's personal lives?" It was what his father had always said, and it was one of the few things he'd been correct about. Provided Lucien turned up fit and ready to drive, no one cared about the rest. The media attention was part of the job, and thankfully the media didn't treat it like a reality dating show. Fans sometimes got a little wild in their attentions; he'd had some DMs that overstepped the boundary but he shrugged them off as part of being a public figure.

"Did you notice much difference in the media attention when you moved from S3 to S1?"

"Loads." Lucien braked heavily as a semi-trailer changed lanes ahead of him. He followed the truck for a while, as they both went past the slower driver in the other lane, then went around the truck.

"Nicely done."

Lucien ignored the compliment to his driving. "Why haven't we talked about this before?"

"This?"

"The difference between S3 and S1. You must've noticed it too."

Victor nodded. "Definitely. I went from being an unknown assistant engineer to having the responsibility for the whole car. It was intense."

"Sure, but you must've noticed the difference in media attention too?"

"I guess so. There are a lot more cameras in the pitlane for S1, but I don't do interviews. That's the job of the drivers and the Team Principal."

Lucien nodded. It made sense.

"And I suppose we've never talked about it because we didn't do the change at the same time. You'd already done two years in S1 when I joined Gamble Racing."

"And I'd moved on to SE."

Victor laughed, all of a sudden, and Lucien risked glancing away from the road. He wanted to know what was funny about the way they'd missed working together. There was no clue on Victor's smiling face, so he slipped back into driver mode.

"This is probably the most time we've ever spent together when we aren't working," Victor said.

"Except for the night you spent asleep in my bed."

Victor's blush was everything. His face went pink all the way to the tips of his ears. "Why would you say that?"

Lucien thought it was rather obvious, but he decided to give Victor a little relief. "You wanted to know what I felt when the media thought Ondrej was the first openly gay S1 driver."

"Yes."

"I shrugged it off because I hadn't really mentioned my own situation much. If it ever came up—you know, being gay—I was happy to talk about it, but it never did. Anyone could've asked; I've never hidden it and you've seen my social media... It just shows that most fans don't care about a driver's relationships or whatever. They care about how the car felt, and why I'd missed the apex on turn two, or what happened during an incident. Besides, Socrates is right there, married to Mike. No one is ever the first."

"What do you mean?"

"Every record that gets broken, every time someone achieves something that hasn't been done before, none of it comes from nowhere. They are all building on what came before. The first car came after the first carriage. Everything is built on something before."

Victor made an odd noise. "You are talking about innovation, not firsts."

"Isn't it the same thing?" Lucien was tired of talking around in circles. "Look, I don't know. Yes, I was a bit jealous when the media were so excited about Ondrej being the first, when I'd been right there for the two years before, and Socrates before that, but it's not Ondrej's fault. I know I'm too quick to anger on these things, on everything, so I just—"

"What? Tried to suck it up and deal with it in private?"

"Yes. I literally don't care if anyone knows I'm gay."

Victor patted Lucien on the shoulder, and he breathed in, enjoying the touch of a friend. "People only talked Ondrej up as the first because he made a big statement."

"The press love having their job done for them!" Lucien

laughed. "Look, I can see why Ondrej did it. For Love." He deliberately made it sound sarcastic.

"It's nice that he did that."

"Yeah, I get it. He wanted Hudson to be with him all the time, and with cameras everywhere, people notice when someone attends every race." Lucien completely understood the urge. "You've seen other drivers kiss someone after a race win. Imagine having your husband right there and wanting to kiss them without people making a big deal about it. I get it."

"Do you think it was more about that, then?"

Lucien nodded. "Yeah, being able to kiss someone special and have everyone just accept it without having to explain, yes, yes, I'm gay, on top of it. It's boring and it detracts from the thrill of winning. I completely understand why Ondrej wanted to make a statement before his actions caused a drama. It's so frustrating that we need to, but I get it. I guess if I had a relationship with someone, I'd probably do the same, so I could focus on enjoying a win with that person without pesky questions."

"Makes sense. That doesn't sound like something that would cause anger?"

Lucien realised he'd sped up quite a bit and he backed off the accelerator. "I'm trying to control my outbursts, that's all."

"Overcoming childhood trauma is an ongoing process."

"Says Mr Therapist's Kid." Lucien breathed in, then out, as the familiar ball of red heat rose up through his chest, spearing into his head. "Fucking hell."

"Hey." Victor rested his hand on Lucien's shoulder—

again—a warm reassuring presence. "You can give yourself some leeway in this process. No one expects perfection."

"I don't want to be perfect. I just don't want to be like him." Lucien spat out the last word, knowing Victor would understand that Lucien meant his father.

"Lucien. You are nothing like him. A few flashes of anger don't make you like him."

"What?" Lucien saw a driveway up ahead and pulled over into it because his eyes were too hot. They prickled and burned.

"You are nothing like him. Did he ever try to stop being angry? Would he care about the well-being of a friend and make them sleep when they needed it? Did he ever apologise for anything?"

Lucien turned off the car. His hands were trembling. "Can you drive for a while?" He stepped out of the car and the cold winter air punched him in the face. He stumbled towards the wooden fence post at the edge of the gate in front of him and grabbed onto it, half-bent over, just breathing. Nausea rose, acidic in the back of his throat. His chest felt like he'd been crushed under a truck. What was happening to him?

"Hey, just breathe." Victor rubbed circles in the middle of his back. "It's okay. You are okay."

He wasn't. But slowly with every breath and every gentle reassuring touch from Victor, he started to feel like he might be able to believe Victor.

"You are nothing like him. You are my friend. I would never be friends with anyone like him. I don't put up with that type of mean bullshit."

Lucien's heart clenched tighter and tighter with every

determined word from Victor. For years, his therapist had been telling him he wasn't like his father because he wanted to change, because he saw the problems with his father's toxic behaviour and he didn't want to replicate it, and because he cared for other people. But none of that had really stuck until Victor validated it all by saying he wouldn't be his friend if he was a shithead like his father. The truth in his Victor's words finally let him believe it. He'd worked hard not to be an asshole, and someone else— someone whose opinion mattered to him—saw it. Saw him.

"I am nothing like him." Lucien's whisper wasn't convincing, but it settled the bile rising in his throat. He stood up tall. "I am not like him."

"You are my friend." Victor kept his hand in the middle of Lucien's back. Such a light touch, almost imperceptible through his shirt. It was too cold to be standing outside in this wind, wearing only a shirt, but he'd leaped out of the warm car without thinking about grabbing his jacket.

"And you wouldn't be friends with an asshole."

"I wouldn't. Absolutely. I would never be friends with an asshole."

The frigid wind was the only thing stopping Lucien bursting into flames. Lucien's body was going to burst out of his skin. Everything was prickly and weird and too hot and too cold all at once. He spun around and kissed Victor. Not a light fun kiss, but a fully aggressive 'I need to fuck you right now' kiss. Finally he had the taste of Victor on his lips and his whole body leaned into the kiss, slowly relaxing with every needy thrust of his tongue into Victor's mouth ... Except Victor was tense and unmoving. Shit. Lucien launched himself backwards, away from

Victor, and his spine hit the wooden fence post with an oomph.

"I'm so sorry."

"It's okay."

"It's not. I just assaulted you." Lucien couldn't breathe. His lungs were too tight.

Victor had that calm expression that always impressed Lucien. "No. You just took me by surprise. I'm not exactly your type."

"Would you kiss me back if I said you were my type?"

Victor's throat moved up and down as he swallowed. "But I'm not."

"What on earth makes you say that?" Lucien had no idea what Victor had based this on.

"I've seen your social media. Every photo of you on break is with some beautiful, sculptured, man."

Lucien was losing the plot; he couldn't understand what was happening. The rush of emotion made everything confusing. "You've been social media stalking me?"

"No. I mean, I follow you, that's all."

"They were just hook ups." The photos were more about the places he visited than the people he shared his bed with. Lucien only wanted to fuck them or be fucked; he liked all types of sex. He didn't want to talk to them or kiss them. He didn't care about them, except to enjoy some fun together, and he certainly wasn't going to listen to their opinion on anything. Oh. The difference hit him like the impact of slamming into a tyre wall at 200 kilometres per hour, winding him. He almost instinctively said that he was okay, just like he would on the radio after a crash.

Victor folded his arms. "See. Look at your face. The very idea of me as a romantic prospect has you stunned."

"Victor. Only you could have this discussion on the side of a road in this fucking cold wind and use romantic prospect to describe ... this."

"Okay?"

"I don't want to treat you like a hook up. You are worth more than that to me. I want to kiss you and treasure you. I want to pour all my needs into you and know I'm cared for."

"Oh."

"Yes. Oh." Lucien was breathing hard, as if he'd been pushing himself on a treadmill. Neither of them said anything for what felt like an agonisingly long time.

"Can I kiss you?" Victor asked and Lucien nodded. He really wasn't going to mess this up by being too aggressive again.

"Can I?" Victor asked again.

"Please kiss me." Lucien wanted another taste of Victor, and he took a half-step towards him but stopped when Victor held up his hand.

"Wait. Not here." Victor glanced over his shoulder at the traffic passing along the road behind them.

Lucien didn't give a flying fuck about who might see them. Surely Victor knew that; they'd talked about only a while back. "Wherever you want."

"Tonight. I want to wait until we are somewhere warm, and we can kiss properly without freezing."

"Promise?" Lucien could ignore a little bit of cold, even though he had gooseflesh all down his bare arms and he'd started to shake now the rush of heat had faded.

"Yes. Now hand over the keys and I'll drive the last three hours."

Lucien did as he was asked and slid into the passenger seat. The rumble of the engine, the warmth of the heater, and the comfy leather seats added to the peace that had come from having Victor affirm that Lucien was nothing like his father. All this emotion, and promises of a proper kiss, were quite tiring.

CHAPTER 11

I t was dark when Victor drove up the driveway in front of the Dochgarroch Inn. The sun set early in December in Scotland, and the light had already been fading when he'd taken over to drive the last section. Lucien had fallen asleep soon after they'd pulled back onto the road. Every now and then during the drive, Victor had touched his own lips, remembering the way Lucien had kissed him. Fuck, he kissed like he wanted to celebrate winning, and even though it'd surprised Victor to the point of immobility, he'd loved every moment of being taken over like that. As if Lucien couldn't stop himself and he just needed to kiss Victor like the kiss was the only thing that mattered in the whole world.

"We are here." Victor touched Lucien on the shoulder, and he jerked awake.

"Huh?"

"Welcome to Dochgarroch Inn." Victor parked the car outside the oldest part of the inn and tooted.

"I'm awake. Hell, you don't have to be so noisy." The

way Lucien sat up straight and shook his head was cute and it took a fair amount of control not to grin goofily at his friend. His smoking hot friend who'd kissed him and had looked ... keen ... when Victor had suggested more kisses. With a long breath out and a reminder that he couldn't get out of the car and see his family while sporting an erection, Victor turned off the car and reached for the door. Family. It helped to stare at the Inn and not look at Lucien.

"Wait." Lucien's voice had a commanding note that didn't help Victor's situation at all.

"Okay?"

"Don't open the doors until your family can see. I want them to enjoy this car as much as you do."

The reminder of his family was exactly what he needed, and he tried not to adjust himself in an obvious way. "So, we just sit here until they come out into the cold?"

"Text them." Lucien rolled his eyes and Victor took the hint because he needed to make himself wait. He had family to deal with before he could even begin to explore this changing dynamic between himself and Lucien. He picked up his phone and sent a quick text to the family group. For a few long minutes, they sat awkwardly staring at the door with Lucien's leg jiggling up and down, and Victor not wanting to ask if he was nervous. It was obvious and he didn't want Lucien to snap at him then regret it. Finally, the front door to the inn arrived and Victor's family piled out, led by Uncle Craig.

"Is that your Dad? He looks just like you, but bald." Lucien's teasing comment sounded a little wobbly.

"No. That's Uncle Craig, Ma's brother. My father is the slender grey-haired man who is just coming through the door now." The whole family stood on the front step of the inn.

"Open the doors now." This time, Lucien's voice was suave, as if he'd gotten over his nerves to regain control of the situation. Everyone's eyes opened wide as the gullwing doors opened, stretching above the car's roof. Lucien was right, it was worth the wait to see their reaction. Lucien stepped out of the passenger seat and Victor realised he was staring at the way Lucien's jeans stretched over his ass as he stood up. Victor cleared his throat—patience—and got out of the car too.

"Victor!" Ma bundled him into a hug, then Pa's arms joined in. "It's so good to have you home. It's been too long."

"Leave the boy alone. He's been busy at work."

His parents stepped backwards. "Too busy to eat? Have you lost weight?"

Not much, and yes, he'd been too stressed to eat properly lately. "No, Ma. I'm the same as always." Victor glanced over at his shoulder to Lucien who was chatting to Uncle Craig about something. From the way he was gesturing, it had to be the car.

"We miss you." Pa said.

"And I missed you both."

"What about us?" His sister Collette stood on the step next to her husband, Gordon, as she called out and Victor waved to them. Rory galloped towards him and threw his arms around Victor's waist.

"Uncle Victor. The car is super cool. Can I get in it?"

"Yes. And yes, I've missed everyone. It's nice to be home for a few days."

"Who is your guest?" Nicole yelled out as she walked over towards Lucien. She sported a light blue streak in her black hair and had a cute undercut.

A little rush of heat touched Victor's cheeks. "This is Lucien Grenville." Hopefully the evening dim hid his reaction.

Lucien smiled. "Thank you for inviting me to Christmas with your family."

"It's our pleasure. Victor has never invited anyone home before." His family knew he was bisexual, and Victor appreciated the way they kept things gender neutral.

"Ma." Victor protested, slightly too loudly because the memory of their kiss still hovered on his lips. "We are just friends. Lucien hasn't anywhere else to go."

Lucien laughed. "You don't have to make me sound so pathetic."

"It's not pathetic."

"Any friend of Victor's is always welcome here. We have plenty of room for guests." Victor's Ma said. "Lucien, please call me Melanie, and this is my husband, Peter. I see you've already met my brother, Craig."

"Yes."

"It's okay if you don't remember everyone's names." Victor wanted to rescue Lucien from his overly friendly family.

"If I can remember all six hundred people who work for Gamble Racing and all the names of the mechanics in my SE team, then I'm sure I'll be fine. Melanie, Peter, Craig, and ahhh—" Lucien pointed at Victor and everyone laughed.

"Come inside. It's cold out here."

Victor had to nudge Rory out of the car so he could grab their suitcases from the storage compartments, while Ma bundled Lucien inside the inn. He closed the car and locked it, before heading inside too. The warmth of the open fire in the lounge reminded him that he was home.

"This place is cool." Lucien's eyes danced as he looked around the lounge. It was interesting to try and see the place from Lucien's view; impossible, really, since Victor had spent every summer holidays as a kid here back when Craig and Zac had run the place and every holiday break here now.

"Yeah, in the 90s, Zac built a big extension to the inn that is used for guests, and the original part of the inn is now Collette and Gordon's home. That's um—"

"Your sister. I met her outside."

"Yes. She's married to Gordon, who seems to have disappeared, but he's probably over in the actual hotel part of the inn. And their son, Rory, is the kid. Um, they run the place now that Craig is retired."

Lucien leaned in close. "And Zac?"

"He died of lung cancer a couple of years ago. It's just Craig now."

"I'm so sorry to hear that."

Victor swallowed. "It was a tough time for everyone. Zac was family." He'd been the best uncle and Victor still missed him deeply. Having happily married gay uncles had really helped him in his own journey of working himself out.

"Is that them?" Lucien pointed to the oil painting hanging over the hearth. Craig and Zac stood outside the inn, overlooking the locks at the end of the loch.

"Yes. And that one is the famous engineer David Mattson. He used to stay here when they were building the canal that goes from the Dochgarroch Locks through the lochs across to Banavie and Neptune's Staircase."

"There's a place in Scotland called Neptune's Staircase?"

"It's a series of locks at the other end of the canal."

Lucien nudged Victor with his elbow. "What interesting facts you know."

"What?"

"It's cool. Really."

"Okay." Victor was pretty sure that Lucien was teasing him. "We should go there sometime. It's clever engineering."

"Where would you go if you wanted to see engineering stuff that interests you?"

"I'm a mechanic engineer. Most of the stuff I'm interested in lives in car museums, although some of the original steam engines are neat."

"I'd be keen to take you to see stuff that makes you excited."

Victor raised one eyebrow, trying—and failing—to return Lucien's enthusiasm with a little sarcastic distance. "Would you?"

"Careful. Before you talk about what makes you excited, remember that your parents are just over there."

Victor was on fire. "Lucien." He growled under his breath and was rewarded with a smile that made Lucien's eyes twinkle.

"How's work? Did you figure out those engine fires

yet?" Pa joined their conversation with the only topic that could possible strip all the heat out of his body.

"No. It's ... infuriating."

"Do you want to talk about it?"

"No. Yes. I just don't understand. It's almost like each fire started in the exhaust, but it makes no sense, and we have no sensors in there, so we couldn't find anything on the data."

Pa didn't scoff; he was too kind for that. It just felt like it. "You and your data. Did you try cutting the exhaust pipes open and having a look?"

Victor held his breath for a moment. Why hadn't he thought of that? His brain screamed at him. It was so fucking obvious.

"Relax. You can do it when we get back to the workshop." Lucien said.

"But it's so simple. Why didn't I think of it?"

"Sometimes the simple things are the hardest to see." Pa waved over at the old bar at the edge of the lounge. They'd kept all the heritage features when they'd converted the original inn into a family home. "Come and have some local whiskey before we head through for dinner."

Victor nodded, numbly, and didn't move until Lucien slung his arm around his waist.

"Come on. Give me the tour."

"You want a tour? Of?"

"Of this super cute historical building that your family lives in. You didn't tell me any of this."

Victor glanced at Lucien. "Are you saying that to stop me thinking about work?"

"Yes. There's literally nothing you can do for a couple

of days. Stop stressing. The exhausts aren't going anywhere."

"Socrates could do it."

"Honestly?" Lucien sounded disbelieving.

"Well, he could." It was a good solution to the problem. Victor trusted Socrates to do a good job with the task and then he'd have more information quickly. Time was critical with not long to go before the new season started; it felt like everyday he couldn't figure this out would impact on next year in a cumulative way.

"Yes, that is technically correct. But do you want anyone else to do this? Surely if it matters, it means you should do it yourself."

Victor nodded. It was true. "I suppose it could wait." It burned him, having to wait, except Lucien was right. He really wanted to do this himself.

"Yes. Now your challenge is to think about, literally, anything else for a few days. Enjoy spending time with your family."

Victor fought the urge to jump back in the 300SL and drive all the way back to Syresthorpe and work. "Fine. Come and have a tour."

"You are still thinking about this, aren't you?"

"Yes. Of course." Victor had to plan carefully because any cut had the potential to destroy evidence and since he had no information about what he might find, he had to work out the lowest risk plan for any cuts they might do.

"You owe me a kiss." Trust Lucien to say the one thing guaranteed to stop Victor from thinking about work.

"Yes, I do." His mouth went dry and he licked his bottom lip, which made Lucien's eyes brighten. Just as

Victor started to lean towards Lucien, Collette handed them each a tumbler with a bronze liquid in the bottom.

"Here, Ma says you need a restorative after your long drive." She glanced between them both. "Are you two more than friends?"

Of course, Victor's face burned hot at the suggestion, and Collette cackled.

"No." Lucien's calm response soothed Victor like a splash of cool water on his heated cheeks. "Not yet, anyway. We are in the negotiation phase."

"Lucien." Victor sucked in a short breath.

"The what?" Collette's eyes danced with glee.

"The negotiation phase. You know; will we? Won't we? We've already shared a bed, and we spent most of the trip up here skirting around whether you are my type of not."

"Hell. Don't you have any boundaries?" Victor refused to look at his older sister who was coughing as if she'd swallowed her whiskey too fast. "Collette, I slept, just slept, in his bed. Once. It wasn't—"

"It might have been." Lucien leaned all the way in and brushed his lips across Victor's cheek. Holy shit. Victor was going to expire.

"Well, it sounds like you two boys have plenty to talk about." Collette's smirk as she walked away made Victor sigh.

"I'm never going to live this down now. Do you know how much my family love to tease me?"

"You are so easy to tease. I get it."

"What?"

Lucien took Victor's glass and placed it on the old bar

beside another glass, then held his hand. "Victor, you are my type, and you owe me a kiss. Take me somewhere."

"Now?"

"There's no time better than now." Lucien lifted Victor's hand and pressed a kiss to his knuckles.

"Not here."

"Then where?" Lucien kept kissing his knuckles, so Victor couldn't even think. He just stared at his hand, and the way Lucien's mouth softly kissed each knuckle. The chatter of his family faded into a faint background noise. Everything, except Lucien's lips on his skin, disappeared.

"Dinner is ready. Come on through." Pa clapped him on the back, and he almost punched Lucien in the mouth in surprise at the sudden interruption. "There'll be plenty of time for that later. Let's eat first."

"Yes, Mr Tsui." Lucien didn't let go of Victor's hand, merely straightened up and faced Pa while still holding Victor's hand like a precious object.

"Please, call me Peter. I don't want to feel like I'm at work."

Lucien smiled. "Peter. Now tell me, what do you do for work? Victor was very vague."

"I'm a retired electrical engineer."

Lucien's eyes lit up and Victor knew what was coming next. "And what are your opinions on electric vehicles?"

CHAPTER 12

Lucien was glad he'd slept for the last stint in the drive here because dinner with Victor's family was loud and fun and energetic. It was all the things Lucien had always imagined being part of a family would be like—just like on telly—and suddenly it seemed possible for him. They finished each other's sentences and laughed at each other's jokes and teased with kindness. When he was with Socrates, Mike, and Xenia, there was a similar vibe, but he always felt like an interloper with them, an intruder on their small family. Victor's family included him without making a big deal of it and maybe it was just that there were more of them, so his presence wasn't so obvious.

Kissing someone because he liked his family was a foolish reason to kiss Victor. Lucien didn't care. He was quickly becoming obsessed with the idea of kissing Victor and holding his friendship and his family close to his chest. It was all so new, this idea of a family who stuck up for each other. His father had only cared about getting into the Series leagues, but he hadn't cared about anything else.

Kurt didn't care about Lucien the child, or Lucien the person, only Lucien Grenville, the driver and brand name. Lucien couldn't resist these people who cared about him; not his ability to drive a car fast. Him.

Since sharing a bed with Victor, having his warmth beside him all night, the comfort of his steady breaths, Lucien had started to notice Victor. The way the corners of his eyes crinkled when he grinned. The way he frowned when he paced back and forth in the workshop. The remnant panic on his face when he'd put out yellow flags on the day Lucien had taken one of the Ferraris for a drive on the test track in the rain. Lucien hadn't seen Victor's initial reaction—since he'd been driving—but he'd seen the way Victor had resolutely scolded him for driving in the wet. There'd been no need for such a big overreaction, but Lucien had come to realise that the panic came from a place of caring. Victor cared for Lucien and Lucien really couldn't fuck this up. Again.

Lucien stepped into a guest room with Victor by his side. The room held one double bed, plush with pillows; the epitome of a decent hotel room, even with a bland painting of the local scenery hanging on the wall. Nothing was garish or offense. It also had not much personality.

"We are sharing?" Lucien asked. He wanted to. So much so that he was hard just at the idea of it. But the memory of Victor's shocked body when he'd kissed him without asking held him back from doing anything. He wanted Victor to choose him.

"I can sleep elsewhere if this makes you uncomfortable." Victor frowned at the double bed, and ran his hands through his thick black hair, leaving Lucien to clench his hands into fists at his side. He wanted to do that, wanted to feel the strands of hair against his skin. For Victor to be worried about Lucien's comfort, when Lucien was the one who'd assaulted Victor made Lucien's stomach twist around. He didn't deserve such forgiveness. His therapist's voice nagged at him. Yes he did. He was allowed to make mistakes, provided he was careful to apologise and take steps to ensure he didn't mess up again. He was allowed to learn and improve, or so his therapist said. If only he truly believed it.

"What were my family thinking?"

Lucien swallowed. Perhaps Victor's family saw the desire Lucien had for Victor. Maybe they saw the way Lucien's body came alight around Victor, how he was alert to Victor's every movement and word. He'd started to practically vibrate with need whenever Victor was in the room. How could anyone not notice?

"Don't stress. We've done this before, and I don't want to be any trouble for your family." Lucien knew he was making excuses. He should stop being a dickhead and be honest with Victor. He wanted to sleep in the same bed as him, to kiss him, and hold him. And the weirdest part of all, was that Lucien really wanted to fuck Victor, but he also wouldn't mind if they didn't. He couldn't wrap his mind around how that worked. Usually sex was a fun physical release, nothing more, and this version where he wanted Victor but he also cared about him as a friend was … a lot.

"It won't be any trouble for them. The inn is never full in the lead up to Christmas, so another room would be easy enough."

"No. It's late. And plus—" Lucien paused on purpose, hoping to see Victor's ears go pink again.

"Plus?"

"You owe me a kiss."

Ahh, there it was; the flush of pink rushing across Victor's skin to the tips of his ears. Lucien wanted to wrap Victor's hair around his fingers and pull him close and kiss him.

"I do?"

"Absolutely. And I think we should count it as our first kiss." Lucien wanted to wink but he kept a neutral expression—or rather he hoped he'd managed that. If the strumming need inside was any indication, he was probably salivating as he stared at Victor's mouth.

"But we've already kissed?"

"No. That doesn't count. I threw myself at you without consent. That's not a kiss. I want a fully consensual—sensual—kiss. One that we've both agreed to and isn't just me being fucking weird and demanding."

Victor's flush deepened in colour. "That kiss wasn't weird. It took me by surprise, that's all."

Lucien clucked his tongue. "You shouldn't have to deal with a surprising kiss that make you all stiff and awkward. You deserve to be kissed when you want it. A kiss should make your body responsive."

Victor blinked a few times. "Is that what you want?"

"Yes. I think—" Lucien watched Victor very carefully. "I think you should kiss me. I want you to take the lead here and show me what you like."

Victor tilted his head to the side. "And if I want you to take over and kiss me like before?"

"What do you mean?"

"I want you to kiss me like I matter. Like you did before when you HAD to kiss me."

Lucien's ears filled with a roaring noise—fuck, he wanted that too—but instead he shook his head. Before he'd realised that Victor hadn't reacted, he'd loved that moment of utter desperation to pour himself into Victor. He couldn't. Not this time. Not without establishing Victor's consent first. Hopefully there would be other times when he could do that, but first... First, he needed to take his time.

"No. Let's start slowly." He would show restraint because Victor deserved to be cherished. He held out his hands and waited for Victor to touch him. Their fingertips brushed. Victor's eyes widened slightly, his lips parted, and Lucien traced his fingers over Victor's palms, across his wrists, until Victor stepped forward, pressing their bodies together. Fuck, Lucien was giddy with his presence. He slid one hand up Victor's arm, over his forearm and biceps, squeezing his shoulder slightly to massage away any remaining tension in Victor's body. Victor held his gaze, his eyes dark with desire, and when Lucien slid his hand up Victor's throat to cup his face, Victor leaned in and brushed his lips against Lucien's mouth.

This was the kiss he'd wanted. One where he was aware of every brush of their mouths together, where the whole world faded away in the very best way. This time, Victor relaxed against his body, and oh God, it was better than Lucien could've imagined. He was soft, pliable, and he tasted a bit like the whiskey they'd had after dinner. Sharp, warm. Lucien wrapped his other hand around Victor, placing it between his shoulder blades. Victor rested his hands on Lucien's hips, a steadying touch, when all Lucien wanted to do was lose himself in this kiss. Trying not to rush took concentration. He nibbled at Victor's bottom lip, loving the little growl when he sucked harder, and then he went back to careful light touches. Victor's fingers dug into Lucien's waist.

"More. Give me more." Victor's voice pitched low.

Lucien dragged his lips across Victor's cheek, over the rough stubble that had grown through the day and whispered in his ear. "You aren't passive here. Give me more."

Victor pulled him closer, grinding his hips against Lucien. The rush of pleasure when their erections met was almost too much and Lucien's hands trembled as he tried to keep his touch light. And this was while fully dressed. Jesus, when he finally got his skin against Victor's, he was going to melt or combust. Both. Victor slid one hand up Lucien's spine and gripped the back of his neck. They were of a similar height, so when Victor kissed Lucien, they met easily. Victor took charge, pushing his tongue into Lucien's mouth, and when he stroked his tongue over Lucien's own, Lucien's knees softened. Being kissed with such confidence sent desire spiking through him. They kissed and kissed, savouring, tasting each other, exploring, until Lucien couldn't breathe. He grabbed at Victor's shirt, tugging it upwards, and Victor pushed him on the chest. Lucien staggered backwards. Had he been too much?

"Don't apologise. Just get naked." Victor's command made Lucien's already hard cock twitch. It rubbed against his clothes—almost painfully hard—and he nodded. How could Victor have known he was going to be apologise for being too much? But Victor stared at him, waving his hands impatiently at Lucien's clothes. He undressed as fast as humanly possible, barely aware that Victor was doing the same, and tumbled onto the bed. Victor crawled over him. "You are so incredibly ... fit."

"The perks of being an athlete." Lucien bucked his hips upwards, needing to have his cock touch Victor's bare skin. His friend—friend!—was beautiful. He wasn't as hard fit as Lucien, slender rather than ripped, but with broad shoulders and almost no hair on his chest, just a dusting of a few hairs with pert brown nipples that begged to be played with.

"Come here to me." Lucien wanted Victor's weight on him, but instead, Victor lay down beside him, gently touching Lucien on one shoulder to roll him towards him. Victor traced his fingers over Lucien's shoulder, up his neck, and slowly along the curve of Lucien's ear.

"I've always loved your tattoo." Victor trailed his fingers down Lucien's throat, towards his tattoo. Most of it was hidden by the way he was lying on the bed, but when Victor's fingers followed the outline of the cheetah's paw spread over his chest, and the scratch marks that had a steampunk heart hiding inside the slashes from the cheetah's claws, Lucien held his breath at the tender touch. And when Victor stopped his investigations and cupped the back of Lucien's skull, pulling them together for another luxurious slow kiss, Lucien wanted to pounce like the cheetah on his sleeve tattoo. They kissed until Lucien was trembling with the outpouring of care and the building need for more. Lucien wanted to wrap his legs around Victor's hips and pull their bodies together. He needed to thrust his hips and slide his cock against Victor's skin. But that little—annoying as fuck—voice in his head reminded him that he wanted Victor to be comfortable. He had to go at Victor's speed. He kissed him back, trying to say all of this with his lips and tongue.

Suddenly, Victor released the grip on the back of Lucien's head and slid his hand all the way down Lucien's spine, leaving a trail of heat, over his hip and... Fuck. Victor grabbed both of their cocks, gently joining them together with searing heat. He stroked very slowly with his fingers curled around Lucien's length. The flood of sensation at the way they were connected had Lucien's eyes rolling back in his head. This was worth the wait. The pressure of their cocks together had him arching his spine, needing to have more of his skin against Victor's warmth. He could. And so, he shifted his leg, wrapping it around Victor's thigh, and pulling them closer together.

"You are leaking." Victor sucked in a tight breath. The barest hint of a whistle between Victor's lips helped. Victor was just as affected by this as Lucien. Just as needy.

"Yes." Lucien clutched at Victor's hair, loving the way the strands were soft on the back of his hands, and kissed him again until they were hopelessly tangled. Victor rubbed his thumb over the end of Lucien's cock, taking some of the precum and using it to glide his hand over them. Lucien added his hand to Victor's, and they stroked together. It was fast and hot and too much, and Lucien growled as their rhythm became jerkier and desperate. Hopeless for each other.

"I'm going to come."

"Together." Victor kissed him again, swallowing all the

noises Lucien was making. He roared into Victor's mouth as he came—too soon, too fast—just from a few kisses and a desperate hand job. It was a lot. A huge burst of energy that flattened him, wrung him out, and made him feel like he'd fallen from a cliff and was gliding through the air towards a soft cloud. And when Victor jerked against him, coming with a shout, Lucien knew his life would never be better than this moment of wild joy. He kissed Victor again, then flopped onto his back.

"Holy shit."

"Yeah." Victor let out an unsteady breath. "I'm sorry."

"Why? That was amazing."

"I wanted to make it last longer."

Lucien rolled on top of Victor, uncaring about the sticky mess all over both of their stomachs and kissed him on the forehead. "You were perfect. And we have all night."

"All night?"

"I'm an athlete. I have a lot of stamina." Lucien rested his forehead against Victor's and just breathed in his warm delicious scent.

"You'll be the death of me."

"Then you'll go to your grave a happy man."

Victor grinned. "Oh my God. The confidence of you."

Lucien kissed him again, the softest of sappy kisses, but he didn't care that Victor might notice how mushy he was being.

"Let me get a cloth." Victor half-heartedly pushed Lucien's shoulders.

"I can do it."

Victor grinned. "Bloody drivers, always having to win. We can care for each other without it being a competition."

"What?"

"I'm teasing. It's okay. You are my guest. Let me clean you up."

Lucien rolled off Victor and sat up. "Fine." He enjoyed the way Victor's back muscles stretched and his ass moved as he walked across the room to the ensuite. Lucien waited until Victor was gone before he cupped his balls and sighed happily. It was probably the worst sex of his life—technique wise—but somehow ranked as the best. He let go of himself and leaned back on his elbows; just in time as Victor came back into the room with a damp cloth. It was warm when Victor stood beside the bed and gently washed his stomach and now softened cock. The cloth soothed as Victor cleaned him up.

"Now your turn."

"I already cleaned myself." Victor waved his hand in the vague direction of his naked torso.

"Aren't you naughty?" Lucien was a bit miffed that he didn't get the chance to care for Victor in the same easy way Victor cared for him.

"Excuse me?" Victor glared at Lucien with one eyebrow raised.

And it was a lot easier to tease him than to show how much he wanted to lavish Victor with attention. "Denying me the chance to look after you. It's a bit naughty."

Victor blinked once, and Lucien winked at him. Victor shook his head. "You are a problem. Now get under those blankets before you get cold."

"Do you promise to join me and keep me warm?"

"Do you flirt with all the boys like this?" The flash of confusion across Victor's face sent a wave of cold regret over

Lucien's throat. He hated the way Victor didn't believe that Lucien wanted him. He leaped off the bed and took the cloth from his hands. With a flick of his wrist, he threw the cloth across the room, and pulled Victor into a hug. He kissed his chin, his nose, his cheeks, showering him with simple affection, then when Victor relaxed, Lucien kissed him gently on the mouth.

"Only for you." He whispered, then he tumbled into bed, pulling Victor with him, who landed on him with a surprised huff of breath. "Come to bed, Victor. It's time for sleeping."

"You are impossible, Lucien."

Lucien smiled. He loved the way Victor said his name with such exasperation. "Yeah."

CHAPTER 13

When Victor woke, the other side of the bed was empty. He scrambled to sit up and turn on the bedside lamp, then growled when he saw a notification on his phone.

LUCIEN

Gone for a run.

It made sense. Lucien's season started in a month. Sometimes Victor forgot that Lucien was an athlete, although he'd very much enjoyed touching his incredibly fit body last night. His lean muscles and quick reflexes marked him as more than a gym junkie because his body was fit for purpose. In a couple of weeks, all the Gamble Racing drivers would go on a preseason fitness retreat for an assessment by the team's trainers including Lucien's personal trainer Hettie. She was such a whirlwind of a person and did triathlons with Ondrej's trainer Amy. He'd met them at various team meetings through the year.

Victor stopped stressing about waking up alone. They were just friends, who'd kissed—a lot—and slept in the same bed. Twice. Not that he was counting or anything. A loud knock on the door vibrated through the room.

"Yes?"

"Victor. It's Ma. Are you two love birds coming down for breakfast? It's past eight already."

"Ma." Victor rolled his eyes. "We—" Aren't love birds? Or were they? They'd come together last night, which had to count for something. Right? He was being silly. This doubt wasn't based in anything Lucien had said; just his own imposter syndrome. Instead of protesting the very premise of Ma's question, he got out of bed, and threw on enough clothes to cover his body, then opened the door. "Ma. Come in."

"Are you both decent?"

"It's just me, Ma." Victor swallowed down his sigh at Ma's disappointed face.

"Oh. I thought you boys were a couple?"

Victor shook his head, unable to deal with her disappointment but also he wasn't even sure what the answer to her question was. "Ma. Lucien has gone for a run. That's why he's not here."

"I see. I'm sorry about the assumption."

"Which one?" Victor grinned. Hopefully she didn't notice that his mouth wobbled a little at the edges. He was being a bit ridiculous. Lucien had given him zero reason to doubt ... anything.

"Honey. What's the matter?" Okay, she noticed. She pulled him into a hug. "Talk to me."

"Ma. I don't need to talk."

"Why do all my children think I'm trying to do therapy on them?" Ma chuckled.

Victor stepped out of the hug. "You can't help it. Look, come in. Sit down." He grabbed a glass and filled it with water for her. "Ma. I know it's different for me to invite someone home for Christmas, but there's really nothing happening. Much. Yet. Um, it's early days. I don't know what this ... thing, um, might, yeah. I'm babbling. Just. It's fine, Ma."

"Do you like him?"

Victor's breath caught in his throat, somewhere between a gasp and a sigh, neither in or out. "Yes. Of course I do. He's my friend."

"And?"

"Ma. I invited him here because he has no family. He's my friend and he was lonely. I thought it would be nice for him..." He didn't say the rest, because it was not Ma's business to know that Lucien had probably never had a proper family Christmas. Plus, he didn't know for sure, he'd only inferred it from having known Lucien's awful father.

Victor's Ma frowned. "But I've seen the way you look at each other. Are you sure?"

"He doesn't look at me like anything. What are you talking about?" Victor knew how he looked at Lucien—when he thought no one was looking—as if Lucien was a tasty treat that he wasn't allowed to devour. He'd spent years pretending, and now they'd kissed, he would never be able to hold it back again.

"Have I overstepped?"

"No. Ma. Relax. You are just a little eager to have to me partner up with anyone, even my friend."

"Right." She gave a long glance at the messed-up bedsheets, as if they didn't tell a whole story about how Lucien and Victor had spent the night. "You want me to back off and leave you to sort it out yourself? You don't need help?"

"I don't know, Ma." He wanted to smile and tell her that they'd kissed and that it was amazing, but it was still so new that he didn't know what to do about it. It could just be a temporary holiday fling for Lucien—that was more his style judging by his social media—and if so, Victor would end up losing his heart in the most devastating fashion.

His mother sipped her water and looked at him as if she could see his jumbled thoughts. "I assume you two met at work since he was very enthusiastically talking about cars with Pa last night at dinner, but I haven't seen him on the tv show you are on."

Victor laughed. "Do you mean the sport channel that shows all the races?" The latest season of the long running reality version of each S1 season hadn't aired yet, and Victor had been trying not to be nervous about it because they loved to create drama. As if S1 didn't have enough politics and drama already. The show had been great for the sport, though, bringing in new fans, even if sometimes it felt a little manufactured. Fuck—they were probably going to make a whole episode about his cars catching fire. The memes had been bad enough.

"What's the matter? Honey, you look terrible."

He shook his head. "No, I just realised something to do with work." His palms were all sticky.

"Want to talk about it?"

He wiped his hands on his boxer shorts. "No. Fuck. It's

hard to explain. I have to fix something before I end up humiliated. Fuck. That sounded a little dramatic. This work problem is doing my head in."

"Victor. It's not like you to worry so much."

"I'm the chief engineer for an S1 team. I worry all the time. This job comes with huge amounts of pressure. I'm way too young to have this job."

"Your boss thought enough of you to give you the job."

Victor wished he could have confidence in that. "It's complicated." The buzz of being selected for such an honour had quickly worn off when the pressure to perform had become all too real. Yes, his car was fast, but it wasn't reliable enough, and every issue cost the team money. Gamble Racing wasn't one of the big teams with huge sponsorship, or the income from having done well in the constructor's championship. They couldn't afford for his car to be a twitchy, hard to drive, disaster.

"How so?"

"The team got a new sponsor and demanded that my predecessor was sacked as part of the deal." Victor swallowed, ignoring the way Ma shrugged. "Yeah, anyway..." He'd already told his parents this story. "You know how the new sponsor gave my boss a list of people who he wanted to replace the last Chief Engineer, and my name—"

"Was top of the list?"

"No. I do appreciate the vote of confidence though. No, Ma, I was the fifth choice. The other four all said no. I'm not the one they wanted. I'm just the one they ended up with." That was why he had to figure out why his cars kept blowing up before he got sacked too. Their new sponsor Mr Sanchez Senior wasn't the type of person to put up with failure and he wanted to absolute best for his son, Paulo, who drove for them.

"Honey, perhaps the others were too expensive."

Victor squeezed his eyes shut and rubbed his hands over them. It was either that or laugh hysterically. "Price doesn't matter to our sponsor. He's a fucking billionaire who bought an S1 seat for his kid. He could have anyone at any cost. Listen, it doesn't matter. I don't know why the others turned down the offer of this job. Could be a bunch of reasons." The most obvious was that taking a team from last place into the midfield was a huge challenge. One he thought he'd been ready for, until reality sunk in, and he realised it wasn't just about building a fast car. It also had to be reliable and driveable.

"Not everything is about money, I suppose."

"Mr Sanchez wanted a fast car for his son. I delivered on that promise, although the car isn't the easiest to drive. Paulo adjusted well though, and he got his first S1 point in just his second race. Everything was solid for the first half of the season, then it went to crap." Victor ran his hand through his hair. "I need to stop my cars blowing up, or I'm not going to have a job. And I love this job."

"Get over yourself. You are the best goddamn engineer that Sanchez could've bought. You are brilliant and you built a fucking fast car. I wish I could've driven it." Lucien's strong voice rang through the room and Victor dropped his hands. Lucien stood there in a sleeveless shirt and tiny shorts. His skin was wet with sweat and gooseflesh stuck out all over him, making the cheetah of his tattoo look more prominent, which made no logical sense. Apparently he was beyond logic whenever Lucien was nearby. Victor wasn't sure if he wanted to wrap him in a blanket to protect him from the cold or lick him all over. Fuck. His mother was in the room, he had to think about anything that wasn't how gorgeous Lucien looked.

"Maybe you should drive it." His voice wobbled a fraction. Hopefully no one noticed. "Like you said, the no testing rules don't apply to last season's car anymore."

"You don't need me, or anyone, to validate that you built a fast car. Just look at the results. I drove in S1 for two seasons in slow cars. Twenty points in my first season and one ... One fucking lonely point in my second season." Lucien stepped closer to him and jabbed him in the chest with his finger. "And if my results aren't enough, take Ondrej. He drove with me in Whitehall's sack of shit car. Guess how many points Ondrej got last season? One. That's why they sacked Whitehall. Because we drove all season in the shitty slow car and the team got two whole points."

"Okay?"

"Now—" Lucien jabbed him again. "—tell me how many points Ondrej earned in your car this season."

"One hundred and twenty-one."

Lucien's stern expression softened for a second. "Ondrej—the same driver in a different car—earned one hundred and twenty points more this season in your car than he did last season in Whitehall's car. Now tell me how many points your cars earned this season?"

"One hundred and ninety-four." Victor hated that he needed this validation, but he fucking loved that Lucien saw it all so clearly. His chest puffed out and he glanced at his mother who was nodding along, smiling at Lucien's passionate defence of Victor's car.

"And where did Gamble Racing finish on the constructor's championship?"

"Fifth." Victor breathed in. "It was a good mid-field result."

"Last season, Gamble Racing came last. The season before, they came second last. Suddenly you arrive on the scene with a fast car, and the team leaps up from last to fifth. No one is going to sack you."

Victor nodded. Perhaps it wasn't so bad after all.

"What about the last few races?" It burned him that he couldn't resolve this, but perhaps he was focusing too much on the problems and not seeing the wider issues.

"Socrates thinks it's the engine manufacturer's issue and nothing to do with you."

"He's wrong. Several other teams use the same engine, and they didn't have the same problems." He couldn't shake the irritating sense that he was missing something important.

Lucien glanced at Victor's Ma. "I'm sorry, Mrs Tsui, but your son is being a fucking pain in the ass."

"It does sound like he's focusing on the negatives..."

"Yes. And he ought to be thinking about next season. How is next season's car going, Victor? Will it be ready for pre-season testing in, what, less than two months?"

"Yes. It's ready. I can work on two things in parallel, you know." Victor wasn't being a pain in the ass. He was merely caring about doing his job well, and he needed to understand the source of this issue before it continued to be a problem next year.

"Great. And will it be as fast as last year's car? Or will Gamble Racing languish back in last place again?"

"Faster. I've been working on a suspension design that will…" Victor suddenly realised what Lucien was doing. "Stop distracting me. I can solve this. I will figure out why my cars keep failing, and I will stop it from happening this season."

Lucien started clapping and Ma let out a little whoop. "Good for you, son. Now, come down and join us for breakfast. Collette is making her famous drop scones."

Ma swept out of the room and as the door clicked shut, Lucien hugged Victor and swung him around in a circle.

"What?"

"You are magnificent."

Victor shook his head. "And you fucking goaded me into saying all of that. How dare you."

"How dare I?" Lucien set him on the floor and kissed him. "It's all true. Now I need a shower, and so do you." The look Lucien gave him could only be described as smoking hot. His throat suddenly thickened, as did his cock.

"I do. How was your run?"

"Beautiful. Truly. I can't believe you got to grow up here. It's stunningly beautiful, with the sun rising over the lake and shit. Wow."

"This way. Time for a shower before you cool down too much."

Lucien tipped his head back and laughed. "Yes. That's why Hettie would want me to shower with you right now. Can't you just hear her telling me not to let my muscles cool down before I've stretched properly?"

"Hey, I'm only doing my best to make sure you stay fit and healthy."

"Good." Lucien kissed him on the cheek and stripped off his clothes, right in front of Victor, and walked, butt naked into the ensuite bathroom. Victor stared. He didn't know what would happen between them once this trip was over, but right now, he didn't give a shit because he was about to have a shower with fucking Lucien Grenville. Third in the driver's championship in this year's Series E competition. Best of all, Lucien cared enough to remind him of who he was—a really good race car engineer and designer—and most of all, Lucien was the best fucking kisser in Victor's whole life. Yes. He scrambled after him.

CHAPTER 14

Lucien stripped off his running clothes while he waited for the water to heat up, dumping them in the corner of the very bland hotel ensuite with white tiles and white towels, and boring fittings. He could've been anywhere in the world. It didn't matter, because the scenery outside the inn more than made up for the dull, clean, room. Perhaps that was the point. Thinking about the aesthetics of the room was a decent distraction from the irritating way that Victor didn't realise how fucking brilliant he was. Lucien couldn't believe he'd had to remind him of his achievements.

"Can I join you?" Victor asked.

"I'd be annoyed if you didn't. Didn't you just suggest this was a trainer sanctioned shower?"

Victor laughed. "I'm pretty sure you suggested that."

"Get naked. Get in here. I want to kiss you again." Lucien stepped under the steaming water, loving the way it warmed his rapidly cooling skin. Running in the brisk—fucking freezing—Scottish winter air had been brilliant.

The clean air was sharp in his lungs as he'd stretched his legs and the scenery was truly outstanding. Now he'd stopped running, he was starting to cool down too fast and he needed the water to warm him up. His cock didn't need any encouragement, and he gave it a quick stroke, keeping his eyes closed as the water ran over his body.

"Did you mean it?" Victor's voice was raspier than usual, and Lucien opened his eyes. A flush spread over Victor's face.

"Mean what?" Lucien dropped his hands to his sides.

"When you said I was magnificent?"

"Absolutely. Now get in here." Lucien tipped his head backwards, letting warm water run over his face. The ensuite shower wasn't huge; nothing like the waterfall one he had in his Monaco apartment. Luckily neither of them were basketballers. He emerged from the stream of water, smiling.

"What's so funny?"

"I was just thinking that it's lucky we are ordinary sized men, not basketballers." The joke didn't remove any of the naked desire shimmering around him.

Victor grinned. "Yeah, that would quite a tight fit."

Fucking hell; the last thing Lucien needed to be thinking about now was a tight fit. He waved his hand. "Hurry up." He didn't care that he'd essentially told Victor he needed to touch him right now. Now. Victor slowly lifted his shirt up his torso. Lucien loved the reveal of Victor's body, from his lean stomach without defined abdominal muscles, to his brown nipples on his chest, and...

"Is that a tattoo?"

"You've seen it before, Lucien." Victor pulled his shirt over his head, hiding then revealing his dimpled smile and dark brown eyes with their intelligent gaze. Finally, Victor dumped his shirt on the floor beside Lucien's running gear and stood there—too far away—in nothing but a pair of shorts. As if that wasn't already too much, Victor traced the outline of his cock through the fabric.

"Stop teasing." Lucien said.

Victor dropped his gaze to Lucien's own hard cock, just for a split second, and Lucien gasped at the heat in Victor's gaze. Victor raised his face and stared at Lucien's mouth as he dropped his shorts to the floor and stepped into the shower. Lucien reached out for him, wanting to pull him closer for a kiss, when Victor dropped to his knees in the shower and wrapped his mouth over Lucien's cock. Fucking hell. He tried to say something cute about this being the best way to end the teasing, but only a croak came out.

Victor flattened his tongue and took Lucien deep. The sudden heat of his mouth and the sight of him on his knees was too much. Lucien flung one hand out and grabbed the wall, just breathing, as sensation flowed through his body. Water dripped off his torso onto Victor's black hair. One little drip went down the bridge of Victor's nose and hung on the end, hovering in the small space between his nose and where his lips were curled around Lucien's cock. Watching that drip of water made it all feel real when the pleasure was so good it felt unreal. Surreal.

"I should tell you how good you are more often." If he teased, he might last longer than … now. Victor hummed, sending vibrations shooting through Lucien's body. Lucien threaded his fingers through Victor's hair and tugged slightly.

"Up."

Victor slid off with a pop that had Lucien blinking. "Too much?"

"I need to kiss you." Lucien didn't need Victor on his knees, he needed to hold him. He needed this to be different to every other meaningless fuck he'd had before, because this was Victor. "Come here."

Victor gave Lucien's aching cock a long lick, then stood up and kissed Lucien. Heaven. Throw in the taste of his own precum from Victor's mouth, and Lucien wasn't going to last long. Again. He held Victor by the back of his neck, and tipped him slightly backwards, dipping him as he kissed him. Victor clutched onto Lucien's shoulders, his fingers digging into Lucien's flesh, and Lucien loved the pressure of it. Hell. He kissed his way down Victor's throat, and suddenly, that little tattoo on Victor's chest came into view again.

"Holy shit, Victor." Lucien remembered that Victor had said he'd got the tattoo after Australia to commemorate having his own design in an S1 race, but Lucien hadn't noticed the details until now. "Is that your car?"

Victor flushed, from his face, all the way down his throat towards his cute little tattoo. Lucien traced it, and when Victor didn't answer, he flicked Victor's nipples.

"Fuck. Yes, it's my car." Victor was panting. "I was so proud of myself for designing a proper S1 car. I couldn't resist."

Lucien kissed the car. "You are magnificent."

"Okay?" Victor shook his head, and Lucien licked his nipple and the car tattoo again.

"Is this weird?" The doubt in Victor's tone slayed him and he stood up straight, hands off, and stared at his friend.

"Because we are playing in the shower?" Or because Lucien wanted to lavish praise on Victor. Perhaps he was coming on a little too strong—again.

"Yes." Victor shifted from one foot to another.

"I want you to be comfortable. Please tell me what I can do to help."

Victor frowned. "It's just ... well, look at you and look at me. And you keep saying nice things about me."

"They are true. You are magnificent."

Victor shook his head, sending water droplets flying everywhere. "I'm overthinking this?"

"Yes." Lucien breathed out slowly. "But honestly?"

"Please be honest."

"It wouldn't be you if you didn't think about every permutation. You're a data guy." He wasn't very strong when it came to data, but when he was driving, in races, there were moments when Lucien needed to take calculated risks, weighing up the chance of a pass against the potential for a crash, and this was one of those moments. Lucien had to tell Victor why him and why now.

"What will it take for you to believe that I want you, Victor? Shall I suck your dick until you come all over my face? I've wanted to do it for a long time, even before you told me I wasn't like my father, that you wouldn't be friends with someone like him."

Victor just stared at him for far too long. Lucien's

breath burned in his lungs. Waiting for an answer was agony.

Finally ... Victor nodded slowly. "I believe you."

"You believe that I want you? You'll stop with this nonsense that you aren't my type?"

"I'll try."

"What will it take—"

"I want you to do it like you did on the side of the road." Victor interrupted, talking rapidly, his gaze firm with a flash of determination that Lucien adored. "Kiss me as if you truly can't stop yourself and you absolutely have to have me. Don't hold back. Please."

Lucien's mouth was dry. He was caught between rampant need and the memory of Victor's stiff reaction.

"Please. Convince me."

With a slow nod, Lucien threaded his hands into Victor's wet hair and pulled him close for a kiss. He started gently, teasing until Victor reached up and placed his hands on Lucien's shoulders, and still he kept things light. Victor moved closer, his whole body pressed against Lucien, with their hard cocks pressed between them. Victor moaned, a needy, breathy, decadent moan.

"More. Please."

Lucien bestowed the most epic of all kisses on Victor. And Victor—thank fuck—melted in his arms. It was nothing like the last time and the relief at having Victor show that he wanted this kiss was incendiary. Lucien gripped on tight to Victor and used all his skill to kiss him, just like he'd asked. Hard, fierce. Full of desperate wanting. It was time to show Victor how much he wanted him. He sank to his knees, kissing Victor's tattoo again, then dragging his lips down over Victor's stomach.

"Lucien." Victor's hoarse cry as Lucien filled his mouth with Victor's cock was everything. The cry was nothing compared to having Victor's cock in his mouth. The hot length filled his mouth, all silky skin and strength. He used all his skill to suck Victor down deep, then bobbed enthusiastically.

"So good. Fuck." Victor's fingers dug into Lucien's shoulders. The water from the shower ran into the corners of his mouth and he thought he might choke on the combination, but Victor's moans and breathy curses made everything else irrelevant. He slid one hand up Victor's thigh and played with his balls. He sucked and bobbed his head and licked because this magnificent man deserved to know how great he was. Lucien was so attracted to Victor, his heart was going to burst with it, and he lavished attention on Victor's cock because he didn't have the words to describe how much he wanted him. Lucien showed Victor.

"Fuck, Lucien. I'm going to come."

Lucien relaxed his jaw and took Victor as deep as he could. He used his hand to stroke up Victor's shaft to meet his lips. Victor cried out and came with a burst of release that flooded Lucien's mouth with the tangy taste of his seed. Perfection. He swallowed, then gently kissed Victor's cock all the way down to the base, then spent some time kissing his balls too.

"Lucien."

"Now do you believe me? You are magnificent and I want you."

Victor's eyes were a little glazed over, so Lucien stood

up and grabbed the soap. He washed Victor all over, then made a show of washing himself, stroking his still-hard cock, as Victor rested against the wall of the shower.

"Do you like this show?"

Victor nodded, his gaze heavy and hooded. It didn't take long for Lucien to come as well, in long strands that were washed away by the shower. Lucien leaned in and pressed a slow gentle kiss on Victor's mouth.

"Believe me. Now come back to bed with me for more."

Victor bit his bottom lip. "Lucien. We are supposed to be going down for a family breakfast with Collette's famous drop scones."

Lucien shivered. "Well, then. I suppose I could give myself a little time to recharge, eat something, and then drag you back to bed."

"Are you ever serious?"

"I'm dead serious. It's Christmas Eve and bloody freezing outside. Why shouldn't we spend all day in bed?" Lucien had the best ideas sometimes, and this one was one of his top ten. Top three.

"You are insatiable."

"Yes." Now that Lucien had had a taste of Victor, he wanted more. So much more. If he'd known how much fun it would be to have sex with someone he knew and liked, he would've done it years ago. The water started to cool, so he turned it off and stepped out of the shower to grab a couple of towels. He wrapped one around his waist, then started to dry Victor.

"I can do that myself."

"I know, but I want to." Lucien fluffed the towel through Victor's hair, and slowly worked his way down, drying all his skin. Victor tried to help, and their hands tangled together in the towel.

"Please. Let me." Lucien gently pushed Victor's hands away and finished drying him. He'd never bothered with this amount of care with anyone else before; usually whoever he fucked knew the deal and once they'd each had their release, that was that. This urge to lavish attention and care on Victor was different and new, and he really didn't want to think too hard about what that might mean in the future. He breathed out. The future didn't matter. Victor was here right now, needing to be shown how worthy of attention he was.

"There. All dry." Lucien quickly dried himself. "Let's put on some decent clothes and have breakfast with your family."

Victor ran his hand through his hair. "Who are you?"

"Lucien Grenville. Series E driver and someone who is about to go to breakfast with his boyfriend's family and watch them pretend that they can't see your post-sex glow."

"My what?" Victor blinked.

"You look like you've been thoroughly fucked. Everyone is going to know what we've been doing."

Victor closed his eyes and tipped his head backwards for a second, then let out a huge sigh. "Lucien."

"It'll be fine." Lucien didn't care if anyone noticed and he wasn't inclined to hide how smug he felt at Victor's soft, sated, expression. He didn't need a gift for Christmas; this expression on Victor's face was enough of a present for him. And the selfish part of him wanted everyone to know that he belonged to Victor, that he was the one who'd given Victor that satisfied look.

CHAPTER 15

Victor walked into breakfast with his head held high, even though he was sure everyone would know what he'd been doing with Lucien. Collette confirmed it. She took one look at him and wolf whistled. Lucien bowed.

"Thank you."

"Stop." Victor hissed at Lucien who nudged him. He didn't need to say 'told you so'. It was written all over Lucien's grinning smug face.

"Yes. Collette. Stop. It's pretty weird to wolf-whistle at your brother's boyfriend."

It was the second time Lucien had called himself that and an unsteady flush rushed up Victor's spine.

"Last night you were just friends." Collette's glee was echoed on the faces of everyone sitting around the breakfast table and Victor wanted to hide; maybe have a hole in the floor open up wide, so he could just slide down into the earth away from their knowing expressions. It was one thing to be with Lucien in the privacy of their room, and another thing entirely to have it openly discussed with his family, especially when it was all so new. So very new. Victor wanted to relax into the freshness of kissing Lucien before he had to talk about what it meant. He had no freaking clue if this was a holiday crush—something Lucien often did, if his social media was any indication—or whether this was the beginning of a change in their friendship, and dare he say it... perhaps a longer-term relationship?

Lucien waved his hand. "We are still very good friends. Very close friends." He practically purred and Victor wished his heart didn't kick up a notch so happily.

"That's enough everyone. Lucien, you too." Victor glared at everyone. "Yes, I invited Lucien here for Christmas as a friend. That's it. I had no expectations that he might..." Victor was sure his face was bright red since his cheeks burned, "um, want to kiss me, and I'm surprised by this turn of events."

"We aren't surprised, honey." Ma's smile was too wide. Had he been so terrible at hiding his feelings for Lucien that she'd known before they'd even met? Just from talking on the phone? Victor loved his family but sometimes they just got too close into his business for his liking.

"Can you all just leave it for a while and give me some space?" Some space to enjoy it without expectations. He didn't want to get his hopes up that this boyfriend thing would last longer than this holiday. He sat down at the table and helped himself to some of the drop scones piled up on a platter in the middle of the table. He drizzled them with golden syrup and started to eat. Lucien sat beside him and wrapped his foot around Victor's ankle. The comforting touch settled the swirling confusion in his stomach, although it did nothing to slow his heartrate.

"Please pass the pancakes?" Craig asked with a sly little grin.

Collette grinned. "Drop scones. Uncle Craig, just because Zac was American doesn't mean we have to use the wrong term for them."

"He loved winding you up about that."

Collette picked up the platter and handed it to Craig. "To Uncle Zac, whose American name for drop scones was annoying as shit, but we always forgave him for that because he was awesome. I miss him too, Craig."

Craig nodded tightly. "Yes. Thank you for these delicious ... pancakes, Collette." They both laughed.

"To Zac. To family. And to new beginnings."

"Collette. Drop it." Victor growled at his sister. "Do you have to antagonise everyone?"

"Let me have some entertainment, Victor."

"We all miss Zac." Nicole tucked her phone under her napkin.

Craig cleared his throat. "Every time someone talks about Zac, it helps. Even when they are being facetious." He stared pointedly at Collette who winked back at him.

"Zac was my mentor. He taught me everything about running the Inn, and I miss his booming voice and his wrong names for things, and this is our second Christmas without him. It's not fair, so if I want to tease him about calling drop scones the wrong thing, even when he's gone, then I will." Collette's voice wobbled and Craig stood up and walked over to hug her.

"Talking about him keeps him alive in our hearts."

Craig kissed the top of Collette's head. "But I'm always going to call them pancakes."

Collette laughed, shaking her head. "Fine."

"Tell us about yourself, Lucien?" Ma asked.

"There isn't much to tell that isn't already on the internet."

Rory raised his hand.

"You don't need to do that. We aren't at school." Collette might tease him relentlessly, but she was so gentle with her son and it made Victor relax a bit.

"Oops. I'm not allowed to look at the internet when we are eating."

Nicole had the good sense to slide her phone under her napkin again. Victor glanced at her, and she sent him that little sister 'don't you dare say anything' look. What—or who—was so important on Christmas Eve that she had to break the family no phone rules? He breathed out. It wasn't his business, and if he wanted people to stay out his business, he could do the same for his baby sister.

"What Rory is trying to say is that not all of us have the time to spend on looking up Victor's 'friend' on the internet. Right?"

"Yes. Why are you on the internet? Are you famous?"

Lucien chuckled and held up two fingers an inch apart. "A little bit famous."

"Cool. My uncle Victor is famous too. I've seen him on telly when we watch the car racing, but he's boring. He doesn't talk on the cameras and just sits with the others staring at computers."

Everyone laughed.

"Hey—" Victor started to defend himself but stopped

because they'd only keep teasing him more and he didn't exactly feel like a success, although Lucien's way of reminding him of the number of points his cars had earned this season sent a flush of heat down his spine.

"That's a pretty good description of Victor's job." Lucien leaned forward, closer to Rory. "What would be the best job to do in the racing team?"

"Driving the cars, of course."

"I think being the guys who change the tyres would be cool. They have that big wheel gun. Makes a neat noise." Lucien made the noise.

"No." Rory shook his head. "The drivers have the best job."

Lucien leaned back in his chair and put his hands behind his head. "Do you want to know why I'm famous?"

"Yes." Rory's eyes widened and everyone at the table stared at Lucien, even though most of them knew the answer already.

"I drive the cars."

"Awesome. Will you take me for a ride?"

Collette was shaking her head, while her husband Gordon looked amused. He was a big quiet Scotsman who countered Collette's brashness.

"Not in a race car. They only have space for one person."

"Oh." Rory pouted.

"I can take you for a drive in the 300SL if you want." For someone who had no family, Lucien was so good with Rory, treating him like a miniature adult which Rory seemed to appreciate.

"Maybe when you visit me at my workshop, Lucien can

take you on the test track in one of the two-seater race cars, like the old Le Mans car that Socrates has in his collection." Victor had a sudden urge to bring his family to the workshop and show them the real part of his job; the part that wasn't sitting on the pit wall stressing about the data during the race. The unseen parts of his job were the most important ones.

"Lucien just said race cars only have one seat."

Lucien smiled. "That's very clever of you. The fastest cars are single seater, but there are some other classes that have two seats. Our boss has one that might be fun to take out on the test track. It's about as close as you get to the single-seater experience of a Series E car. Not quite as fast, if that's alright with you, Rory?"

"I don't think that's a good idea to promise my son a ride like that." Gordon's soft accent floated across the table.

"It's fine. He can wear one of my old fire suits from my karting days, and I'm sure I've got a helmet that'll fit." Lucien's offer would have any racing fans salivating. It was the type of offer that money couldn't buy because most drivers were too busy to do stuff like this unless it was for team promotional opportunities. The media usually got one of the S1 drivers to take a local celebrity for a fast lap in a production sports car before each race; and most teams were happy to take part once a season to promote their commercial cars.

"My friends at school will think I'm so cool."

Victor tried to send a non-verbal message to Collette that her son would be safe with Lucien.

"Do you crash very much?" Nicole asked. "What is the legal position if you crash with my nephew in the car?"

"Nicole is studying law at university." Victor whispered.

"I'm not going to crash doing a slow test lap with a child in the car." Of course, Lucien wouldn't go at the limit with someone else in the car, although Victor wasn't about to mention that Lucien's version of slow would be likely too fast for most people's comfort level.

"But you need a fire suit and a helmet?" Collette's voice pitched upwards.

Lucien nodded. "Yes. It's standard practice. I wouldn't go too fast because his body isn't trained for high speeds, and I'm one of the best drivers in the world."

Victor understood Lucien's implication that he'd set the speed to suit the passenger; best didn't just mean fast, it meant understanding the conditions and adjusting to them.

"Arrogant much?"

"Settle down everyone." Pa spoke clearly and everyone turned to stare at him. "No one is going to do anything that risks hurting anyone. We are a team in this family, we look after each other."

The yearning in Lucien's eyes cut into Victor's heart. Pa's often spoken statement was so normal for Victor that he barely heard it anymore. To watch Lucien's reaction to a family who cared for each other was a pertinent reminder of how lucky he was to have this family.

There was a general mumble of agreement and then the conversation moved on. Gordon and Collette talked to Ma about the new menu and a local sheep farm that had started working towards organic status. Victor tried to eat his drop scones, but it was hard as he kept glancing at Lucien to see how he was doing. He ate without seeming to be stressed about the drama he'd caused by offering to take Rory for a spin around the test track. After a while, Lucien beckoned to Rory, who slid out of his seat and walked over to stand next to Lucien.

"Do you want to see my worst crash? Don't show your Mum though, she'll never let you drive with me."

"Lucien. You can't ask a child to have a secret from his mother."

"Oh. No, no, no, don't do that. That would super bad." Lucien waved his hands. "Sorry, I don't really spend any time around kids."

"Can you show me the crash?" Rory asked.

"I don't know. Should I?" Lucien asked Victor.

Victor shrugged. "It depends if you want to scare him."

"That would suit you, wouldn't it?" Lucien winked. "You couldn't possibly let your nephew get a lap with me before you do."

Victor nudged Lucien with his elbow. "Who said I wouldn't demand to be first?"

"You are too nice for that. You'd want Rory to look cool for his friends."

"Yeah, I would." Victor's pulse had skipped a beat when Lucien said he'd selfishly put himself before his nephew, but of course Lucien was teasing, so he breathed gently again. "Which crash were you thinking of? Canada at the start last year?"

"No. That was a bad one too. I was going to show him London this year." Lucien winked. "I should show him how a proper car looks."

"Yeah, that one was scary. Saved by the halo." Victor ignored Lucien's teasing. He'd been setting up at Spa when the Series E class were racing on a street circuit in London and had watched on screen, holding his breath, as Lucien's car had been clipped by another car. Crashes were always scary, and more so, when it was a driver in their team that everyone adored. Lucien's car hit a sausage kerb at full speed, launching his car into the air. It'd flown through the air, crashing into the tall metal barrier designed to keep the cars away from the crowd. The car had bounced back, rolling until it landed partly on the tyre wall, with only the halo stopping Lucien's head from being crunched by the barrier.

Lucien's mouth quirked up on one side in a cheeky half-grin. "You see, I walked away without a scratch because we have excellent safety equipment."

"The whole S1 pit garage at Gamble Racing cheered when you walked out of the car."

"It was a bit awkward, dangling half upside down on the barrier, but always good to walk away from something like that."

"Can I see?"

Victor glanced at Collette who frowned. "Ask your mum first."

Rory rushed around the table. "Mum, can I watch one of Lucien's car crashes?"

"Yes. Hopefully it'll stop you from wanting to get in a car with him."

Lucien laughed, wrinkling up his nose. "Come here then." He pulled out his phone and typed in something, then showed the screen to Rory. Victor still held his breath for that milli-second while Lucien's car was airborne. It didn't matter that he knew Lucien would be fine. The crash was scary as heck.

"Why aren't they helping you?" Rory asked.

"It's an electric car, so they have to check that the battery is safe before they touch the car."

"In case the car is live?" Pa asked.

"Yes. The battery is contained in a carbon fibre case that is supposed to unable to be penetrated, but with all the electrical components, the whole skin of the car has sensors to indicate if there is an electrical fault and there's a process to earth it before the marshals touch the car. We wouldn't want anyone to get electrocuted."

"What about you?"

"I'm inside a capsule. It's almost the same as the one used in S1 and can extract a driver without having to move their spine if that's necessary after a crash."

"Can I see it again?" Rory asked.

"Sure." Lucien played it again, and this time Rory gasped when the car lifted off.

"Why did the car fly?"

Lucien slowed down the footage and showed Rory the crash in slow motion, indicating the sausage kerb and using his hands to describe how the car lifted up. "It was just unlucky that the barrier was right there. Normally a crash like that, the car would roll through a gravel patch and slow down. It always hurts a bit when you hit the barriers."

"Does your test track have those kerbs?"

"No."

"I think I still want to go for a ride with you." Rory said. Victor waited for it, because the serious consideration from Rory was bound to make Lucien...

"There's no doubt you are related to your Uncle Victor. He's got that need for speed combined with cautiousness."

"Thanks." Victor wasn't sure that was a compliment. "At least I'm not reckless."

Lucien tilted his head. "I'm not reckless anymore. I haven't pushed past the limit since S3."

"What does that mean?" Rory asked.

Victor really wanted to know Lucien's answer to that, because it would open up an interrogation from his family if he mentioned the impact that Lucien's father had had on his career and his ability to drive a car without crashing. More than that, he wanted to see Ma's reaction to how Lucien described this. Was it wrong to be curious about Lucien's psyche?

CHAPTER 16

Lucien didn't think the technical answer to the question about finding the limit of a car was going to be much help for Rory, since most eight-year-old kids had probably never driven a car. He'd already been racing karts by that age, but he hadn't exactly had a typical childhood. "Have you ever run down a steep hill?"

"Yes."

"Then you'd know that moment when you are going as fast as you can without falling over?"

Rory smiled slowly, then waved his arms around, pretending to stop himself falling. Everyone chuckled quietly, not at Rory; more of a kind, knowing noise of appreciation for his demonstration. It was so lovely to be with a family who cared for each other in such an obvious way.

"At that moment, if you go a tiny bit faster, then it can easily turn into a disaster," Lucien continued. "You fall down and hurt yourself. Any slower and you know you can push for a little bit more speed. When you get that balance right between speed and disaster … That's the limit. Every driver is always trying to find the limit and stay there."

"For the whole race?" Nicole asked.

"Ideally." Lucien tended to go past the limit more often than he held back, hence his higher than average crash percentage. "It's not that easy to achieve, especially not in a twitchy car." Lucien winked at Victor, just so he could see him protest.

"Hey. We ironed out those problems early in the season." Bingo. Victor's retort sent a burst of heat across Lucien's skin.

"You did have a rookie driver," Lucien tilted his head as if making a concession to his point. "Who is to say whether the twitchiness came from the car or Paulo?"

Victor raised his eyebrows, as if to say that he could tell what game Lucien was playing, which made it even better. Lucien loved the way Victor responded to being teased by demonstrating his confidence in his technical abilities. Victor often seemed to struggle with doubt, but when teased, Lucien was able to draw out the innate ability underneath—which was why he did it. Often.

"It was the car."

"Are you sure?" Lucien leaned forward, wanting to see how Victor was going to defend himself. He'd given him a quick excuse by blaming the driver, but Lucien was certain Victor would be truthful and talk about how his initial design was hard to drive with a lighter back end and too much front end downforce which had led to too much oversteer while cornering, meaning the car tended to spin at speed. He'd sent Victor a text about it after watching the first pre-season testing nearly a year ago, and Victor had confirmed the problem.

"Yes. Ondrej has a lot of experience in S1. If he said it was twitchy, and why, then obviously I'm going to listen to him and the specific way the car reacted into and out of each turn, then we made adjustments to the downforce setup."

"Do you guys talk anything that isn't cars?" Nicole interrupted.

"No."

"Not really." Victor spoke at the same time as Lucien and Lucien couldn't resist grinning at him.

"There was that time when we talked about... No, that was about cars too." Lucien rubbed his chin and Victor laughed.

"I'm sure we talked about ... No, I suppose the shape of turn one at Imola is also talking about cars." Victor's eyes twinkled.

"What about when we discussed ... Hmm, no, you know what? Maybe Nicole is right. We only talk about cars." Lucien almost leaned in close to Victor and whispered something about talking about kissing in his ear, but Victor made an exaggerated gesture with his arms that kept Lucien out of his space.

"Surely not, Lucien. We must talk about other stuff. What about that time when Socrates took his helicopter for a flight during the summer break this year, and no one knew where he'd gone. He was missing for several hours. That involved a lot of talking about non-car things." Victor's brown eyes glinted and Lucien tried not to grin because Victor's choice of story was so perfect.

"True. That was a time when we didn't talk about cars. Although technically, he wasn't missing. He'd just gone to buy a—"

"Car. And hadn't told anyone what he was doing." Victor started to laugh, and Lucien couldn't stop himself from joining in. Soon enough they were both in tears, leaning against each other, while laughing way too much. It wasn't even that funny. It was mostly the delight when Victor stopped worrying about his work and relaxed enough to joke with Lucien. Lucien wanted to treasure these moments.

"Oh, look how cute you two are." Collette's comment cut Victor's laugh short and Lucien wanted to growl at her. He'd forgotten about the rest of the family listening to them be silly together. Plus, it annoyed him that she stopped Victor from enjoying himself. Didn't she under-stand how rare it was to see Victor let go like this?

"Who is Socrates?" Rory asked.

"Our boss. He won the World Championship twice before he had a bad accident." Lucien was glad for all the safety improvements now. A crash like the one that had ended Socrates' career would hardly bruise someone now. Back then, they hadn't the same neck protection or the same strength training to deal with the G-forces of a sudden impact. Socrates had slammed into a concrete wall at over 200 kilometres per hour and ended up with a concussion that had affected his vision. Those old cars didn't have the same driver protections, and Lucien always drove with the knowledge that drivers before him had sacrificed their lives to get him the safety protocols that kept him safe now.

"Can I see it?" Rory asked.

Lucien shook his head. "No. It's not good to watch crashes where someone is badly injured. Only people who are trained in analysing crashes like that should watch them, so they can make improvements to safety in cars and on tracks. I only showed you my London crash from this season because you know that I'm okay."

"Your boss was not okay after his crash?"

"Socrates was in hospital for a long time after that crash. I'm not sure of the full list of his injuries, but he had a bad concussion that affected his vision sometimes. The crash ended his driving career, and that's why he started Gamble Racing. Us drivers are a bit obsessed with cars and most of us end up staying in the sport after we retire." Lucien wasn't sure what he would do; he still had a good decade left in Series E before he needed to decide. He wouldn't mind another crack at S1 one day, but first he wanted to win the SE title.

Nicole coughed. "But your boss flies a helicopter?"

"His vision is mostly fine now, for everyday use. It wasn't good enough to drive an S1 car at the limit, so he had to retire."

Victor slung his arm around Lucien's shoulders. "I think we are talking about cars again."

"Well, darling. It is my favourite topic." Lucien couldn't resist leaning against Victor, and he tucked his head against Victor's neck. Being with Victor's family, and their fun banter, was such a great experience. Victor stiffened for a second, then relaxed again.

"Can you get me a ride in the helicopter?" Rory asked.

"What? A fast car isn't enough?" Lucien grinned.

"Can't blame a kid for trying!" Gordon said.

"Socrates would love an excuse to take his helicopter up for joy ride." Lucien knew that if he asked, Socrates would probably fly up here today just for the lark of it. He wouldn't ask because if Socrates could see him and Victor now, he'd be insufferable. He was going to be that way soon enough, once Christmas was over, and they all went back to work where Socrates would be able to see the change in the way Lucien acted around Victor. Like a dog in heat, but less gross... hopefully.

"Mum. We need to go and visit Uncle Victor at his work."

Gordon cleared his throat. "We will try and find a time when the Inn isn't too busy and Victor isn't travelling with his team."

"I want to see the helicopter and ride in a car with Lucien. It sounds like a cool place."

Lucien sat up straight again and smiled. "It is a cool place. Socrates is basically a big kid who has a lot of cool toys, and he likes to share them with people so they can enjoy them too."

"What else does he have?"

Lucien shrugged. "Aside from a car collection, a helicopter, two small planes, an entire estate, some racehorses, and his own test track? Oh, and three racing teams?"

"When you say it like that, it sounds pretty excessive." Victor took his arm off Lucien's shoulders and Lucien wanted to grab it back. Lucien almost made a jest about S1 being the team of excess with the amount of fuel they used in each race as well as all the travel. S1 was really the worst team for climate change and while Series E was the future —and carbon neutral—but something about the way

Victor sat kept him from pushing too hard. Was this progress?

"We should probably stop dominating this discussion with our obsession with cars. What are the plans for the rest of today?" Lucien asked. He wanted to get the spotlight away from Victor so he'd relax again.

"I have some preparation to do in the kitchen for tomorrow. There are a few rooms booked for the Christmas lunch in the hotel restaurant. Gordon?" Collette asked her husband.

"No plans."

"We could take people for a drive in the 300SL?" Victor asked.

"Yes please." Victor's father and Gordon and Rory all answered in unison, and Lucien chuckled.

"It's only a two-seater, so it'll have to be one at a time." He'd probably have to think about ensuring they had enough petrol to get home again too.

"Not too fast."

"I always obey the road rules." Lucien wasn't about to throw an antique car around on country roads. The risk wasn't worth the pay off, besides, most people's idea of fast was quite slow on his scale. He wouldn't have to go too fast to impress them.

"We need to decorate the inn with holly. We should go for a walk and collect some this morning." Victor's mother, Melanie, had a good suggestion.

"Excellent. Maybe some fresh air will stop these two talking about cars," said Nicole.

"I doubt it, but we can try and expand their minds a little." Melanie winked, and Lucien nodded in acknowledgement. Unfortunately, he didn't know much beyond cars and racing. He didn't even know what holly looked like; although it was probably something Christmas related, so he figured he'd recognise it once he was shown some. He had seen enough Christmas movies to know what happened in other families; he'd never admit to watching sappy movies with happy families just to hope that he might have that one day. He barely admitted it to himself.

"If everyone is finished, please take your plates through to the kitchen." Craig's direction had everyone moving, and Lucien followed along at the end of the group. He ended up walking beside Victor's father.

"Tell me, Peter—" Lucien didn't have a question and suddenly it seemed rude to ask if he was content to be the quiet one in the family.

"Yes?"

"Am I being insufferable?"

"No. Why?"

"The whole conversation at breakfast revolved around me. That's the definition of insufferable."

Peter scoffed. "You are new. Everyone is curious."

"Are you curious?"

"I have heard Victor talk about you for years now."

Now Lucien was curious. "And?"

"You aren't what I expected."

Lucien held his breath.

"I thought you'd be … more."

"More, what?"

"More temperamental. More insufferably cocky."

Lucien eased out the breath he'd been holding. "Okay?"

"When Victor got his first job, we used to watch the

races on the sports channel. They didn't show Victor very often, but there were a few races where you crashed and acted like ... well, like a damned fool. Kicking the car's tyres. Punching a wall. Throwing your helmet on the ground. I expected you would be a lot—" Peter paused and Lucien didn't want to know what he would say next. He stared at the floor, unable to meet Peter's eyes as he reminded him of a what an ass he used to be. "More."

"I was very hot headed when I started out in S3."

"We stopped watching all the races because we hardly ever got to see Victor and it made Melanie very uncomfortable to see someone in Victor's team behaving so out of control."

"Fair enough. I had a lot of issues when I was younger."

"And they are improving?" Peter's question felt like it was asking more than the words. Did he want to know if his son was safe?

"Absolutely. It's been a long road. I've got a good team around me now. I have a therapist and a sports psychologist helping me deal with my anger problem."

"You readily admit to having an anger problem?"

"Yes. I can hardly lie and pretend it doesn't exist when the evidence is literally on global television."

Peter patted him awkwardly on the shoulder. "Many people do deny such things."

"Not me." Lucien growled, then forced himself to settle the rising red mist before it grabbed hold of him. "Do you know why I picked the London crash to show Rory?"

"Because it was spectacular and you walked away?"

"Yes, that. But mostly because if the same thing had happened to me three years ago, I would've punched the other driver in the head and called him rude names. It was completely Van Dijk's fault. He shunted me into the sausage kerb."

"And yet, you didn't go near him."

"No. If you watch the crash again, you'll see that when I am extracted from the car, I stand next to the barrier for a couple of moments, just breathing. People who notice that; well, they think that I'm injured when I'm doing that. I was physically fine. I clung onto that tyre wall to stop myself from marching over to Van Dijk and decking him. I can't be that person that I used to be." Lucien was caught between being proud of himself that he'd stopped himself and frustrated that he was always going to have to make a conscious effort not to be a complete tool.

"Show me."

Lucien pulled his phone out of his pocket and leaned against the wall as he typed in the crash (again) to his search engine app. He didn't need to have the link saved because he hadn't looked at it since it happened half a year ago. Today was the most often he'd looked himself up online in ages. He turned the face of his phone towards Peter and watched Peter's face. Victor's father gasped; presumably when the car hit the kerb and took off—then he frowned.

"Gosh. That's quite an impact."

"Yes. It hurt a bit." Lucien heard the radio call, all tinny through the small speakers of his phone. "Are you okay?" "I'm okay. Sorry." He dangled there in his seven-point harness until the marshals came, checked the car, then helped him out. He wasn't sure he breathed properly in those few minutes.

"Oh, now you are out of the car. I see what you meant."

"Yes?"

"Look." Peter turned the phone towards him and went back on the video a little bit. "Look, you scramble to your feet, then stare at the other car, before grabbing the tyre wall. It does look like you are just a little wobbly on your feet, but I can see your perspective too." Peter handed him back his phone and clapped him on the back. "You did really well in controlling an outburst against the other driver. Was it his fault?"

"Absolutely. He got a five grid place penalty for the next race."

"And if you'd hit him?"

Lucien shrugged. "Likely we would both have had some type of penalty." It wasn't about that for him, although his team would argue otherwise, it was about not being like his shithead father. Victor was so lucky to have a father like Peter whose quiet humble presence and continual reminders to be kind were born out in the way he acted. He walked his talk.

"You did well." Peter's simple praise made Lucien feel ten-feet tall. He waited for Peter to hand back his phone, then slipped it into his pocket. If he could keep this gentle warmth, like being fed soup on a cold day, he'd tuck it into an envelope and carry it with him everywhere. Hopefully Victor understood what a gift his father was. Surely he did; he was too self-aware to take his father's kindness for granted.

CHAPTER 17

"Y ou've worked us all too hard." Victor hugged Ma then stepped back and showed her his hands. They'd spent the morning harvesting boughs of holly from trees planted near the inn for lightning protection—a local myth that was weirdly backed up by science—something about the shape of the leaves, according to Nicole, with the long spines on each leaf working as a miniature lightning conductor. Once they'd gathered enough holly, they'd all brought them inside to the main dining room where Gordon had set up long tables for guests to make their own wreaths. Victor had helped guests by bringing them boughs of holly when they needed them, and at some point, he'd gifted his gloves to one of the guests, so now his hands were covered in tiny scratches from the sharp plant.

"You were the one who decided not to wear gloves." Ma admonished him.

"I didn't take my gloves off to prove how tough I was." Victor wanted to roll his eyes like a petulant teenager.

Sometimes Ma's teasing frustrated him because he wasn't very good at easy retorts. He always took things too seriously at first.

"I know, honey. I saw how you gave your gloves to the nice old man staying with his wife in room twelve." Then she said things like that which managed to balance it out and make him feel like he was overreacting for being annoyed at the teasing.

Victor shrugged. "It is a spirit of Christmas."

"And it's the family philosophy for running the inn. For generations we have cared for weary travellers who have found their way to Dochgarroch and we've cared for them. It's instinctual."

"Are you saying I gave our guest a pair of gloves because it's bred into me?" Victor wanted to call bullshit on that one. He was kind to people because his parents had instilled kindness as a core tenant. "Next you'll say that I had no choice but to help a guest because it's in my DNA."

Ma laughed. "Of course."

"I think that's ridiculous. I helped the guest because that's what we were always taught about running the inn. The guest's needs come first."

"And now your hands need tending to. It's hard to look after other people if you aren't looking after yourself too."

"Yes." Victor couldn't tamp down this damned irritation inside him. He wasn't even sure if it was Ma that he was annoyed at. The whole holiday was a distraction from the work he needed to do, and where the hell was Lucien?

"What's the matter?"

"I don't know."

"Is it Lucien?"

Victor breathed in through his nostrils. "I guess?"

"You know that I don't offer advice for no reason; only when you need to hear it. It's always offered with love."

"What is your advice?"

Ma rubbed his shoulder. "Relax. He's your friend, first and foremost. Whatever happens next, you both have a foundation of caring for each other through your friendship."

"But what if this destroys the friendship?"

Ma frowned. "Why would it?"

"What if it doesn't work out? Won't it be awkward afterwards? I don't want to lose his friendship."

Ma hugged him. "Victor, honey. You are so much like me sometimes. It's like looking into a mirror."

"What?" Victor didn't see why that was relevant to anything.

"I thought that becoming a therapist would help me understand how brains work. It would give me some control for the constant overthinking I did."

"And?"

"Sometimes understanding a problem doesn't always give a solution. Maybe all the stressful overthinking I do is simply nature, and I can't nurture it out of me."

Victor nodded. He had the same inability to control the way his brain cycled the same information over and over until everything felt like a disaster in the waiting. "I have this issue at work, and I can't let it go. I can't get past it. Now it feels like it's stopping me from doing the other, more important, tasks for my job." Like getting next year's car ready for pre-season testing in a couple of months. "My brain just goes around and around and it's exhausting. And now you are telling me there's nothing to be done. It's literally my nature."

"How much of any action is innate nature versus the nurture of a parent or of oneself? It's a continual balance."

Victor clenched his teeth together. "It's Christmas Eve. Spare me the philosophy." He immediately regretted grumping at Ma and tried to send her an apologetic look. She nodded.

"I'm pretty sure Melanie wants you to agree that it's nurture, not nature." Lucien slung his arm over Victor's shoulder. "I suppose even therapists need the validation that they'd done a good job."

Ma smiled at Lucien. "All humans like to be told when they've done well. There is nothing wrong with external validation, provided it isn't your only source of confidence. Why give the power of your happiness to other people?"

"Very true. Sometimes it's hard to avoid."

"What do you mean?" Ma asked and Victor frowned at her.

"Ma. Where is the line between therapy and curiosity?"

Both Ma and Lucien laughed. "It's okay, Victor. Your mother is allowed to interrogate me. I'm sure she wants to know if I'm capable of caring for her son and that I'm going to treat you properly."

"Fucking hell." Victor buried his face in his hands. Lucien had no filters. Victor didn't mind that his mother was curious about Lucien, she found people fascinating and he definitely understood being fascinated by Lucien, but it was too soon after they'd kissed for the first time and he wasn't sure about anything. Throw in Lucien's lackadaisical ease about it all—calling him boyfriend, teasing his Ma—

and it was all a lot of change to process in a short amount of time.

"For years, my worth was measured on the racetrack. I was lauded when I won and punished when I didn't. It took a long time to figure out that I'm more than just a driver who only matters when I win." Lucien shook his head slightly. "Knowing the truth doesn't make it easier though. I still find it hard not to let winning become proof that I'm a good person."

"Interesting."

"Ma." Victor warned his mother.

"Victor, honey. It's lovely that you are so protective of Lucien, but you do realise he's a grown man who can make his own choices about this conversation."

"I quite like his protectiveness. Victor, shall we go and get ready for dinner now?" Lucien's comment jarred Victor. He thought Lucien wanted to talk to Ma about ... his deadbeat father and all that stuff. But he wasn't going to disavow Lucien if he wanted to leave.

"Okay. See you later, Ma." Victor gave her a quick hug.

"He's a good man, Victor. I'm just not sure he believes it." Ma's whisper was correct, proving once again that she was good at her job.

"I know. But like you often say, it's his own journey, Ma." Victor stepped away from his mother and turned to Lucien. "Shall we go?"

———

They'd barely made it inside their room when Lucien pushed Victor against the door. He didn't kiss him, just stared deep into his eyes with a questioning expression. Victor wanted to squirm against Lucien's body to guide their cocks together and feel that delicious pressing heat again. Once would never be enough.

"You have such an interesting relationship with your mother."

"Oh?" Victor must have a concussion with the way his brain jerked back to reality. What on earth did Lucien mean by asking that?

"She's so caring and pleasant and yet you keep her at a distance. Why?"

Victor didn't think he did. Not much, anyway. He struggled to get enough blood in his head to answer Lucien, because he needed—desperately—to remove that curious expression from Lucien's face and replace it with desire. He cleared his throat. "Ahh... One theory is that I have middle child syndrome; which may or may not be a thing depending on which study you read. The oldest child bears the responsibility of doing well for the parents and often also for caring for younger siblings. The youngest child is the baby of the family who enjoys all the fun, and the middle child gets overlooked on both fronts." The theory was that middle children had to work harder to get noticed, and that meant they tended to be either more charming or naughtier. The theory didn't work for him, he was basically a rule follower, a goody two-shoes. But he'd always wondered if he kept a little distance because he felt over-looked and when his parents paid him attention, it always caught him by surprise. He always wondered '*why are you noticing me now?*' Had he done something wrong? Usually the answer was no, but the instinct was hard to shake since he was out of practice at being noticed.

"Or it could be that I was sent to boarding school as a teenager, so I'm just not used to the attention from them." Victor probably should see a therapist of his own—not Ma —to figure out this puzzle, but it never seemed that important on the scale of things.

"Fuck, you are so sexy when you talk all geeky." Lucien leaned forward and kissed Victor. A firm, hard, demanding kiss that had Victor whimpering for more. This was what he'd been hoping for, and he relaxed under the ministrations of Lucien's mouth. He reached out and held Lucien by the hips pulling him closer, loving the way he was squashed between Lucien's firm hot body and the hard cold door. Lucien kissed in such a decadent fashion, as if he really loved kissing. He showered Victor in attention and Victor adored it. Middle Child Syndrome or not. He could get addicted to the way Lucien kissed with such obvious enjoyment. Victor needed more. He tugged Lucien's shirt out of his jeans, desperate to touch his skin, and when his palms connected with Lucien's warm skin, he sighed. Lucien cupped his cheek.

"Look at you."

Victor held Lucien's gaze—not ready to ask what Lucien could see in his expression—and spread his hands over Lucien's back. The scratches on his hands stung a little and he ignored them.

"Why are you frowning?" Lucien brushed his forefinger over the crease on Victor's forehead. "Did I do something wrong?"

"No. I want this. I want you." Victor's throat thickened.

"Only if you tell me why you are frowning?"

Victor sighed. "It's not about you."

"Do you think I make everything about me?" Lucien was frowning now. Victor shook his head. This man and his constant battle to be more than the selfish fuck he'd been raised by; it slayed Victor to watch Lucien struggle to believe he was a good person.

"This is getting out of hand." Reluctantly, he removed his hands from Lucien's back and held them up. "This is why I was frowning. Touching them hurts a little bit."

"Victor. Why weren't you wearing gloves?" Lucien stepped back and held Victor's hands in his own as if they were precious to him.

"I wore gloves for most of the day, but at the end one of the guests didn't have any and he wanted to make a wreath, so I lent mine to him."

Lucien lifted Victor's hands to his mouth and gently pressed kisses all over his scratched hands, with such tenderness that Victor couldn't understand how Lucien couldn't see his own caring nature.

"You have such beautiful hands."

"I do?" Victor just had hands. They functioned, which he could concede was a type of pragmatic beauty.

"You do. And now you've gone and hurt them." Lucien's little kisses were going to destroy Victor. Every single one pierced his heart.

"I'll heal." He wanted to dismiss this moment, to make it less intense somehow.

"Your kindness is always getting you into trouble."

Lucien licked the inside of Victor's right wrist and Victor's knees buckled.

"What does that mean?" It didn't exactly sound like a compliment but that didn't make sense. Victor was caught off balance by the sensual way Lucien used his tongue on Victor's tender skin, and the words he teased him with.

Lucien smiled. "Years ago, you made friends with an angry young man, and now look at you."

"I don't follow your logic."

"You were kind to me and now we are both in trouble."

"We are?"

"Yes. The trouble..." Lucien drew out the word, then blinked slowly. "The trouble is that I really want to keep kissing you. My friend..." Lucien breathed in and out with a little ragged noise, leaving Victor wanting to kiss him again. "And I don't know if that's a good idea, or a fucking brilliant one?"

Victor didn't know what to say. A weird whimpering noise came out of his mouth, which was quite embarrassing.

"The trouble with kissing you is that it's making me feel things and I—" Lucien sucked in a deep breath, his nostrils flaring. "I think I prefer sex when it's less complicated. And I'm torn between wanting to strip myself bare and have you fuck me, and worrying that I'll..."

"Ruin our friendship." Victor worried about the same thing. "I worry too. What if this changes everything between us and I like you too much to lose you through a silly mistake."

Lucien held his gaze for a moment, then leaned closer, resting his forehead against Victor's forehead. They stood there for a long time, just breathing, with Lucien cradling Victor's sore hands. It was probably already too late to be having this conversation.

"Goddamn it. I really want to kiss you again. Can I?"

Victor cleared his throat. "We are grown men. I'd like to think that we can manage to stay friends afterwards if we just try hard enough." Just because part of him screamed that this would be impossible, didn't mean that he couldn't want to believe it.

"Let's agree to do that."

"You just want me in your bed." Victor's chuckle came out all breathy and weird.

"Yes. I really do."

Victor didn't have time to take a breath before Lucien was kissing him again. Their hands pressed against his chest as they kissed; open mouthed, fast, desperate kisses that said all the things that Victor couldn't say. That he wanted Lucien as more than a friend, that he wished he believed that he was Lucien's type—against all the evidence—and he'd always found Lucien incredibly sexy. How many times had he watched footage of Lucien walking in pit lane, unzipping his racing suit? The way his hand trailed from his throat down to his waist as he undid his suit was so goddamn hot. That he got to kiss him now seemed like a dream.

"You are thinking again."

Victor couldn't deny it.

"Does that giant brain of yours ever turn off?" Lucien nibbled at Victor's bottom lip, rendering him unable to speak. He stared deep into Lucien's golden brown eyes instead.

"I wonder if I could find a way to help you stop thinking."

Victor growled. "I like thinking."

"Think about this." Lucien stepped back, released Victor's hands, and pulled his shirt over his head. Fuck. Victor loved seeing him like this, all those lean muscles rippling, and his incredible tattoo with the steampunk cheetah covering his bicep and the words 'wicked fast', with the cheetah's paw outstretched across his pectoral muscle, having just scratched Lucien with sharp claws. Victor reached out and traced the tattooed scratches on Lucien's chest. Gooseflesh rose where his fingers touched Lucien's skin and he leaned in to kiss Lucien again. The taste of him on his tongue was like the heady rush when drinking vodka too fast on a cold day and he had to slow down before he swooned.

"I've always wondered if the mechanical heart was a symbol." Victor knew it was likely that Lucien had deliberately done this as a symbol; that the cheetah was ripping open his chest to expose a mechanical heart, one without the ability to love.

"Of course it is. Use that clever brain of yours."

"You are capable of feelings." Victor ducked his head and kissed the tattoo, dragging his lips over Lucien's skin. The tattoo tasted just like the rest of Lucien's skin —delicious with a weird hint of the holly they'd spent all day carrying—he knew it would because he'd been curious about the taste of tattoos years ago. Would they retain a hint of ink? He'd been wondering this before he got his own tattoo, not that he could kiss his own nipple to figure out the answer anyway, but he was hardly a virgin and there had been that memorable one-night stand in Baku after the S3 race there two years ago when he'd met an older man in a bar and satisfied his curiosity on the taste of tattoos and well... a whole bunch of other things.

"You are thinking too much again." Lucien licked along the outer edge of his ear. "I love when you get all hot and bothered and your ears go pink."

"You do?" Victor was glad of the excuse not to talk about what he'd been thinking about.

"I do. Now what was so interesting that you stopped playing with my tattoo?"

Victor's face burned hot and Lucien chuckled.

"This is going to be good. Were you thinking about what you want to do with me?"

"Fuck." Victor didn't think his face could get any hotter but now it was an inferno.

"Now I have to know. Please." Lucien licked his bottom lip. The little flash of pink dragging over his plush lower lip only added to the fire burning inside Victor. He'd lost track of whether the heat was desire or embarrassment or some weird combination of both where they fuelled each other into an inferno radiating out from his chest to consume him.

"It's embarrassing."

Lucien cupped Victor's chin and lifted his face up, then traced one finger across Victor's blazing cheeks. "I can see that. Your fantasies are safe with me."

If only it has been something like that, not a weird train of thought that ended up being about someone else, but Victor wasn't about to lie to his friend now. "Remember when you won the S3 race in Baku and we all went to that bar?"

"Yes." Lucien paused. "You want a threesome?"

"What?" That wasn't what Victor meant. He'd had no clue that Lucien had celebrated in such a way.

"That night, I had a threesome with two super-hot men. It was like a chain, and I was in the middle."

Victor's brain emptied. "Um..." His stomach churned at the image. Did he want that? Fuck, he could picture it with Lucien driving his cock into Victor while Victor did the same to some random person; being bisexual meant anyone could fill that role in this fantasy. Hell. He was going to expire on the spot; spontaneous combustion or something completely unscientific.

"I had no idea you were so kinky. How did I not know this?"

Victor felt like he'd been thrown off a cliff. This discussion had gotten completely out of control. "Wasn't that. I didn't know that had happened that night. I just meant that, um, I went back to that same bar a couple of years later, when I was still in S3 and you were in S1."

"Okay?"

"I met someone." Victor cursed his need for honesty because this was about the most awkward conversation he'd ever had in his thirty years on this planet.

"And had a threesome?" Lucien's frown deepened.

"Fucking hell. No. We just had standard sex, a one-night stand."

"But you were thinking about him while licking my chest? I don't understand."

Victor ran his hands through his hair. "This is so

embarrassing. I was licking your tattoo and thinking about how tattooed skin tastes just like skin, not like ink or whatever, and how I knew this because of that night back in Baku, and then my brain just spiralled because it was fucking weird to be thinking about someone else while my tongue was on you..." If he believed in God, he'd be quite happy to be taken to hell on the wings of an angel or something dramatic to make him disappear.

"And now you want a threesome?" Lucien slowly smiled until he was laughing. Victor smacked him on his bare chest.

"No. I just want you. Damn it."

"Good. Because while a threesome is really hot, I don't want to share you with anyone." Lucien's admitted jealousy sent a fresh rush of heat down Victor's spine.

"Same."

"Come here." Lucien held out his hands and Victor placed his own onto them. Lucien cradled Victor's hands gently, careful not to hurt his scratches, and walked backwards to the small ensuite in their room. He ran the tap until it was warm, then used a cloth to gently wash all the scratches. Victor could barely breathe as Lucien cared for him with such tenderness. The complexity of this man who risked his life for his job, laughed and teased about threesomes, and freely gave his time to cleaning Victor's hands was overwhelming. His insides were all soft and gooey at being cared for, and his cock was rigid at the thought of being fucked by Lucien in such a public display of need. As Lucien dried off his hands, Victor shuddered.

"Did I hurt you?"

Victor shook his head. "No. I just want ... you. I want you."

"Now?"

"Yes." He pulled his hands away and ripped off his clothes. "Stop teasing me and please just—"

"Kiss you? Blow you?" Lucien tilted his head, his lips curling at the edges. "Fuck you?"

"Yes. Please. Now." All this talk of threesomes and not wanting to share and being looked after, had Victor trembling with need. He had to have Lucien now. No more talk. No more kissing.

CHAPTER 18

Lucien adored teasing Victor like this—more than the way he teased him as a friend—and seeing him strip off his clothes with fumbling fingers, desperate to be naked for Lucien was the ultimate outcome. He followed him out of the ensuite back into the main room. Victor threw himself on the bed, sprawled on his stomach with his ass in the air. Fuck, what a sight. Lucien stepped up behind him, leaning against his thighs.

"You still have pants on." Victor whined, his voice all rough.

"Yes." Lucien placed one hand on the flat of Victor's back, and with the other, he reached around to hold Victor's thick erection. The moan Victor let out was decadent. Lucien stroked him, loving the smooth skin under his palm. The drip of moisture leaking from the head of Victor's cock told him how close Victor was, and he used his thumb to explore the tip of Victor's cock.

"Please."

Lucien leaned over Victor's body, letting his chest

touch Victor's back, and whispered into his ear. "What do you need, Victor?"

Victor moaned, so deep that it was almost a growl.

"You have to tell me what you want. I need to know. I need your consent." He wasn't—ever—going to do anything without Victor's explicit permission again. He'd stepped over that line once and he had to retain control over his anger, or any other emotion. He wasn't going to let himself hurt someone just because his feelings got out of control.

"Please fuck me."

"Do you have a condom?" Lucien wasn't sure that he did, and the likelihood that he had lube was even less. Fuck. This wasn't good, unless Victor was prepared. Lucien certainly hadn't planned to have sex while on holiday with a random friend. Best friend? He wasn't exactly swimming with choices for friends. There was probably a condom or few in his suitcase, leftovers from his pointless trip to the Maldives, but he wasn't about to go hunting for one now on the off chance that he hadn't tidied up from his last trip.

"No."

"Then we can't." Lucien stood up and rolled Victor over. Before Victor had a chance to protest, Lucien went down on his knees and sucked Victor's length into his mouth. He'd already been so close—begging for Lucien's cock—and now it wouldn't take much to bring Victor to the edge. For himself too, judging by the way his own cock rubbed his jeans uncomfortably. The salty taste of Victor's precum was fucking delicious and he licked and sucked and took Victor deep into his throat. He used his shoulders to push Victor's thighs wider and slid his hands up the insides of Victor's legs, until he cupped Victor's balls.

"Fuck. I'm close."

Lucien hummed around Victor's cock, loving the noises Victor made. Lucien flattened his tongue and took Victor as deep as he could without gagging, loving the way Victor's balls tightened in his hand, and Victor's gasps became shallower. Suddenly, Victor grabbed Lucien's hair and pulled. Hard. It surprised Lucien, and his head jerked upwards with his mouth sliding off Victor's cock with a loud pop.

Victor shouted insensibly, followed by a few babbled swear words. "Lucien."

His name rang through the room as Victor came, spurting onto Lucien's throat and chest. It was glorious. Victor's face, with his eyes squeezed shut and his mouth open, was incredible. Lucien wanted to see that expression a million times. Victor flopped back on the bed, and Lucien would've been content to let him rest, except he could never resist teasing his friend.

"You can't sleep yet."

Victor half-heartedly lifted his head. "Huh?"

"No sleeping. Not yet." Lucien waited.

"Oh, fuck, I'm so sorry. That was so good. I completely forgot about you." Well, if that was a compliment, Lucien would take it. He'd given his friend such a good blowjob that he'd forgotten...

"Yes. We're supposed to be at dinner in half an hour and you've made a mess of me."

"Dinner?" Victor frowned, then scrambled on the bed.

"Shit. Dinner. What magic did you weave that I've forgotten everything?"

"Not everything, I hope?" Lucien licked all the way Victor's torso, then bit his nipple. Not hard, just enough that he'd gasp. Victor's eyes rolled back in his head, so Lucien did it again, then licked the tiny tattooed car.

"Tastes like skin."

Victor puffed out a breathy laugh. "Lucien."

"Should I keep going?" Lucien could tease this gorgeous man forever, drinking in his ragged breaths. The way he said Lucien's name made him feel like he stood on a podium. King of the world. Fastest driver on earth.

"I'm never going to get to dinner if you keep doing that."

"Let's have a quick shower." Lucien would deal with his own erection in the shower. He leaped up and walked towards the ensuite. Once he reached the doorway, he glanced over his shoulder, before undoing his jeans and pushing them down his legs. Victor jumped off the bed and ran across the room, then wrapped his arms around Lucien's waist. His hands were a little rough; partly from the way the holly had scratched them, and partly because he moved them quickly. Victor rested his chin on Lucien's shoulder, kissing his neck as he stroked Lucien's cock.

"Fuck, Victor, that's so good." Lucien had already been at the edge watching Victor's pleasure and now the unsteady, needy, way that he stroked Lucien's cock was pushing him closer and closer to... Lucien grabbed the door frame, needing the support, and his fingers clutched the wood until his arm muscles shook. With every stroke of Victor's hand on his cock, he clung tighter to the door. His breath was ragged, out of time with Victor's tight hand, and then Victor sucked on his earlobe. The combination of his hot breath in Lucien's ear and the sharpness of his mouth was all it took.

"Holy shit." He let out a long groan as he came hard enough to see stars. Victor kissed down his neck, and across his shoulder blades, and Lucien let his head hang forwards in the aftermath of a really fucking good orgasm. His breathing slowed and he was overcome with the urge to lie in bed with Victor and cuddle him. What? It must be a friendship thing, because he'd never wanted to do that with anyone else.

"Let's get cleaned up and go to dinner." He really didn't want to. Hanging out with other people was the last thing he wanted to do when he could cuddle in bed with Victor and explore all the ways they could bring each other to orgasm without needing a condom. He was clean, but he didn't want to broach that conversation so early in this ... whatever this was. Friends with benefits? A proper relationship? Gah. He normally mentioned it before he hooked up with someone and now they'd done this a few times without talking about safety. Lucien didn't know how to be in a relationship. He was going to make a mess of this before they'd even started; probably already was fucking this up. His head hung heavily.

"Do we have to go to dinner?" Victor apparently agreed.

"They are your family. Do you think they'd be upset if we just stayed in our room?"

Victor ran his hands down Lucien's back, over his ass muscles, all the way down to his feet, where his pants were still around his ankles, and helped him step out of them. He'd completely forgotten that he had only been half-way through getting undressed when Victor had pounced on him.

"I think they'd be delighted either way. Staying here would prove that they were right, and…"

"Going to dinner with them looking at us is going to prove them right too." Lucien shook his head as he stepped into the shower to turn it on.

"Yeah. They already think that me inviting you here means that we are boyfriends."

Lucien held his hand under the water, waiting for it to warm up, and turned to face Victor. "Aren't we?"

"I guess so." Victor had that 'I'm trying to figure out a puzzle' expression of his that Lucien usually enjoyed seeing, mostly because he loved the next moment when Victor figured something out and he would almost smile to himself in the cutest way. Okay, crap. Lucien was in deep here. And probably had been for a while now, if he was going to be honest with himself.

"I'd like to be your boyfriend."

"You would?" Victor ran his hands through his hair. "I mean, you've called me that a couple of times already, so I suppose it's not a surprise."

"Victor. We've literally fucked. You are my friend. I'm not going to walk away from this easily." The water was finally warm enough, and he adjusted the temperature, then got into the shower. Water streamed over his head, and he grabbed the soap to wash all the come off his body.

"Are you annoyed at me?" Victor took the soap from his hands and started to wash him.

"How can I be annoyed when you do this?" Lucien spread his arms wide. "It's hard to be annoyed when I'm being lathered in attention."

"Lathered. Ha." But Victor wasn't laughing.

"Jesus, fuck, Victor. Do you want a proposal? Stop doubting this. You've been my friend for years, even when I was too much of an asshole to deserve friendship, and now we've kissed. You are my type—"

"Because I give you attention?"

"Can you stop being fucking irritating? You are my type because you are my friend. I adore spending time with you. You make me laugh. You care about me. You fucking make me want to care for myself. Don't you understand what a bloody gift that is? Hell. I would, quite literally, be dead if I hadn't had your friendship when I first came to S3. I was a reckless young man being pushed by a toxic old man who wanted to live my life for me, through me, whatever. And you saw through the drama to the real me. I pissed off so many people in that first year. I'm sure I was the most hated person on the team."

"No. That was your father, but to be fair... Yeah, a lot of people couldn't separate you from him, and the mechanics did find having to fix your car frequently on race weekends quite frustrating." Victor stopped soaping and Lucien grabbed the soap from his hands. He lathered it up and spread the soapy bubbles all over Victor's torso.

"I've wanted to kiss you for a long time now."

"No. That can't be right."

Lucien grabbed Victor's arm and washed it, then did the other, dragging his fingers down his bicep and forearm. "I didn't deserve you, so I would've denied it if you'd asked.

Hook ups with random strangers is a lot easier than falling for my best friend. Shit." Lucien sank to his knees and washed Victor's legs.

"Can you relax a bit?"

"What?"

"You are being quite aggressive with your hands."

Lucien rocked back on his heels and held his hands up, away from Victor's body. "Sorry." Obviously he wasn't boyfriend material if he couldn't even wash Victor without doing it wrong. Anger still guided his body whenever any emotion threatened to become uncontained.

"It's okay. My doubt shouldn't be your burden."

Lucien stood up and kissed Victor. "Please don't doubt this."

"How? I can't help comparing myself to all the cute men on your social media and I'm just..." Victor waved his hand in front of his body.

"Victor. I don't need you to be a gym junkie, or to be an athlete who is as fit as me. I adore you as you are." And his cock agreed, already getting hard again just from being close to Victor's naked wet body. He moved closer, pressing his body against Victor so he could feel the truth.

"Oh." Victor swallowed.

"Let me wash you." He wanted to show Victor the truth, that he was falling for him—even if he probably shouldn't—and he wasn't ashamed to let him know. Victor nodded slowly, and Lucien bent to finish the task he'd started. He washed every inch of Victor's skin, taking care to be gentle with his touch, thrilled by the ways Victor sighed sometimes, or wriggled when Lucien touched a ticklish spot, but most of all, he wanted to show Victor the truth. He had always thought he didn't have a type—willing consent was his only benchmark—except only the pretty ones who consented ended up on his social media. He'd curated a type unconsciously, but it wasn't everyone and it wasn't really real; it was more about Lucien the driver brand. Fuck. He'd never be free from that expectation. It was unfortunate that Victor measured himself by something that wasn't the whole truth.

And now, Victor was the only person he wanted to be with. He stood up, satisfied that Victor was thoroughly soaped all over, and then he moved so that Victor was under the shower. The water streamed over Victor's body, sending lather running over the planes of his chest, and down his body to the floor.

"Take all the time you need." Lucien figured it out—finally—and all Victor needed was time to adjust to this change. He'd pushed too hard, too soon, for Victor to be his boyfriend, when they'd literally only kissed for the first time yesterday. He'd jumped in feet first, like he always did, racing towards an imaginary finish line, and he'd left Victor behind on the starting grid still trying to decide if he wanted to be in the same race.

"What?"

"I'm a race car driver. I've gone too fast."

Victor raised one eyebrow. "What are you saying?"

"If wanting to kiss you is the starting grid, I've rushed ahead into the let's be boyfriend's stage and will soon be heading for the chequered flag."

Victor grinned. "Only you could explain a relationship like it is a race."

"A sad truth. Anyway... I don't want to rush you, so I'm going to back off now."

"Does this mean that it's my job to think about the data and make strategic decisions?"

Lucien barked out a laugh, all the air in his lungs rushing out. "Um, I think we've taken this metaphor as far as we can. I just meant that I have a tendency to leap into things, and I guess you are good at thinking about every scenario, so maybe we have different ways of approaching this?"

"This being if we want to be friends with benefits or actual boyfriends?"

"I want to be your boyfriend." He'd just have to figure out how to do that as they went along. He'd never been anyone's boyfriend before. A flutter of panic rose like sawdust in his throat and he shoved it away. It couldn't be that hard. He just had to be faithful to Victor—not a hard-ship—and ... um ... listen to him. No, the key would be not to lash at him in anger because he knew deep down that Victor would always forgive him and that felt like too much of a burden for someone else to carry for him. Thank fuck for good therapists; he'd talk to his personal one as well as the team sports psychologist about how to manage a relationship while focusing on work. Other people did it. There must be a system or something that he could use as a starting place.

"It's hard to believe that when your face is all scrunched up and frowning."

"It is?" Lucien rubbed between his eyebrows and sure enough his eyebrows were knitted together in a deep frown.

"Oh. Well, I was just thinking that I've never been anyone's boyfriend before, so—"

"Really?"

"I'm not, like, a virgin." Just a relationship virgin if that was a thing.

Victor laughed. "Oh my god. I know that. This evening you told me about a threesome in a bar and I've seen your social media posts."

"Those don't tell the whole story."

Victor looked bemused. "Yeah, okay. I'm parking that one for later. Let's stick to the actual issue. You've never been in a relationship? Just hook-ups?"

"Yeah." Was there anything wrong with that? He was only twenty-five. Middle aged for an athlete, but still young for life stuff. "I'll figure it out. I have the internet."

"Fuck me, Lucien. You can't learn how to be a good boyfriend by reading some random blog post on the internet. God knows what you'll read."

"Why not? I like you and if I'm going to be your boyfriend, I don't want to fuck it up just because I'm ignorant. Plus, I know how the internet works. I'll have to read lots of different sources and then figure out which ones apply to us."

"Right. All you need is more data." Victor had the same expression as when he stared at his burnt-out engines, all in pieces on the shop floor.

"Yes. See. No dramas at all. Now let's get dressed and go to dinner." Lucien kissed Victor and it soon turned into a long luxurious kiss. His favourite sort.

"You wild beautiful man. How can I resist you?" Victor mumbled against Lucien's neck.

"You shouldn't resist me."

Victor stood up with a gasp and stared at Lucien, eyes wide and nostrils flared.

"What?" Did Lucien really want to know what Victor had just thought of? Yes. He would never get bored with the way Victor's brain worked.

"If you are going to do research on how to be a good boyfriend, please don't ask Socrates."

Lucien peered at Victor for a second, then tried to hold back a laugh. "But he'd enjoy it so much."

"Too much. We'd never hear the end of it."

"He'd turn it into the funniest speech at our wedding."

Victor shoved Lucien on the chest with both hands, and Lucien stepped backwards until his back hit the wall of the shower.

"What?"

"How can you joke about our wedding? Can you hear yourself?"

"But isn't that the logical conclusion of being boyfriends?" Lucien winked and Victor scrubbed both hands through his hair. Lucien wanted to beg him to do that again; the way the water mixed with Victor's masculine competent hands, and the threads of his black hair shifting against his skin was fucking everything. He wanted to grab each one of Victor's fingers and suck them into his mouth, just to hear Victor moan.

"Lucien."

"Fine. No asking Socrates for advice. No joking about weddings. What else do I need to know to be a good boyfriend?"

"If I say no teasing, you won't believe me, will you?"

"Hell no. Teasing you and seeing you flush is one of my favourite things, and I think you like it too. I'm pretty sure that even I know that being a decent boyfriend is about doing enjoyable things together."

Victor shook his head slowly. "Buckle me in. Being your boyfriend is going to be a wild ride, but I'm in. Tease me whenever you want."

Lucien wrapped his arms around Victor and squeezed him tight. "Yes."

"And now we are late for dinner." Victor didn't move though. He lifted his face and kissed Lucien gently on the lips. They stayed like that until Victor shivered.

"Fuck, the water is getting cold. Time to get out." Lucien reluctantly let Victor go and reached around him to turn off the water. He stepped out of the shower and grabbed a couple of towels, holding one out for Victor and wrapping him in it.

"The easiest way to be my boyfriend is to keep being yourself. You are a good friend to me, just keep doing that."

"With the added benefit of excellent sex." Lucien grinned as Victor blushed all over. "Come on, we are already late for dinner and everyone is going to know what we've been doing."

Victor's face went even brighter red. "I told you this would be wild. I suppose you are going to announce this to everyone."

"Of course. I'm so keen to be your boyfriend." Lucien really was. It felt like the beginning of brand-new exciting adventure.

CHAPTER 19

Lucien pressed a kiss between Victor's shoulder blades, then carefully extracted himself from the bed without disturbing Victor's sleep. Last night's dinner had been hilarious. He'd tried to listen and make sure he didn't dominate the conversation—which was easier now everyone had become bored with hanging out with a semi-famous race car driver and just treated him like any other person—and it'd been nice to sit beside Victor and enjoy the way his family obviously adored each other's company. He threw on some running clothes and grabbed his shoes from beside the hotel room's door, before heading outside for a run. Technically, Hettie had given him a day off for Christmas Day so he didn't need to run, but he'd woken up restless, needing to do something with his body.

Before he'd started racing in Series E, the season had started in November and gone through to June. Now it started in late January, so the teams could—theoretically—enjoy Christmas without needing to do race preparation. He'd been fortunate to join the circuit when the calendar aligned a bit more closely with the other Series races, so it was more in line with what he'd been used to in S1. It was easier to adjust to a new racing system when many parts were the same; the travel and the training.

Unlike Christmas, which was completely outside his life experience, something that he'd heard about from other people and from movies or whatever. The idea of spending Christmas Day with a proper family who did Christmas traditions and stuff... Phew, that was so far away from his experience that he needed to go for a run and get rid of some of this nervous energy. Nervous? He closed the door quietly, then bent down to put on his running shoes. Yes. This had similar vibes to race day, except on race days, he had a routine, and he knew what to expect. It was the weight of the team's expectations that created nerves. Before each race he would walk the track with his teammate Alex, their race engineers, and a few others from the team, and then they went through all the set up for the race. By filling every minute from waking up until the grid start with preparations for the race meant that he didn't have time to get nervous. He took that energy and used it to focus his thoughts as he sat on the grid start, ready to win. Once he was in his car, staring at the track through his halo, every nerve fled, and he was ready. Calm and wicked fast.

Today's nerves were different; they came from not knowing what was going to happen, or what to expect, or how he should behave. He couldn't, technically, win at Christmas Day so it was silly to worry, yet he wanted today to be perfect. He wanted to be the perfect boyfriend for Victor, with his emotions under control.

The air was sharp and cold as he stepped outside the

inn. He should've stretched inside where it was warmer. Too late now. He went through his pre-run routine, then began. Every step helped ease the churn in his stomach, and so he ran and ran until his lungs burned. He ran too far before he turned back towards the inn and by the time he'd arrived back where he started, he was done. His legs were dead and his lungs struggling for oxygen. But at least he was too knackered to be nervous anymore. He stumbled inside and walked up to his room. The door opened easily and he put his shoes near Victor's, just like proper boyfriends with their shoes neatly together—his heart fluttered a little— then he walked over to Victor who was still asleep. He couldn't resist kissing him on the temple. How lucky was he that this man wanted to be his friend? His boyfriend. Now he just had to make sure he didn't fuck it all up. First, a shower, and then he was about to experience his first ever family Christmas day. He shook out his hands, wiping them on his shorts. Judging by the way butterflies were dancing in his stomach, he'd need to go for another run. He certainly didn't feel like eating anything. He would because he was an athlete and Hettie would have his head if he didn't have proper nutrients after a long run like this one. After a few short breaths, he stripped off his rapidly cooling sweaty running clothes and had a shower.

"Merry Christmas." Victor sat up in bed and the blankets fell to his waist. Lucien stood awkwardly in his under- wear. He'd stared at his suitcase for too long unable to work out what he should wear today and now his skin was cold. Socrates had suggested a range of things from formal—his shirt needed an iron—to casual but right now he'd kill to have Socrates, or anyone, tell him what the appropriate thing was to wear to a family Christmas Day.

"Yeah."

"What's the matter?"

Lucien may as well be honest; he had nothing to gain from pretending everything was cool. "I'm nervous. I've never been to a family Christmas Day before."

Victor just nodded solemnly and Lucien was so grateful that Victor knew about his shithead father and he didn't have to explain why or anything. "Every family probably does it slightly differently. We get up early and the kids all open their Santa stockings." Victor flushed a little bit.

"Are you embarrassed about that?"

"No. Just that my parents still do stockings for us kids even though we are grown."

Lucien clapped his hands. "Oh my God. That's so adorable. Will I get one?"

"Fucking hell. If you want, I can ask Ma."

"I don't want to be any trouble."

"You are always trouble." Victor rolled over and grabbed his phone, his thumbs flying over the screen. It dinged with a reply. "She already made you one and wants us to know that we are late. Rory wants to see what is in your stocking."

"Shit." Lucien was already messing up and he hadn't even known it.

"It's fine. We aren't strict about this. People do their stockings whenever they wake up, then we have a late brunch together. It's timed so the hotel guests are sorted out as a priority. We set up a basic breakfast for any guests who are awake, then we feed ourselves."

"Okay." Lucien let out a long breath. He hadn't fucked up yet. "Then?"

"After brunch, we all work in the restaurant serving the guests their Christmas lunch, and after that's all cleaned up, we sit in the lounge together, eating, and swapping gifts. It's quite informal." Victor shook his head. "Fuck, when I was at uni, I went to Christmas with my girlfriend Carol, well, she's not anymore, obviously—"

"Relax. We both have, well, history with other people. Tell me about Carol."

"She's happily married now, but um, this is about Christmas." Victor's eyebrows knitted together, and Lucien pressed his finger to the crease.

"Tell me." He leaned closer, resting his face against Victor's hair, and breathing in the sandalwood scent of his shampoo. He didn't give a flying fuck about Victor's past relationships; it would be highly hypocritical of him to care about who Victor had slept with. This relationship business, and Christmas, was all new to him and he needed to know what to do.

"I went to her family's place for Christmas one year and it was awkward as fuck. They all sat in the lounge and had all the gifts under the tree. This slimy old uncle pretended to Santa and handed the gifts out one at the time. Each person had to open their gift with everyone looking at them, and gush their thanks to the giver, before the next gift was handed out."

"Okay?" Lucien had spent his Christmas Days with his father, usually being berated for not giving him enough wins during the year. That was the only gift his father ever wanted; success that he could gloat about. Sitting around with family—even a slimy old uncle—sounded nicer than being in the same room as a toxic old prick.

"It was so stilted and awkward and it took forever. We are more relaxed. There will be lots of laughter. Collette is really good at finding gifts for people, so everyone always looks forward to what she gives. Craig just gives everyone a bottle of local whiskey. You'll fit right in, and people are going to love getting Gamble Racing merch."

Lucien breathed out slowly. "I'm glad Socrates gave me a box of stuff to hand out." There was one thing in there that Lucien was really looking forward to giving to Victor. Socrates had used the 3D printer in the workshop to make a model of Victor standing next to Ondrej and the car with the trophy from the first podium Victor's car achieved at Austria this year. The trophy from Austria was bigger than a racing helmet and in the shape of the track which made it a lovely reminder of the location in the 3D model.

"Relax. It'll be fun."

"Tell me about the restaurant thing."

"We help out in the hotel restaurant because Gordon and Collette always give the staff the day off, so we dress up in staff uniforms and serve the guests their Christmas lunch."

"And you were just going to spring this on me?"

Victor had the decency to look contrite. "Yeah, sorry. We do it every year, so I guess I forgot that it's all new to you."

All of this was new; from the happy family, and how they helped out guests, and worked together. Always together. Lucien didn't expect Victor to understand, so he aimed for a teasing note instead.

"Is there anything else you've forgotten to tell me?" Every detail helped because he had no idea what a typical Christmas Day with a family meant, let alone a family who was also trying to run a boutique inn in the middle of nowhere at the same time. "Do you have to feed everyone dinner too?"

"No. Guests get a lunch with all the trappings, then the kitchen does a simple buffet option for dinner that is mostly cheese, crackers, fruit, and wine."

Lucien nodded. "And we eat after the inn's guests?"

"Yes. Mostly it's leftovers so it can be a bit random, but the point is to be together with family, not a fancy meal. We are very relaxed. You've already survived a couple of dinners with everyone, it'll be the same today."

"Okay. Next question. What do I wear?" Lucien hated being this far out of his depth. It made his stomach twist, and he couldn't possibly try and eat until he had enough answers. Hettie's voice nagged at him, that he had to eat soon, otherwise he'd lose muscle mass. Soon. When his guts stopped flipping.

Victor grinned; which didn't help at all.

"Now I am worried. Why are you grinning like that?"

"Like what?"

"Like you are about to spring a nasty surprise on me?" He needed to do something to stop him freaking out. "Don't tell me your family are secret nudists? I mean, I do have the best body in the room, but I'm not sure I'm keen to see your parent's naked bottoms."

Victor spluttered. "What the fuck, Lucien? How does your brain? You know what? Never mind."

Lucien swept Victor into a hug because he just adored Victor's responses to his teasing. Yes, he'd said that to skirt around his own nervousness. It'd worked. And he was grateful that Victor had, inadvertently, helped.

"Well?"

"Reality is a lot less weird than whatever you are imaging. Naked parents, what the everlasting hell?" Victor cleared his throat and rested his hands on Lucien's shoulders. "We have matching t-shirts. Collette gets them made, and we wear them while serving for lunch too. The guests love it. It's a little bit cringey."

"No. It isn't cringey. It's adorable. Dorky, but definitely adorable." Lucien would wear the heck out of a matching family Christmas shirt. He'd be part of a proper family. His eyes prickled with heat, and fucking hell, he might burst from the yearning for it. How on earth was he going to stop them from seeing his nasty brutal anger—he didn't know how to contain that all the time—but he was planning on keeping that tamped down tight. These lovely people who accepted him into their family didn't deserve to see the worst of him.

"Okay. I'll get our shirts. Collette gave them to me last night." Victor tried to move and Lucien held him tighter.

"First, a kiss. Good morning, boyfriend." Lucien loved the flash of a grin on Victor's lips just before he leaned in and kissed him. He tasted a bit rough, like a long night's sleep, but it didn't matter. Lucien had showered after his run and brushed his teeth; fresh enough for them both. Mostly it didn't matter because Lucien adored kissing. Always had. It bothered some of his hook ups in the past because it was too intimate, but that was the reason Lucien loved it. And to kiss Victor—his first boyfriend—was so special. He could shower him in kisses for hours. He ran one hand up Victor's spine and cradled the back of his head, loving the way Victor relaxed into his hold. Victor held Lucien's biceps, and with every stroke of their tongues together, Victor pulled Lucien closer.

"You are very distracting." Victor ran his hands up and down Lucien's bare arms. Lucien was more than willing to distract Victor from … whatever they were supposed to be doing, so he kissed him more, sucking on Victor's tongue until he moaned. He couldn't help it. He kept one hand firmly holding Victor's head, and with the other, he explored freely, running his hand all over Victor's naked body. Over his ass, and then along the softer parts of his waist and stomach, until he cupped Victor's balls.

"More." Victor begged.

"You want this?" Lucien mumbled against Victor's mouth, then sunk his tongue inside Victor's mouth as he wrapped his fingers around Victor's hard cock. He stroked lazily until Victor pulled back from their kiss.

"Faster." Victor slipped one of his hands between their bodies, and spread his palm over their leaking cocks, before he moved Lucien's fingers until both of their hands were wrapped around both cocks. Fucking hell, Lucien's eyes rolled back in his head. Having Victor take control and show him what he wanted was even better than listening to him beg for more. They had just enough precum to lubricate their hands as they stroked together, mouths resting on each other's cheeks, breathing ragged. Lucien was about to lose it.

"Victor." He tightened his fingers in Victor's hair and kept up the rhythm with his other hand. Victor's eyes were dark and wild with lust—he was so fucking hot when he looked like that—and Lucien sucked Victor's bottom lip into his mouth.

Victor shouted something that might have been Lucien's name or a swear word or a garbled combination, and he came. The feel of Victor's coming with their cocks held together was all it took, and he followed Victor into mutual pleasure. He was dizzy and it took him a second to catch his breath. He rested his head on Victor's shoulder, nuzzling against his neck, floating a little inside.

"Holy shit." It came out as a hoarse whisper. Lucien was quickly becoming addicted to the way Victor shouted nonsense when he came. Being able to make his very sensible boyfriend lose all his stiffness and relax like that was so special.

"Merry Christmas, Lucien."

"Best one ever." He kissed Victor on the tip of his nose. "I suppose I'd better shower again."

"Yes, we are probably the last ones to come down and open our stockings."

"Shower with me?" Lucien probably couldn't come again, not after such a long run and before he'd eaten to replace all the energy he'd used up, but he could try and give Victor another round.

"You say all the sweetest things."

CHAPTER 20

Victor loved watching Lucien serve the guest's their lunch. This year's shirt was a replica of the prank jumper worn by actor Ryan Reynolds several years ago. It looked like a big Christmas present with red and green paper and a gold ribbon that was tied in a big bow just under his ribcage. The Inn's logo was on the back with a slogan that said, 'Our gift to you is us'. Typical of Collette, it was innocent enough on face value with just enough of a hint of something rude that it could be interpreted either way.

"Did you know that Reynolds sold that original jumper for eight hundred and fifty thousand to charity? Isn't that cool?" Lucien sidled up to Victor with a grin. "The people at table four told me. They recognised it."

"Did they recognise you?"

"No. Only race car fans recognise me." Lucien bumped his elbow into Victor. "Soon more people will recognise you."

"Why?"

"The audience for that streaming show about S1 is probably bigger than people who watch the actual races. You'll be all over it."

"No. They only did one interview with me in the Gamble Racing weekend."

"About?"

"It was early in the season, so it was about the step up from S3 and living up to the legacy left by my predecessor."

"Legacy? His cars were slow. What are they talking about?"

Victor frowned at Lucien. "He built the cars that took Socrates to his World Championships. Yes, he didn't keep up with everyone else, and his last few seasons really weren't great, but you can't dismiss his initial cars."

"You didn't gloat at all? Your cars were so much faster than his."

"It's not really my style." Victor's toes tapped in his shoe as he remembered the interview and the way his stomach had churned. "It was a pretty intimidating experience."

"What? Talking to media. Didn't the team give you training first?"

"Not really. Socrates just said to relax, that the show just wanted to chat about ordinary things. And then they slammed me with a whole bunch of history that I wasn't across. I took on this job so late in the season with only a few months to build a whole car for the next season. I didn't have much time for anything else."

"And you still achieved a fast car."

"Are you two talking about cars again?" Nicole pulled

her phone out of her pocket, checked it, then put it away again.

"What is so interesting in that phone?"

"Just a project I'm doing."

"For uni?"

"Something like that."

"On Christmas Day?" Victor had been to university. He knew that wasn't how it worked.

Nicole shook her head. "It doesn't matter."

"I think it does." Lucien was looking at Nicole with a curious expression. "I can hear it in your voice."

"Just go back to talking about cars, will you?" Nicole grumped at him.

"Hey, you were the one teasing us about that." Victor was impressed with Lucien's perceptiveness. "Also, you can talk to us about whatever you are waiting for."

Nicole shook her head, then her phone dinged, and she pulled it out of her pocket, fumbling slightly. She read the message and her mouth dropped open. "Oh."

"Good or bad?" Victor wanted to wrap his little sister into a hug and protect her from whatever bullshit had been sent to her. And then she laughed. A hysterical laugh that didn't tell him anything.

"Holy shit." Nicole whispered, then clamped her hand over her mouth.

"Nicole, you are worrying your brother. Please tell him how he can help." Lucien's stern voice cut through the air.

"She did it."

"Who? What?" Victor was so confused and then Nicole's phone rang. She answered with a squeal.

"This is really happening, Kunaal." Nicole danced in a

circle. Okay, so this was good emotions. "Iona did it. ... Yes, we are good to go for launch."

Victor felt a tug on his hand.

"Come over here. Leave her alone with her news. Besides, table two is waving at you." Lucien nudged Victor, who didn't give a damn about table two.

"Okay." He watched his sister who was twitching and jumping with excitement. "I was worried that something was wrong, but she seems good."

"I don't know what is happening, but if I had to guess, she's more than good."

Nicole laughed again.

"I'm sure she'll tell you when she is ready."

He nodded. "Yes. She's my little sister, you know, so I want to protect her from the world. You understand."

"Theoretically yes. It's like when the press says something bad about a teammate and you want to tell them they know nothing?" Lucien asked.

"Yeah, I suppose a family is a bit like a team." He whirled around, aghast that he'd been so insensitive. "I'm so sorry for forgetting about your—" He'd meant to say family, but that didn't really describe Lucien's situation.

"For forgetting that I don't have a family. It's okay, Victor. My team is enough family for me. I have you and I have Alex, and I even have a weird uncle in Socrates."

Victor coughed. "He would make the best uncle, always saying the things that no one else can get away with." Victor could see Lucien being like that as he got older. It was the easiest thing in the world to imagine coming here for Christmas every year and listening to Lucien tease his family, like the curious uncle who loved everyone and wasn't afraid to show it. His chest tightened a bit. He'd had the same already with Craig and Zac growing up and it's been amazing. Heat built behind his eyes. "I'd better go and help table two."

———

Lucien perched on the edge of his chair at the back of the room as everyone crowded around the Christmas tree. It was decorated with twinkling lights and an eclectic bunch of hanging things, handmade treasures, and nothing really matched, yet it worked together. His leg kept wanting to bounce and he had to push it against the floor. Victor's father, Peter, and Rory sat cross legged on the floor beside the Christmas tree. It'd been a weirdly happy lunchtime, working in the restaurant, making guests feel welcome and fed. He wondered if that's how the mechanics felt after a good pitstop; that sense of satisfaction in being part of a team without the glory—and pressure—of being the driver. Was that how Victor felt seeing a car he'd designed doing well?

"Shall we start with this one? It doesn't have any names on it." Peter picked up the box of merch and Lucien stood up, awkwardly clearing his throat. Victor grabbed his hand and pulled him down again.

"Relax." His whisper soothed, as much as the simple touch of his hand and he plonked himself down in the seat. "Um, let's leave that one for a while and start with another one."

Peter nodded and put the box down, picking up another gift. "This one is for Rory from Victor."

"But you didn't bring any gifts in your luggage." He leaned over and whispered in Victor's ear.

"I posted my gifts a month ago."

"Clever." Lucien's chest puffed out with a bit of pride at his boyfriend who'd thought about everything and planned for today. Rory opened the gift and gasped. It was a Lego Series One car.

"Thank you so much Uncle Victor."

"It's remote controlled, and my boss had some Gamble Racing stickers printed, so you can use them if you want too."

"So cool. It's like a Lego version of your car."

"Technically, no."

Lucien pressed his palm over Victor's mouth. "Let him enjoy it. No one needs the technicalities today." Victor nodded, his lips sliding over Lucien's skin which was oddly too hot for this room, especially while everyone was looking at them. Victor pulled Lucien's hand away.

"I know everyone thinks I'm car obsessed."

"You are!" Half the room yelled that out and the other half laughed.

"Anyway... I thought this would be fun for Rory, that's all."

"It is fun."

Peter whispered something to Rory, who nodded, then said, "Thank you, Uncle Victor."

Peter cleared his throat. "Okay, the next gift is from Collette to Nicole." They continued this way, handing out gifts in rapid fashion, often overlapping the teasing between people. The room was loud and with every laugh and gift, Lucien relaxed. He could do his gift now that he understood how it all worked. And he'd gathered a little pile of things for himself. A bottle of whiskey from Craig. A mug with the Inn's logo on it from Collette and Gordon, and a lovely scarf from Victor's parents. This was the best Christmas he'd ever experienced—with real gifts and happy people who enjoyed being with each other—and he didn't even know how to tell these people what a gift it had been to be included so easily. They'd probably not understand, and he didn't want to put a dampener on the festive mood.

"Okay, can I do my box of gifts now?" Lucien asked. Peter and Rory were too busy chatting to Nicole as she unwrapped something that looked like a ... fluffy pony toy?

"Just go and sit next to Rory. He'll help you with it all."

Lucien nodded and carefully picked his way through the room, through the scattered pieces of wrapping paper and piles of gifts and people, then sat down beside Rory.

"Want to help me with this one?"

"Like Santa's helper?"

"I guess so." Lucien didn't know anything about Santa except what he'd seen in movies. Why on earth children thought there was something special about some dude in a red suit was a mystery to him. But then, he'd grown up believing that if he didn't get into his car from the right side, he was going to crash. Ironically, it had taken Victor to show him his data for him to realise that it was just a superstition, something his father believed, and he didn't need to believe it anymore. He spent the rest of that season getting in his car from the wrong side—when his father wasn't looking—and Victor kept track of the data for him. His crash stats didn't change. It wasn't until his father died that his ability to keep the car on the track improved; and he freed himself from all that superstitious nonsense. He didn't need lucky underwear, or to always get dressed in the same order, or pray to his right tyre—a weird NASCAR tradition because they only went the same way around all the time. He could just be himself, confident in his ability to push the car to its limits and not go beyond.

"Should we start?" Rory tapped him on the knee and Lucien looked up to see everyone staring at him.

"Yes. Okay. I haven't wrapped anything..." He stopped before he told everyone that this was his first family Christmas day and he'd only known about wrapping gifts from movies, not that he had to do it for today. "Rory, how about you take something out of the box, and we can all decide who should get it?" It seemed the fairest way to do it, when he didn't really know what Socrates had packed. Hopefully Socrates had included enough things for everyone in the room; Melanie and Peter, Collette and Gordon, Nicole, Craig, and Victor. They all leaned forward as Rory knelt beside the small cardboard box and opened the top. He pulled out two Gamble Racing hooded sweaters.

"What size are they?"

"I don't know." Rory stared at him as if to say, how the heck would an eight-year-old kid know that, and Lucien tried not to laugh.

"Um, let me see the tags." Lucien held out his hands, ignoring the chuckles from everyone else in the room. He checked the tag on each sweater. "This one is child sized ten." He pretended to scan the room, looking at everyone except Rory. "Yeah, I don't think there is anyone here who would fit this one. We might have to give it to charity." He pointed at the ceiling, pretending he'd had a great idea. "I know. If I sign it, I could sell it and give the money to charity."

"Lucien, just give the sweater to Rory."

"But it's too big. It must be for another child?" Lucien was having too much fun with this.

Rory elbowed him. "You are mean and it's not funny."

"Oh. I'm sorry." His stomach sank to the floor. He was crap at this. "Obviously this one is for you. Shall I sign it?"

"No. Uncle Victor can sign it. I've seen him on TV."

Lucien clutched his heart. "Ouch. I deserved that."

"The other one is sized M." Rory was much better at this Christmas business than he was. He breathed out slowly, with his therapist's voice reminding him to give himself some grace. Of course Rory was better at this; he'd been to more proper family Christmas Days than Lucien.

"Is there anyone out there who is M sized who wants a Gamble Racing sweater?"

"Men's or women's sized?" Nicole asked.

Lucien held it up. "I don't actually know." This was a disaster. He couldn't even give away two sweaters without cocking it up.

"I'll have it." Nicole said. Lucien bundled it up into a ball and threw it across the room to her.

"Next we have this long thing." Rory pulled out a scarf.

"It's a scarf."

"Yes please." Craig waved his hand. "I could do with a new scarf."

They handed out hats and a couple of t-shirts and lots of stickers, and finally, everyone had something except

Victor. A few times, Rory had tried to pull out the 3D model of him and Lucien had whispered to leave it till last.

"The last thing in the box is for Victor. It's from the whole Gamble Racing team." As soon as he spoke, Lucien wanted to swear. He hadn't gotten anything for Victor. He'd make up for it later. "Stand up, Rory and give him the box."

Rory jumped up and navigated through the mess of the room towards Victor. "It's so cool."

"You've had a sneak peek?" Victor asked.

"Yes. All the stuff was tangled around it."

Victor nodded, and slowly pulled the 3D model out of the box. He stared at it for what felt like a long time.

"It's from Austria." Lucien said.

"My car's first podium." Victor stared at the 3D model, created from a photo of Victor and Ondrej holding the third placed trophy.

"Socrates printed in the shop from a photo." It was quite sweet of their boss to think of doing something for Victor, to put his first podium into a statue for him to keep. "The tech is pretty cool."

Victor must be a bit overwhelmed at the gift because he didn't say anything about understanding the way their 3D printer worked. After all, he used it to mock up parts for the wind tunnel on a frequent basis. Victor cradled the model like something precious, just staring at it, and occasionally turning it around in his hands. From the confused expressions around the room, none of Victor's family could quite understand the significance of this gift and why it meant so much to Victor.

"Achieving a podium in S1 is basically impossible. You

need to have the combination of a fast car, a very good driver, the right strategy, and a decent amount of luck. Every season, one or two teams dominate the podium positions because they have built the best car. All the other teams are scrapping it out for the rest of the points; hoping that their driver can overcome the lack of speed in the car, or that they get lucky during the race. For Gamble Racing, who started out as a solid mid-field team years ago, then slowly faded in recent years as Victor's predecessor struggled to keep up with the technology improvements, to suddenly have a car fast enough to consistently get points was a huge deal. And to get their first podium in ... what? Three or four seasons? Massive." Lucien was probably boring everyone. "Anyway, it's a huge achievement and Gamble Racing is really proud of Victor for creating a car that took them off the bottom of the grid onto the podium. You should all be proud of him too."

"We are. We always have been proud of Victor. He doesn't need to win for us to be proud of him," Melanie said. Lucien couldn't imagine it. His own worth was so wrapped up in winning that it was unbelievable to watch this family's steady support system, and he swallowed. Victor's family cared without conditions. Lucien's breath trembled as he slowly released it, and he ducked his head to swipe his hands across his eyes.

"It's a very thoughtful gift from the team." Peter walked over to Victor and gave him a hug. "We didn't need Lucien's speech to see how much this means to you. To both of you."

Victor blinked rapidly. "I always forget what a big deal this was, because my job carries so much responsibility and

I'm always trying to improve." His voice was a little wobbly and Lucien wanted to hold him. "I'll always treasure this. I'd better text Socrates and thank him."

"I'll grab your phone. You left it charging in our room." Lucien jumped up before anyone could say anything to stop him. The weight of emotion in the room made him feel like an interloper, intruding on a nice family scene, and he needed a little space. He held back the sob until he was alone, crying into a pillow in their room where no one could hear him. He wanted to be worthy of Victor's family.

CHAPTER 21

"There's nothing like the roar of an engine under your feet." Lucien relaxed in the passenger seat of the 300SL as Victor drove. They were about half-way home after a relaxing Boxing Day hanging out with Victor's family.

"Rory loved his drive with you. Collette is going to make all the photos into a little keepsake book for him."

"Oh, that's sweet. I love how thoughtful your family is." He couldn't keep the wistful tone out of his voice, and he didn't really care, because this had been his best Christmas ever. "I didn't get you a gift though. Sorry."

"Convincing Socrates to let me drive my favourite car is a gift enough."

"Okay?" He wasn't convinced it was enough.

"Experiences are more important than things when it comes to gifts. I'd much rather have this opportunity than a trinket that has not much meaning." Victor dropped one hand to the gear stick, then put it back on the steering wheel.

"You didn't like the 3D model Socrates made?"

Victor's smile made his whole face glow. "I loved it. It will always remind me of a wonderful experience and achievement."

"Are you saying you like it because it represents the experience?"

Victor nodded. "Absolutely. That's why the best gift you could've given Rory was the ride in this car, and why the photo book matters; because it reminds him of the experience."

Lucien knew what he wanted to give Victor. He'd get the team's media people to set up a photo shoot with this car and the two of them on the test track, maybe with Victor's first S1 car in the background. It would take a bit of organising. Worth it, though.

"Nicole's business venture sounds exciting." He didn't really understand the tech behind it.

"It's a cool concept; a dating app but for friendship."

Lucien pulled out his phone and scrolled through his contact list. "That reminds me. I have to send a few texts on her behalf." He'd agreed to ask a few S1 drivers if they'd be keen to chat in the S1 group on launch day. The app was basically a mash up of old internet forums where people talked about their hobbies, and a dating app with the ability to private message people. He might even sign up himself; he didn't really have any friends outside racing. He sent the texts out and then leaned back in his seat.

"Are you ready for the next stint? We need fuel soon."

"Sure. You can keep going if you are up for it." He closed his eyes, but his phone dinged with Ondrej agreeing to be part of it. He sent Nicole's phone number to him so they could sort out the details. "Ondrej agreed. Just waiting on Alex, and Paulo, and JP."

"You asked JP?"

"Of course. Who better than the reigning World Champion to help launch your sister's thingy?"

Victor made a happy noise. "You are a good friend."

"Thanks." It warmed his heart to be able to do something so basic as ask a few famous colleagues to help another friend. "You could've asked them too."

"I suppose so. I'm not a driver though."

He rolled his eyes. "Yeah, because we are such a special club that engineers can't talk to us."

"You kind of are though, Lucien." Victor's retort made him uneasy.

"Really? No. We are all on the same team." If he was going to get technical, Ondrej and Paulo were on the same team as Victor, while he was in a whole other team. All Gamble Racing but S1 and SE didn't spend much time together.

"Well, not JP."

"No." Gamble Racing did not have a World Champion driver. Yet. As for Victor's point, he wasn't sure how to counter it since drivers did get a lot of the media attention, and he thought he was pretty important to the team's success. Still... one thing was true. "Without a good car, a driver is nothing."

"And without a good driver, a team is nothing." Victor kept his gaze on the road. Why was it that Lucien could feel his reactive energy anyway?

"See, we aren't special. No more than the car. A team

needs both, and mechanics. How many races have been lost in the pit lane?"

"For Gamble Racing, or generally?"

He chuckled. "I didn't expect actual data. It was a rhetorical question."

Victor sighed. "Don't mind me. I'm a bit tense. Every mile we drive gets me closer to an unanswerable question. Part of me doesn't want to get back to the workshop because then I must confront the fact that I might never know why the engines kept catching fire, and part of me can't wait to cut the exhausts open and see if it gives us a new clue."

"Either way, it's inevitable."

"That's not overly helpful, Lucien."

He shoved Victor on the shoulder. "Fuck, Victor. Don't say my name like that. I'm not some kid that needs scolding by his teacher."

"Gross. If I'm going to scold you, at least use a less icky metaphor."

He shifted in his seat, intrigued. "Hmm. In an equal relationship where we are both adults, would you scold me by bending me over your knees and slapping my ass?"

"Lucien. I am trying to drive a priceless car." Victor's voice tightened and his skin flushed, in that horribly attractive way that Lucien couldn't resist.

"Fine, I'll be quiet." Lucien pretended to zip his lips shut. They drove in silence for a while until Victor pulled into a fuel station and parked the car beside a pump. Victor jumped out, careful that the doors didn't scrap on anything overhead as they opened upwards, and filled the car with fuel. After replying to JP's text saying he'd been keen to help Nicole, Lucien stepped out of the car ready to pay for the fuel. He'd paid for the whole journey because he earnt a lot more than Victor, although Victor earned a decent amount too, so perhaps they should've talked about it and shared the cost. Whatever. What else was he going to spend all his money on?

"Want a coffee?" Victor asked. "I can drop into that café next door and grab us something."

"Sure." Lucien went through the motions quickly. The 300SL chewed through fuel; typical for an old sports car. When he walked out of the shop, Victor was nowhere to be seen. He must be still in the café, waiting for coffee.

But when he opened the door to the café, a rush of heat made his stomach clench. Victor leaned against the counter, laughing at something the very handsome barista had said. Lucien ignored the rising red mist and marched over to Victor, kissing him on the cheek. Instinct made him want to claim ownership of Victor.

"Lucien?"

Fuck. The question in Victor's voice managed to infiltrate the raging emotion inside him. Ownership—what a horrific idea. One little laugh with a handsome random stranger shouldn't have him all jealous and out of control. He breathed in and out a few times slowly. "Are the coffees ready?"

"Soon."

He couldn't stand here and watch Victor flirt with a man whose ready smile was exactly the type of man Lucien would've fucked. The type of man who was firmly and most definitely in Lucien's past now.

"Are you alright?" Victor asked, placing his hand on Lucien's shoulder.

"Yes. I'll be in the car." He marched out of there, head held high, but shrinking inside. What a fucking mess. Victor might be his boyfriend, but even he knew that it was weird to react with such a surge of jealousy to Victor talking to a handsome man. The only good thing about the whole interaction was that he'd realised he didn't want another random hook up. He only wanted Victor; with an intensity that he probably ought to get control over. He leaned on the car's bonnet. Victor had the keys.

Soon enough, Lucien was behind the wheel, but the hum of tension wouldn't go away. Being able to name the source—jealousy, confusion, rage—didn't make any difference. By rights, everything should make sense now. The world usually made more sense when he was driving. He pushed the car; glad they were on the motorway now and the excessive speed wouldn't be so noticeable. The weird buzzing in his chest persisted, or was that simply the sound of the engine being asked for maximum effort?

"How fast are you going?"

Lucien roared past several lorries, switching lanes to maintain his speed. "Don't you need to get back to the workshop?"

"Alive. Yes."

A siren sounded behind him. "Fine. Maybe pushing towards 150 miles per hour was a little much." He backed off, easing the car from its max speed down to the road's speed limit. Soon enough the police caught up to them and he pulled over as requested.

The policewoman knocked on the window, and Lucien

waved at her to step backwards. The windows in the gull-wing model were fixed and didn't open, so he opened the door. The policewoman frowned and stepped out of the way of the door.

"Yes?" He got out of the car and stood beside her.

"Stay in the car and open the window."

"The windows in this car don't open. It was designed that way."

The policewoman blinked once and he almost started to explain how the shape of the door precluded the window from being able to wind downward so the designers had fixed it in place, but she probably didn't want a discussion about the aesthetics or design quirks of an antique car.

"Do you know how fast you were going?"

"Not precisely. This car, the Mercedes-Benz 300SL was the fastest sports car in 1957 and has a maximum speed of 161 miles per hour." Reciting the car's data was the easy part. "I know I wasn't pushing it to the limit, so less than that?"

The policewoman blinked. "I am not impressed. Hand over your driver's licence."

He leaned into the car and took his wallet from Victor who held it out for him, momentarily considering giving her his super licence. No, that might be considered inflammatory, and while he was white and could probably get away with it, he'd already made enough unwise decisions today. Instead, he grabbed his British road licence and passed it over.

"Mr Lucien Grenville?"

"Yes, that's me."

"Okay." She checked him against his photo without a

change of expression. "I'm going to check your details in my system and then issue you a fine."

He nodded once. As soon as she'd taken his licence into her car, Victor giggled.

"What?"

"She didn't recognise you at all."

"Why would she? Most people don't even know Series E exists, and I wasn't exactly one of the famous S1 drivers." Being pulled over managed to halt all the raging emotions inside himself. He shouldn't have let his emotions bleed over into his driving. Having to stop and wait on the side of the road for a fine that wouldn't put a dent in his pocket was probably what he needed to settle himself down. He breathed in deeply, his lungs filling with the grubby air from the side of the motorway, hints of truck diesel and the damp cold of fallow paddocks. Luckily it wasn't raining today. The wind was cuttingly chill, and he rubbed his arms. How long was this going to take? He wanted to get back into his warm car.

"Here you go." The policewoman handed him his licence and a printed fine. "Drive safely. Slowly."

"Yes." Lucien was too cold to say anything too cheeky, which was probably for the best. He jumped back in the car and pulled the door shut. "Fuck, it's cold out there."

"Serves you right for speeding on a public road." The censure in Victor's voice had him gritting his teeth again, but he pulled back onto the motorway carefully and kept his speed just under the limit for the road. With the heater blasting and the radio playing some old rock tunes, he started to warm up as they drove along in silence. He mulled over his reaction from the coffee shop, and wished he could hide under the seat of the car, alone with the unbidden tingling in his chest and clammy sweat on his palms. God, this was so fucking shameful.

"It's been an hour. You can stop sulking now."

"Fuck off." It wasn't sulking. It was the realisation that he'd been a dickhead and he didn't know how to stop himself from having these toxic reactions to the most basic of things.

"Lucien." The calm tone hit him in the guts. Shit.

"Victor, I think I need—" What he really needed was an angry fuck to get rid of all this ... stuff ... inside his head. He was going to burst, or something else equally as dramatic, and no amount of breathing exercises were going to help. Before he'd declared himself as Victor's boyfriend, he used to go to clubs to find someone who also needed a release from the world around. It'd been effective but it wasn't what a good boyfriend did. However he framed it, it sounded toxic as hell. '*Fuck me hard until it's all I can feel and all the rest of this junk in my head goes away temporarily. I don't want to* feel *this anymore.*' He ground his teeth together until his jaw hurt.

"This isn't going to work. You need to dump me before I hurt you."

Victor sighed. "Lucien, stop it. I'm not going to dump you, just because you got pulled over by a cop for going too fast. It's literally your job to go fast."

"No. You should dump me for overreacting at the coffee shop."

"Excuse me?"

227

How could Victor not understand? "When the barista was flirting with you." And he'd barged in and marked his territory like the toxic prick he was by kissing Victor on the cheek.

"Were you jealous?" Victor's befuddled expression would've been funny if it wasn't so serious.

"Yes." Lucien whispered. A weird breeze touched the back of his neck, not hot or cold, but somehow both, and he rubbed at his skin.

"Seriously?"

"He was very handsome and you were laughing together."

"Oh Lucien. You wonderful, ridiculous man. Have you been worried about this ever since?"

"Yes. I over-reacted by claiming you with a kiss on the cheek." He glanced quickly at Victor who touched his face in the same place. Fuck. That shouldn't be so hot. He was a disaster.

"It's okay to have big feelings, Lucien. Besides, I really liked it."

"But it's possessive and weird."

"No, it's possessive and hot."

Lucien scanned the road ahead and found an area to pull off the motorway. He didn't breathe until the car was parked safely away from traffic. Once the car was turned off, he turned slowly in his seat to face Victor.

"You liked that? When I barged inside the shop and wanted to hurt that random man for flirting with you?"

"But you didn't hurt him. You dismissed him and focused on showing that I am yours. That's what is hot."

Heat rushed down his spine, pooling low. "I want to fuck you."

"Here?" Victor's gaze darted around at the traffic.

"Anywhere. Everywhere." He didn't care who saw. The way his cock ached for Victor just made him want to show the world how much he needed Victor.

Victor swallowed. "It would be irresponsible of me to ask you how many more fines you'd risk to get us home quickly." And that was why Lucien simply had to fuck Victor.

"It would." He breathed out, and the air trembled a little as it slid across his lips. "I don't think I'm in any state to drive right now." He jumped out of the car, glad that Victor had too, before he slid into the passenger seat, pulling his seatbelt tight across his chest, tight enough to contain him. Victor stepped into the driver's seat. They shut the doors, and Victor turned the key. The engine roared to life.

"I love this car. The straight six engine sounds so good."

"It's smooth." Lucien closed his eyes and listened to the steady rumble of the engine as Victor drove. If only it could soothe the heat inside him. He held his cock, squeezing it through his jeans, to get rid of some of the tension.

"We should be home in just over two hours."

Two hours of agony. Hell.

"Try and sleep. I'll still be here, wanting you when we get home."

"To your place?" His voice cracked and he grabbed the half-full water bottle in the door and chugged the rest of it.

"If you'd like."

"I would like to see your bed." The next two hours were going to be the death of him.

"My bed, or me in my bed?"

"Victor." He wasn't going to make it.

"Relax, Lucien. Breathe. Try and sleep."

He coughed. "I can't sleep with this giant hard on. Are you trying to give me blue balls?"

For a long moment, Victor didn't answer. Then he whispered, "I don't think I need to try."

"Fuck." He turned the radio up loud and stared out the window, trying not to think about the way the beat of the music thumped in time with his heart.

CHAPTER 22

Victor carefully parked the 300SL on the street outside his small cottage in Syresthorpe and glanced over at Lucien who had finally fallen asleep. Nine hours of driving in winter meant they arrived in the dark, after dusk, and he switched off the engine. He wasn't ready to say goodbye to this car just yet, but he'd have to take it back to Socrates tomorrow when he turned up for work. For the first time in his life, he wasn't looking forward to work. Not when he'd spent the last couple of hours trying to focus on driving while Lucien's ragged breathing filled the car until he'd slept and then all Victor could hear was the engine and Lucien's steady quiet breaths.

"Wake up, we are here." He patted Lucien on the shoulder, who jerked awake with a big breath inwards.

"Fuck. How long did I sleep?"

"Maybe an hour and a half? Come inside." Victor made sure everything in the car was set back to neutral—everything in this old car was manual with a great many dials and buttons that needed adjusting for driving—then pulled out the key and opened the door. He gasped. Outside the car was bloody cold.

"Our stuff can wait until morning. Let's get inside before we freeze to death."

Lucien chuckled, sinfully. "Now who is being dramatic."

"Come on." He leaped out of the car, shut the door, and rushed to his front door, fumbling slightly with the house key before he pushed open the door and walked inside his cottage. It was fucking cold too, having been empty for five days with the heat turned off. The door slammed shut behind him and he turned to see Lucien rubbing his hands together.

"Sorry. I can put the heat on, but it'll take a while to warm the whole place."

"Forget it. Take me to bed and I'll warm you up there."

"Promises, promises." Victor grinned, then walked down the hallway with his head held high. He'd barely stepped into the room, when his back hit the wall and he was pressed against it by Lucien. Lucien kissed him, stealing his breath with a kiss that reinforced the possessive way Lucien had claimed him in the coffee shop. Fuck, Victor adored being kissed like this, as if Lucien poured his entire wild need for him into Victor's mouth. His hips bucked against Lucien's lean body, almost of their own accord, and he grabbed Lucien's shoulders. Lucien—oh, so casually—covered Victor's hands with his own, and slowly carried them to the wall, stretching him out, all the while kissing Victor until he wanted to melt. Lucien wrote circles on

Victor's palms, sending sparks of energy flying from each hand down his arms into his torso. He moaned, and when Lucien chased the sensation with his fingers, caressing Victor's arms, he turned his head away from the kiss.

"To bed. Please."

"Not yet." Lucien kissed his cheek, then sank to his knees. Oh, fuck. As he sank down, Lucien ran his hands all over Victor's torso—his damned shirt was in the way—then Lucien slid his fingers under the waistband of his jeans, finally touching his skin.

"Please." He needed ... Lucien's hands against his bare skin and Lucien's mouth on his rigid cock. Now. But Lucien took his sweet time, exploring Victor's legs, pressing his fingers into the long muscles, making Victor far too aware of his own body. Every touch was fantastic even with his jeans in the way. And when Lucien—finally—undid the fly on Victor's jeans, he couldn't wait anymore. He grabbed his jeans, pushing them down along with his underwear, freeing his impossibly hard cock for Lucien.

"I need your mouth."

Lucien blew a little breath on Victor's balls, warm compared to the chill of the room, and just as Victor was about to expire from holding his breath, Lucien licked the entire length from base to tip.

"Fucking hell."

Lucien closed his mouth over the head of Victor's cock, and he had to hold on tight to something, so he didn't collapse as sensation ruled. He gripped Lucien's scalp, pulling his hair.

"Yes, holy fuck, like that."

Lucien grunted, then looked up at Victor, golden brown eyes glowing. Victor couldn't help it, he stroked his finger over Lucien's face, down his temple and along his cheekbone, across to where his lips were stretched around Victor's cock. Lucien's hum of appreciation buzzed through Victor's cock and he groaned. With every stroke of Lucien's tongue, and each dip of his mouth around him, Victor's balls tightened until he was going to come. Lucien sucked him deep into his throat, then wrapped his fingers around the base of Victor's cock, holding him tight.

"Oh fuck, keep doing that or I'm going to come right down your throat."

Lucien made a strangled noise, almost like a laugh, and it vibrated down Victor's length. He pulled Lucien's hair, hard.

"Off."

Lucien, of course, took his damned time, slowly rising along the length of Victor's cock as if it were the greatest treat in the fucking world. He tried to breathe through the tension of being right on the edge—the limit—and when Lucien popped off the end with a noisy slurp, Victor shuddered with need.

"Look at you." Lucien's hoarse voice was rough, coming from a throat that had been well-fucked. It didn't help Victor's situation at all. But then, Lucien stood up—smooth and easy like the athlete he was—and kissed Victor. The taste of his precum, a little salty, in his own mouth made the struggle not to come nearly impossible.

"I need you to fuck me now." Victor was so far gone, he didn't care if his begging sounded desperate. It was the truth. He needed Lucien's cock in him now.

"Lube? Condom?" Lucien's reminder was a good one. They'd discussed their sexual health in the car before coming inside, but agreed that using a condom was a good idea until they could both get tested again together.

"Bedside drawer." Sadly giving the directions meant that Lucien walked away, leaving Victor leaning heavily against the wall, his knees too weak to walk to the bed. Lucien took what he needed from the drawer.

"Nice toy collection." How did Lucien sound so casual? He was dying over here, leaking and painfully ready to come. He was helpless to move, brought right to the edge by Lucien's mouth, ready to explode with a furious need to get over the peak and be free.

"Come here." Lucien patted the bed. Victor pushed off the wall, walking on shaking legs, all four steps across the room, and stood there.

"You look glorious." Lucien traced one finger lightly down Victor's cock, along the pulsing vein, and Victor squeezed his eyes tightly shut. "Now bend over. Let me look after you."

He complied, needing this more than anything in the world, and was immediately rewarded with Lucien's touch. Lucien stripped Victor's jeans off, then palmed Victor's ass, pushing his legs wider, playing until Victor moaned desperately, and finally, finally, Lucien caressed Victor's hole. It didn't take much preparation since he was more than ready.

"This lube is cold."

"Everything is cold." Except his body which had forgotten about the air temperature.

"Shall I warm you up?"

"Yes. Now."

The blunt head of Lucien's cock pressed inside, slowly —too damned gentle—until he was inside. Fuck, it'd been so long since he'd enjoyed this, and as Lucien adjusted the angle to slid past his prostate, he cried out. Lucien held Victor's hips with one hand, and with the other, he wrapped his long fingers around Victor's cock. All the while, keeping up a steady rhythm. Every thrust made his shirt brush his chin, a reminder that he wasn't completely naked.

"You are so good at this." Victor grabbed the blankets, clinging on, as pleasure coursed through him, shockwave after shockwave, as Lucien filled him and stroked his prostate over and over.

"Come for me." Lucien whispered, then stroked Victor's cock twice, rough enough to be amazing. Stars exploded behind Victor's eyes as he came, pretty sure he babbled a bunch of noise and words that definitely included Lucien's name.

"Say my name again." Lucien's voice was ragged, a sexy rumble.

"Lucien."

Lucien came with a shout. "Victor." Then he collapsed on top of Victor, surrounding him with delicious heat, and they lay there for a while until the cold of the room seeped through the happy warmth of each other.

"I'd better clean up." Lucien stood up. "Do you have a bin for the condom?"

"In the bathroom. It's the door opposite this one." His house was a typical old worker's cottage that had a lounge at the front, two bedrooms down one side, one bathroom opposite this room, then a kitchen and dining area at the rear. He rolled onto his back, and watched Lucien walk out of the bedroom, then slowly stood up on wobbly legs. All he wanted was to sleep but he probably should throw the top blanket in the wash and grab another one. He was doing that when Lucien walked back in with a cloth, and gently washed Victor's stomach.

"Come to bed now."

"I'll just grab another blanket."

"I'll keep you warm."

"I know, but it's winter, Lucien. Another blanket is a good idea."

Lucien smiled. "So practical." He kissed Victor on the cheek, threw the now-dirty cloth in the same direction as the dirty blanket, and slid into bed. "Oh fuck, these sheets are freezing. Hurry up and get in here."

He shook his head as he rushed towards the hallway cupboard to grab another blanket. Damn, Lucien could be so cute. Yes, he still had a bit of anger to unlearn, although frankly, he had it under control more than he gave himself credit for. Victor still couldn't believe how much Lucien had beat himself up for that little kiss at the café. He hadn't given it much thought, and the idea that having someone handsome flirt with him made Lucien jealous was really good for Victor's doubt. Fuck. He leaned his forehead against the wall for a second. How lucky was he that Lucien had picked him! Lucien fucked like a sex god and Victor was the person Lucien had selected to benefit from all that skill. He shivered; half from the cold and half from the flash of memory. Best sex of his life. And from someone who wanted to be his boyfriend—who regularly used that word as if it was a gift—when it was Victor who'd been given the gift.

"How long does it take to get a bloody blanket?" Lucien called out. Victor probably should get in bed with his boyfriend. This was real. He could push aside all doubt that he wasn't good enough for someone like Lucien— third on the World Championship in Series E compared to the fifth-choice engineer for Gamble Racing—and enjoy the moment for as long as he could. Before any new doubt —obviously that Lucien would get bored with him—could sink in, he marched back into his bedroom and flung the blanket over the bed. Lucien patted the pillow next to him.

"I'm here." He slid under the blankets, flinching at the cool sheets, and quickly found himself wrapped in Lucien's arms.

"Good." Lucien kissed his neck, light flirty kisses, and Victor closed his eyes, relaxing into Lucien's hug. The soft kisses continued until Victor fell asleep.

"Good morning." Victor woke to find Lucien still asleep, tucked in under the blankets with only his face exposed to the cool winter air. Damn, his house was so cold when he didn't have the heater on all night. The same rush of good luck warmed his heart again this morning; how had he managed to end up in bed with someone so amazing. Lucien was beautiful, not classically handsome, but his features all combined to make him gorgeous. Even with his sharp eyes closed, he still exuded confidence. Yes, a confident sleeper. Victor was well aware of how sappy his thoughts were, but he didn't care. If he couldn't gush over his boyfriend, what was the point?

Lucien didn't reply, just rolled over, and pulled Victor closer. Real life could wait a little bit longer because sleepy cuddles were the best way to wake up. He covered Lucien's hands with his own, wriggling closer.

"Careful. Any closer and I'll be inside you." Lucien's voice whispered sinfully over his skin.

"Yes." What a way to wake up.

Lucien slid one of his hands away from Victor's hold, then nudged Victor's thighs apart. "Like this?" Lucien rested his hard cock between Victor's thighs, branding him with the heat of it.

"Yes, just like that."

"I have a dilemma though." How could Lucien sound so chirpy when he'd only just woken up and honestly, Victor just wanted more of his touches. He didn't want to have to think yet. He hummed in response.

"I have a fitness test with Hettie in Monaco in four days, so I should go for a run."

"Okay?"

"My dilemma is this; Should I run now because it's the best time for running in my fitness schedule, or should I delay my run until later?"

Victor frowned. "Is it really better to run now?"

"According to Hettie."

Victor sighed. He didn't want Lucien to leave. Not yet.

"And since you are a member—" Lucien reached around and stroked Victor's member with fingers that weren't quite held tight enough. "—of Gamble Racing, I wonder what your opinion is. From a team perspective."

Victor let out an embarrassing sound that wasn't really a word, impressed that Lucien could be so lucid, while needing his touch to be a lot firmer. He fumbled slightly as he covered Lucien's hand and tightened his grip on his cock.

"I take it that means you think the run can wait?"

Hmmph. He really needed Lucien to focus now. He stroked himself again, holding Lucien's hand in place.

"It's hot when you take control. Maybe you should fuck me this morning."

Fuck. Yes. If he could last that long. The cosy warmth of the bed and the press of Lucien's body against his spine was a lot. He couldn't stop the breathy whimper.

"Yes. Be noisy. Wake the neighbours."

A hot flush raced over Victor's skin, lighting him up from the outside inwards. "It's double brick." The neighbours probably wouldn't hear anything through the old, very thick, walls.

Lucien chuckled, a reckless urgent sound. "One brick." He squeezed Victor's cock. "Double brick." He thrust with his own cock, sliding between Victor's legs.

"Fuck."

"Yes. That's what I want you to do." Lucien stroked him with short sharp movements that did nothing at all to help Victor in being able to move or talk.

"Stop."

Lucien shifted away completely, leaving Victor cold and alone. He gulped.

"Not completely. You didn't do anything wrong. It was just—"

"You were too close?"

"Yes." From a little bit of a hand job.

Lucien blew a gentle breath across the back of Victor's neck and he shivered. "I suppose if I want to get thoroughly fucked by you, I'd better not tempt fate and wrap my lips around your lovely dick."

Victor bit his lip. He wanted to protest that it was just a standard cock, not worth of such nice words, except he wanted to believe that Lucien truly thought that about him. His chest swelled at the notion that Lucien—who could have any man in the world—wanted him.

"Roll onto your back."

It was the easiest thing in the world to comply. Lucien shifted the blankets, making a little fort for them, then rolled a condom onto Victor's cock.

"Where?"

"I left it on the bedside table for easy access. You aren't the only one who is good at planning for the future." He winked, a sly little grin on his face. Victor grabbed Lucien's head and kissed him. Hard. He stared into Lucien's golden brown eyes and loved the way that their kiss softened and changed his gaze into one of pure longing. Imagine. Lucien Grenville longing for him.

"Isn't kissing just wonderful?" Lucien's voice was as soft as his expression. He'd done that to him. With a deep breath in, he tried to respond, but Lucien's skin still held hints of his aftershave with notes of cardamom and pine needles. It shouldn't be nice, they'd driven all day, and fallen into bed without a shower or brushing their teeth, and yeah, there was that slight morning undertone, but mostly Victor breathed in the essence of Lucien, like rolling in a pine forest with a diesel truck revving in the background.

"You know what would be better?"

"How are you still talking?" Victor clung to the edge of pleasure, barely able to form any words.

Lucien's grin stirred up more heat. "Victor. There's one way you can shut me up."

He didn't want Lucien to stop talking; it was more incredible than anything else. He pushed Lucien's shoulder, rolling him onto his stomach, and knelt either side of his thighs.

"Keep talking." He pulled the blanket around them again.

"Do you like the encouragement?"

Victor hummed and reached out for the bottle of lube on the bedside table. Lucien took advantage of his movement and shifted, rising up onto his knees, making the blanket fall off, but Victor was so hot now, it didn't matter. He squirted the lube onto his palm. It was bloody cold, so he rubbed his hands together, warming it up for Lucien.

"What is taking you so long?" Lucien turned his head, and all the muscles in his back rippled. Hell. Victor grabbed the base of his cock and squeezed tight. He had to last long enough to give Lucien what he wanted.

"Come on, Victor. I need you inside me."

"Soon." It came out all wobbly. The lube was warm enough now, so he spread it on Lucien's crack, carefully around his hole, loving the way Lucien kept his back arched for better access. The beautiful sight made all the hairs on his arms rise up.

"Give me your fingers. Open me up."

Victor did as he was told, hooking his finger enough to brush Lucien's prostate.

"Fucking yes. That's perfect. It's always the quiet ones that make the cleverest lovers." God, how was he still talking? Victor wanted to hear every thought of Lucien's as he fucked him. He slid his fingers out and slowly pressed his cock against Lucien's hole, guiding himself with a full body shiver.

"That's it. I love that pressure." Lucien breathed out, visibly relaxing his body for Victor, which was the hottest thing he'd ever seen. He closed his eyes so he didn't come while still only beginning. He grabbed Lucien's hips and imbedded himself. Fuck, it was so tight, holding him.

"Oh, that's amazing. I'm so full of you. I love it."

Victor swallowed, shaking his head at Lucien's chatter. He moved a little and Lucien groaned, so he did it again, until he was sliding in and out in a steady rhythm. Lucien's chatter turned into a stream of moans and groans and the occasional swear word. He felt like a king, being the one to make Lucien stop talking and beg insensibly for relief.

"Let me." He leaned forward and threaded one hand through Lucien's hair, and with the other, he reached around and took Lucien's cock in his hand.

"Oh fuck yes please." The desperation in Lucien's voice sent Victor right over the edge and he slammed into him hard and fast, coming with a shout. He collapsed onto Lucien's back, panting hard, barely aware that Lucien came into his hand. They stayed like that for just long enough that Victor realised he needed to grab the condom as he slid out, fumbling a bit in a panic.

"Was that okay?" He asked.

"No."

Victor gasped, and he went cold all over.

"It wasn't okay. It was magnificent." Lucien wriggled underneath him, rolling them both over, and before Victor knew what was happening, he was being thoroughly kissed again.

CHAPTER 23

V ictor was late for work. Not that anyone noticed, because he was the only one in the workshop. All the rest of the Gamble Racing staff had taken a longer break over Christmas to spend valuable time with their families, before the season got underway. Lucien had come to the workshop with him, supposedly to keep him company, and Victor couldn't work out if having him hang around was more of a distraction than anything useful. He already had Lucien's opinion on this problem, from a driver's point of view, and while it had been useful, he didn't think there was much more that Lucien could do.

"What do you want me to do?" Lucien asked. An awkward laugh caught in Victor's throat and he coughed. Probably not much, although it was better that someone was here with him as he was about to operate tools that could potentially injure him if something went wrong.

"It's not as simple as Pa said; just cut them open and have a look. The whole exhaust system is complex, and did he mean the tailpipe or the two wastegates, or earlier in the system, and anyway, I need a laser cutter to do anything effective."

"Right, because S1 exhaust systems aren't made of stainless steel like an ordinary car." Lucien understood.

"Yes. Like most of the other teams, we use an alloy of nickel and chromium that is light and thin and can withstand the thousand-degree temperatures."

"Is there a way to work out where the fires started?"

Victor dragged his hands through his hair.

"Yeah, okay. You've obviously figured that out and I'm just asking basic questions here."

"It's not you. This whole thing is frustrating. If it was as simple as knowing where the fires started, then it would be a matter of deduction to work out why."

Lucien leaned on the workbench. "What is your gut feel?"

"I can't engineer with something so … vague."

"But you can. I do it all the time." Lucien held up his hands. "And before you say that I'm a driver, not an engineer, think about this. When I'm in the car, I feel it. I know it. I might not know why something is happening, but I can feel what is happening and communicate that reaction to someone like you who can interpret into something useful."

Victor marched over to the deconstructed engine from Ondrej's car and stared at the burnt wreckage. The problem with fire was that it did a lot of damage quickly and it wasn't always easy to see where it had started. But... He stood there with his hands on his head for a while.

"I don't have any evidence to support this."

"And yet, you have a niggling feeling?"

"Yes. I feel like these three fires all started in the exhaust system. Around here." He crouched down and grabbed one of the charred tailpipes. "It would only make sense if there was a hole or a fracture in the pipe..."

"Like a manufacturing fault?"

Victor put the tailpipe down again. "Assuming that's the case, then it would most likely be along the seam."

"Seam?"

"The whole exhaust system is made in pieces, and laser welded together, then covered in an insulating material to prevent the heat from the exhaust upsetting the rest of the engine. There isn't much space in there, so it all has to wrap together closely so we can have the best aerodynamic skin for the whole car."

"I do remember some of this from when I drove S1."

"Of course. I haven't forgotten that. It's just that talking about it out loud helps me figure it out."

Lucien nodded. "Good. Keep talking."

"If the joints weren't perfect, then you might get some heat escape from the exhaust and if you had something flammable nearby, you'd end up with a fire, but we design it so that shouldn't happen." Victor kept dismissing this as an option because the fire damage to the exhaust system meant that it probably wasn't worth doing an eddy current test to check for damage. How could he tell if the issue happening before or after the fire?

"Shouldn't. Not can't."

Victor sighed. "Let me grab the schematics again."

"Let's think about this from the other direction. If someone wanted to cause an engine fire, how would they do it?"

Victor paused mid-step and turned around. Lucien had pushed off the table and stood with his arms outstretched. For a split second, Victor hoped it meant that Lucien was inviting him for a hug, but then Lucien folded his arms and raised his eyebrows.

"I don't know. Why would anyone want to cause an engine fire? It makes no sense to do something so reckless."

"Forget about motivation. Say you wanted to do it, how would you?"

Victor struggled to make his brain think upside down like that and he just stared at Lucien, internally protesting against the idea. He couldn't imagine deliberately trying to sabotage his car. Fuck. It came to him suddenly, like a punch in the face.

"Shit. I would use a laser cutter to carefully cut a few fractures in the tailpipe and the insulting material, not the wastegates, somewhere close to the engine, not at the end where the tailpipe is exposed at the rear of the car, and then I'd pack something innocuous at the same point. Something that would burn slow enough to create a proper engine fire. It would have to be outside the exhaust system, near the engine, not inside the pipe. Even if you stuffed the tailpipe with something, the temperatures are so hot that you'd only get a short burst of smoke while it burned, then it would go away..." Holy shit. In Austin, Ondrej's car had done exactly that. He gasped.

"What have you just worked out?"

"In Austin, Ondrej's car had smoke coming out of the tailpipe and he came into the pits. But then it just stopped and we had nothing on the data to suggest anything was wrong with the car, so he kept racing. If someone had packed the inside of the tailpipe with something flammable, that would fit with what happened."

"Wasn't that the same race that Paulo's brakes caught fire?"

"Yes, but we solved that. One of the mechanics fitted the wrong type of disc and it couldn't withstand the heat of the race. We've upgraded the systems since then to make sure it can't happen again."

"Devil's advocate here—"

Victor interrupted. "Nothing good ever comes after that saying."

"Hear me out."

"Okay. Fine. Let's hear it." The idea that someone might have deliberately done this to the cars was like something from a movie. It made no sense in real life, but he was all out of ideas, and this felt like—those pesky feelings again—the closest he'd been to solving this.

"What if someone tried packing the tailpipe with something and it almost worked, so they tried something different next time?"

"This isn't the movies. We aren't dealing with a villain who learns from their mistakes until a whole car blows up."

"Aren't we? Do have any evidence?" Lucien's eyebrows were doing a lot of work and Victor wanted to ... well, he didn't actually know what he wanted.

"No. I don't have any evidence. It just seems highly unlikely. You must be aware of how much security we have."

"Fine. But indulge me here. If you were a villain and you tried stuffing the tailpipe and it caused smoke, but not a fire, what would you do next?"

Victor shook his head. He'd already answered that. "I need to scan each exhaust with an eddy current to see if there are any fatigue cracks or other faults that might have caused the fire." In hindsight, he should've done this a long time ago—right after each fault—but he'd dismissed it as useful since the pieces of exhaust were so fire damaged.

"Let's do that."

It wasn't that simple. Isambard was probably the best person on the engineering team to assist with that. "I need to make some phone calls."

"Why don't you do that, and I'll go up to the big house and get some lunch for us both?"

Victor nodded and picked up his phone. Hopefully, Isambard wasn't too far away. He lived in the village, like many people in the Gamble Racing team, except there were still a few days of the Christmas/New Year's break to go so there was a chance that Isambard had travelled to visit family.

———

A few days later, Lucien walked into the workshop to say goodbye to Victor. He was heading to Monaco for a few days for pre-season fitness testing with Hettie and the other S1 and SE drivers. They'd do another one at the end of January; a more intense one that usually consisted of a few days of cross-country skiing, a lot of reflex tests, and neck strength testing. His own season started in the last weekend of January, with the first race being a dual race weekend. The S1 team had a bit more time to get ready for pre-season testing of the car before their season started in March.

He'd barely seen Victor for the past few days and now he had to leave. Victor had his team scurrying around the workshop, and if Lucien hadn't turned up every evening to drag Victor home, he was pretty sure that Victor wouldn't have slept much. They'd established that the exhaust system had faults in them that may or may not been there before the fire. Lucien assumed the faults were deliberate, since the alloy used in the exhaust system was unlikely to fail like that without assistance. He was starting to get frustrated with how much Victor wanted to blame himself for the failures, and not consider the possibility that it might be an external issue. Perhaps nothing as dramatic as sabotage—like Victor said, this wasn't a movie—but perhaps a manufacturing issue or something less sinister. The idea that someone wanted to harm a mid-field team was a bit overwrought. Wouldn't it be more likely that someone might want to stop the top team or driver from winning? Lucien knew he could be a bit self-centred—he was a driver—but yes, it was a bit much to leap directly at a conclusion that made little sense for where Gamble Racing was on the constructor's championship.

Victor was obsessed with finding the answer to this problem and now Lucien had to head to Monaco, and somehow, he knew Victor wasn't going to look after himself while Lucien was away.

He could just call. He breathed out slowly. The time difference between England and Monaco was only an hour. Just call and remind Victor to eat and sleep. If it didn't sound quite so silly, he'd book a session with the team's sport psychologist to try and figure out how to be a good boyfriend while still being an awesome focused driver.

Other people did it. He probably didn't need a manual or a guidebook on it.

"Lucien. Is it that time of day already?" Victor looked like he'd been attempting to make himself bald. His habit of dragging his hands through his hair when he was frustrated meant that his black hair often stuck out on odd angles, especially today, as it looked like he had engine grease all along the left side of his scalp. Lucien wanted to kiss him, right here in front of everyone, but they'd talked about it a couple of nights ago and Victor wanted to maintain a little distance at work. It was work and he was the Chief Engineer. Lucien didn't really see what that had to do with whether he kissed one of the drivers, but he respected that it was what Victor wanted. They weren't hiding their relationship. Lucien wasn't capable of hiding, and he'd put photos of him and Victor and the 300SL on his social media over Christmas anyway. It was more that Victor liked to look professional, and that didn't include public displays of affection in the workshop, apparently.

"It's noon. I just dropped in to say goodbye."

"I wasn't expecting you until three."

"Socrates is going to drive me to London for my flight to Monaco."

"I thought he was going to fly you in the helicopter?"

"He was, but the weather is too bad, so we are leaving now instead." It was a lot safer to drive in wet weather and gave Socrates a chance to take one of his car collection for a spin. "Shall we go for a walk?" Lucien really wanted to kiss Victor before he spent a few days away from him.

"Come into my office." Victor marched off, leaving Lucien to follow along. He didn't want to be Victor's dirty secret. It wasn't like that, was it? Now that he'd thought about it, he couldn't get rid of it. This weird churn in his stomach had to be purely because he was leaving for a few days and he didn't want to be away from Victor yet, not for any other reason...

Once the racing season started, they'd hardly see each other as the S1 and SE schedules didn't overlap much. He didn't like that either although it was necessary. Victor was on the verge of great success with this season's car performing well in the wind tunnel, and Lucien wanted to protect that and encourage him. And Lucien had a job to do and his own World Championship to win.

He closed the door. "Good luck with everything. I'll be back in a few days."

"Lucien. Is it selfish of me to want you to fly Hettie here for your test?"

He smiled, warmed all the way through by Victor's wish. "If it was only me, then it would be no drama." He knew he shouldn't have worried that Victor might want to hide. It literally made no sense—they were both out—although he was discovering that there were a lot of new things about being in a relationship that weren't the same as hook ups. Obviously.

"Oh?"

"Ondrej, Paulo, and Alex all live in Monaco, as does everyone's trainers." Lucien had an apartment in Monaco too. Someone came and cleaned it once a fortnight, which must be the easiest job in the world given that he hadn't lived in it for months. He didn't mind because being a cleaner sounded like an unrewarding job, so he happily paid someone too much money to clean his clean apartment.

Besides, he liked the idea that he could arrive there any time without notice and it would be spotless.

"I see. That makes sense to hold the tests where the most people live." Victor fidgeted with some papers on his desk.

"What is the matter?"

"I really want to kiss you goodbye—" Victor waved at the big glass windows of his office that looked out onto the workshop.

"No one is going to be bothered if you do."

"They'll tease me."

Lucien frowned. "Okay?"

"You don't understand."

"Obviously." Lucien tried not to check his watch. He really didn't have time for this.

"You have a reputation as someone who ..." Victor blushed and looked down at the papers on his desk that he was mangling with his hands.

"Has slept with a lot of men?"

"Yes. People will think that I'm just another one in the long line of them."

People? Or Victor? The red mist began to rise up through his torso and he clenched his fists at his sides. He would not lash out at such obvious bullshit. Victor's doubt could go step on Lego; something he'd experienced over Christmas thanks to Rory.

"Lucien?"

He breathed out slowly and tried to relax his jaw. "I don't give a fuck what other people think. Victor. I don't want you to be the next one in a series of many. I want you to be the last one."

The air shimmered and only the sounds of their heavy breathing filled the space. It took a while before Lucien realised what he'd said. His heart raced, faster than ever before, and his mouth tasted like acid.

"The last?"

"Yes. I want you to be my first boyfriend and I want you to be the last man that I fuck. There will be no one after you. You are it." He went all in—may as well—since he'd already let his emotions rule his tongue and he'd let out a truth that he hadn't even known himself. It felt … good. Honest. And now he really needed Victor to respond. Say something. Anything. His chest was caught in a vice, tighter and tighter with every millisecond of silence. This was worse than being shunted into a concrete barrier at top speed.

"Lucien." His name hung in the air as Victor breathed it out slowly. "Lucien." A second later, Victor rushed across the room and slammed into Lucien, pushing him against the glass window, and kissing him like he was trying to save him from death. Victor's hands cradled Lucien's face, and the kiss was hot. Possessive. Rough. Needy. Lucien kissed him back. Fuck, he loved kisses, and kissing Victor was definitely his favourite type of kissing. The taste of him, the wicked craving in this kiss. It was intimate and urgent, and it stole his breath. He lost track of how long they kissed; tongues lashing and lips together, occasionally the desperate touch of teeth against each other as they tried to deepen the kiss. Lucien wrapped his arms around Victor's waist, then slid his hands down to grasp Victor's perfect ass. He pulled him closer until their cocks ground against each other and Victor moaned. It vibrated through him.

"Fuck, I can't come in my office."

"No." Lucien didn't mind people watching, but he didn't imagine Victor would be comfortable with that. "Or you could."

"What?" Victor rasped.

"Lock the door, pull the blinds, and sit in your chair."

Victor frowned, his face flushed bright pink, all the way to his ears. "What?"

"Think of it as a going away present. Something to remember me by for the next few days." Heat rushed down his spine as he waited. Victor blinked a few times, then softened in Lucien's arms.

"Okay."

Yes. Lucien wanted to punch the air in victory. Suddenly, he understood the cliché of wanting to bottle a feeling and keep it; he wanted to take this moment to Monaco and hold it tight when he was away from Victor. Instead, he relaxed his hold and waited as Victor stepped out of the hug and went to lock his office door.

"Everyone will know. There are no blinds for these windows."

The challenge of it roared in Lucien's chest. "Sit at your computer and pretend that you are working."

"But people know you are in here with me."

"Maybe—" Definitely. Especially after that kiss, but... "They won't be able to see me."

Victor frowned. "Okay?"

Lucien could see the war happening inside Victor. The moment that he decided to comply was so beautiful, and Lucien waited as Victor sat in his office chair and leaned forward with his elbows on his desk. Lucien checked the door, then dropped to the floor, crawling across the floor until he was underneath Victor's desk. It was probably the least sexy foreplay he'd ever tried to do, ridiculous and yet, the ragged way that Victor breathed sent a rush of heat over Lucien's skin. Victor started tapping his fingers on his keyboard. Lucien had no idea if he was actually doing work, or if it was just the noise of it. Whatever. He tucked himself into the space, unsurprised by the lack of cables or mess under here, given Victor's tendency towards being neat and methodical.

"Ready?"

"I can't believe I'm going to do this." Victor dropped one hand under the desk, and Lucien squeezed his fingers.

"We don't have to. I want you to be comfortable. We could go to my room in the big house."

"No. This is … Um, like a fantasy but also freaky, you know."

Lucien wanted to give Victor something memorable before he left for a few days. "In this fantasy of yours, are you talking to Socrates on the phone about something important while I blow you?"

"No. Fuck. Lucien."

He probably shouldn't have mentioned their boss. "Perhaps keep all your attention on my mouth." He released Victor's fingers, resting his hand on his thigh. Victor had lovely hands; masculine and practical with slender fingers. Lucien shifted a little so he could grab Victor's ankles, then he slid both his hands up Victor's legs. He wasn't going to waste time with a lots of foreplay; not while they were in Victor's office and everyone in the workshop likely knew they were there. He didn't want to give Victor too much time to think about other people, or worry that Victor's phone might ring and he'd end up having to leave without giving Victor a moment to remember. The last thing he wanted was to leave Victor with blue balls. Focus, Lucien.

"Tell me Victor..." He undid Victor's fly and gently shifted all the fabric. Victor's hard cock was solid evidence that Victor wanted this, and Lucien traced one finger along the silky length of it.

"Yes?" Victor's voice shook a little.

"Do you like the idea of sitting here in your office, like a boss, knowing that everyone out there saw you kissing the number one Series E driver?"

Victor made a little grunting noise. "Third."

"Technicalities." Number one for Gamble Racing, and this season Lucien would be number one in the world. Before he could go to work, he had a lovely cock right next to his face, begging for his mouth. There was something odd about being tucked under Victor's desk, staring at his gorgeous cock and not being able to see his expression. It was oddly impersonal; detached.

"Are you still alive down there?"

"Just planning how to win the championship this year."

Victor choked on a laugh. "Lucien."

He leaned forward and blew a gentle breath over the round end of Victor's exposed cock, loving the way Victor's stomach trembled. It was the easiest thing to put his lips around Victor's cock and enjoy the taste of him, the smooth skin, the salty pre-come, the hard length pushing against the back of his throat. The way Victor slid forward on his seat, closer to Lucien's face. It had to look obvious to anyone looking through the window. Fuck, Lucien wanted to see. He needed to see Victor's expression, because judging by the desperate noises Victor was trying not to let out, Victor loved the feel of Lucien's mouth wrapped around his cock. Except ... this wasn't as fun as he had hoped. He sucked as hard as he could, suddenly needing to be done with this. It was too much like a hook up without that connection to Victor that he'd come to adore. He pushed Victor's pants further down—awkward with him sitting like that—and curled his fingers around the base of Victor's cock.

Victor groaned. "Oh fuck, Lucien." And suddenly Lucien relaxed, from his throat down to his toes. Yes. Hearing his name in such needy tones made it personal again. Lucien moaned, and Victor hoarsely whispered his name again and again as he came. Lucien swallowed it all down, the taste made more perfect by the way Victor reached under his desk and grabbed Lucien's hair.

"Lucien. Lucien. Oh fuck."

He licked across the end of Victor's cock, then tucked him gently back into his pants, before crawling out from under the desk to stand next to Victor. Fuck, he looked wrecked with his eyes all soft and his head resting back against his office chair.

"Jesus, Lucien. Why was that so hot?"

All Lucien's weird doubts fled. This was what he'd wanted to leave Victor with; completely sated and devastated by his skill. Standing on the podium had nothing on how much of a winner Lucien felt like now. He licked his lip, then leaned over for a quick kiss. Well, a long kiss, because he could never resist a proper kiss.

"I'd better be off then. See you in a week."

"Just like that?" Victor's voice cracked.

"If you want to be a gentleman, you could walk me to my car."

Victor frowned. "How do you do that?"

"What?" Lucien winked.

"Tease me after you've just destroyed me. You are amazing. I can't believe I get to be your boyfriend."

Lucien kissed him again, this time wrapping his hands around Victor's head. A long indulgent kiss.

"Believe it. And think of this whenever you are lonely without me."

"What about you?" Victor glanced downwards for a second.

"I'm fine. It's part of my stamina testing." Lucien couldn't seem to help being sarcastic. Fuck, his chest ached at having to leave Victor—even for a week for work—and it was easier to be playful than face the prospect of being without him. He was being so sappy. It would've made him ill, if Victor wasn't staring at him like he was the king of the fucking world.

"I'm going to miss you."

"Will you?"

"Lucien. Yes. Send me pictures."

"I'll call you whenever I can." He kissed Victor again, then grinned and walked away.

"Wait. I'll walk with you." Victor slung his arm around Lucien's waist.

Lucien kissed him on the cheek. "There's just one problem."

"Oh?"

"We aren't going to fit through your door if we walk

like this." Lucien grabbed Victor's hand and pulled him closer. "I am going to miss you. If I'd known having a boyfriend would be this much fun, I'd have done it earlier."

Victor shook his head, laughing. "Listen to yourself. Lucien Grenville, famous playboy. Nah."

"No. You are right. I had to wait for the right moment with exactly the right person." He kissed him again. At this rate, he'd never leave, and it didn't seem like such a bad idea. He could just curl up in Victor's office and stay. Did he really need a World Championship? Yes. Life always made sense when he was racing.

"Really?"

"Yes. Really. You are my exactly right person." He countered the annoying doubt quickly, then pulled his phone out of his jean's pocket. "Take a selfie with me. I'll put in on my socials, and then Socrates can tease you while I'm away."

"Lucien." That warning note was starting to be Lucien's favourite sound.

"Come on." He snapped a few photos. "This one is the nicest one. Look at you. You look like you've been thoroughly fucked."

"Lucien."

"Fine. I won't post it. I'll just wank to it on the plane."

"Fuck. Lucien. Can you just go now?" Victor pushed him, half-heartedly, and Lucien laughed before pulling Victor in for another kiss. This one was the actual goodbye and he poured all his feelings—the ones he was hiding behind his jokes—into the kiss, stroking Victor's tongue lovingly, until Victor softened in his arms.

"I am going to miss you." Victor whispered against Lucien's mouth.

Lucien rested his forehead against Victor's forehead and just breathed for a while. "Same. Now, go and sort out your car while I do punishing runs up the mountains around Monaco."

"Goodbye, Lucien."

It would the easiest thing to make another joke, and yet he couldn't. Not with their foreheads still resting on each other and Victor's dark eyes holding his gaze. "I'll be counting the hours, Victor."

"Go. You have a championship to win."

Competition stirred Lucien's blood. "Definitely."

"Plus it's only a few days, and then you can come home to my freezing cottage and we can—"

Lucien grinned. "Promises, promises." He gave Victor one last quick kiss, then bolted out of his office while the promise of becoming the World Champion still beckoned. In this single moment in time, Lucien felt like he could have everything. And so he left before he could ruin it.

CHAPTER 24

T he week disappeared in a blur of meetings and lack of sleep. And now Victor had to deliver some bad news to Socrates about the engine fires. Skye had found evidence that the exhaust systems had been tampered with by someone who had access to the team's equipment as it was moved from one racetrack to another; presumably a member of the logistics. Since he couldn't call Socrates while he was flying Victor's precious cargo—Lucien—home from London, he had to wait impatiently until they were safely on the ground before delivering the bombshell news. They still didn't know who —or why someone would want to wreck Gamble Racing's ability to finish Grand Prix races—and as Victor paced back and forth in the hanger, he hoped Socrates might have some ideas. It'd been freezing cold, but with clear skies, when Socrates had taken off a few hours ago, and the weather had held up nicely. Winter around here could change so quickly. Victor nodded to Janic, the mechanic who worked out here, mostly alone, looking after Socrates' helicopter, small Cessna, and an antique Tiger Moth. Eventually the tinny sound of the Robinson helicopter filled the air, and it wasn't long until the helicopter landed safely. Now the helicopter was on the ground, Victor could breathe a little deeper. He tightened his big jacket around his chest.

"Victor." Lucien stepped out of the helicopter with his head ducked low under the slowing rotors and jogged across the tarmac towards him. His loose strides were relaxed with no sign of the minor hamstring strain that he'd complained about on the first day of his fitness test. Each night, Lucien had called Victor, between fitness work and going out to eat with the other drivers and their trainers, and they'd talked about the discovery of The Shadow. Victor had only found out about Lucien's minor injury when Lucien had complained that it wasn't that glamourous to go to dinner with an icepack strapped to the back of his thigh.

"Your leg—" He didn't have time to finish the sentence as Lucien's mouth covered his in a kiss and Lucien hugged him tight, colliding with his body in a savage fashion. Lucien grabbed Victor's hips, and Victor responded by holding Lucien's biceps firmly. Lucien kissed him wildly, an almost brutal urgency, and Victor wanted to howl at the desperate joy of kissing his boyfriend. A week apart and Lucien demonstrated how much he missed him with the fierce use of tongue and lips, as if he wanted to devour him. It was fucking great. Victor didn't hold back, needing Lucien with the same intensity too. His skin was on fire, energy pulsing through him. Hearing someone cough was the only thing that stopped him ripping off Lucien's clothes right here, wherever they were. In Socrates' hangar with other people around...

He caressed Lucien's arms and shoulders, sliding his hands up until they were wrapped around Lucien's neck, and slowly Lucien relaxed in his arms, softening the kiss into one of deep affection. It was incredibly special. Victor adored how indulgent Lucien was, and he especially loved how Lucien could remove all his worries and make it feel like it didn't matter where he was or who was watching; it was obvious to everyone that Lucien wanted Victor more than anything else. Combined with the little growl Lucien made in the back of his throat just before he'd kissed him, it was the sexiest experience of Victor's life.

"That'll do love birds. Save it for later." Socrates thumped them both on their backs. Janic walked past to do whatever he needed to with the helicopter, not that Victor really noticed since he would much rather press his face against the crook of Lucien's neck and feel his stubble against his cheek.

"Yes boss." Lucien turned his head and grinned at Socrates but didn't release his arms from around Victor.

"Is it weird for you?" Victor asked. He had to know if having a relationship would be a problem for his job.

"Because you are kissing one of my drivers?"

"Hey. I'm the one doing the kissing here," Lucien said.

Socrates' eyes twinkled. "Looks pretty mutual from where I'm standing."

"Victor thinks people won't respect him if they know about us."

"I think that ship has already sailed." Socrates raised his eyebrows and Victor tensed. Lucien rubbed his hand gently on the base of his spine. He appreciated the attempt at reassurance. It wouldn't work, as Socrates had basically confirmed that people didn't respect him now.

"What do you mean?" His throat hurt as hot dry air escaped from his lungs.

"Everyone knows." Socrates barked out a loud laugh. "No one gossips like S1. I heard a rumour that you two were seen kissing in Victor's office last week. I heard another that Lucien was going to get Ondrej's seat this season."

"Because we are together? That's silly. As if I have any influence." He was barely hanging on to his job thanks to The Shadow trying to destroy the end of last season.

"This sport thrives on rumours. Just ask old Freddy, or Alicia Blasi. Now there's someone who can sort the trash talk from the really juicy truth." Socrates mentioned the two most prominent S1 journalists. Freddy used to drive in S1, and Alicia had equally as impressive qualifications, being a retired World Rally Champion.

Lucien leaned closer and whispered in Victor's ear. "I noticed that he didn't reply to the respect part of your question. Do you want me to talk to him later?"

Victor gulped. "Thanks for noticing." He didn't care if people knew about his relationship with Lucien, but he cared, probably too much, about being respected by his staff. He was very young to be a Chief Engineer for an S1 team—all his peers were at least a decade older than him—and now that things were going wrong, he felt younger and less capable than ever.

"Go home. Whisper your sweet nothings to each other there. I am going to home to kiss my husband." Socrates started to walk away, then turned back to them. "Oh, Reginald Whitehall is coming to dinner tonight. Victor. I need you to attend. I think it'll be good for your career to listen to him."

"Yes." Victor would never dismiss the chance to talk to an experienced designer. Sure, his last few designs had been slow, but he'd also won World Championships and Victor certainly hadn't. He extracted himself from Lucien's hug, although Lucien kept one hand resting on Victor's lower back. "Mr Whitehall has a lot of experience. I respect that, and I'd love to join you."

"And I suppose you could bring your boyfriend here." Socrates winked at Lucien who grinned back at him.

"I live in your house. I eat dinner with you most nights."

"And it's been so peaceful since you've been away. Please don't harass Reggie about his last few season's cars."

"I had to drive those cars." Lucien stiffened slightly beside Victor. A cold chill fluttered across the back of his neck; he'd forgotten that Lucien and Mr Whitehall had worked together for two seasons and knew each other well. He was about to go to dinner with people who all knew each other and he'd be the new one, the odd one out trying to learn the nuances of everyone's relationships with each other. As if he wasn't nervous enough...

"Then you understand that it's a touchy subject for him. He's still my friend and I don't want him antagonised by a young upstart who can't keep his mouth shut," Socrates said.

"Yes, boss."

"Team orders." Socrates stuck out his hand and Lucien took it, both smiling at each other, as they shook hands competitively. Victor waited his turn, then shook his boss's hand, wishing that he also had such a relaxed relationship with Socrates. He'd have to impress him first, and maybe not be so intimidated by him. Perhaps it was just because both Socrates and Lucien were drivers; they understood each other in a way the Victor couldn't.

"What time for dinner?" Lucien asked. Socrates waved his hand in the air as if to say that such details were beneath him.

"Send Mike a text. Wear something nice." Socrates marched off, leaving them alone in the freezing aircraft hangar. Lucien flicked his thumbs over his phone.

"I guess we should go home and get ready?" Victor asked. He had been hoping to get back to the workshop and see how Skye was getting along with analysing the logistics security tapes. They didn't seem to mind that it was such an arduous task, hunting through hours of footage to try and find the person that most of the team were now calling The Shadow. No one ever accused mechanical engineers of being creative.

"Shall I walk you to your car, my dear?" Lucien bowed with a silly flourish.

"Fuck, you are so adorable when you play like this." Victor couldn't believe the depths of this man. Put him in a car and his focus outstripped everything; and when he tried to control those flashes of anger—the unfortunate training of his childhood—he embodied such internal strength, that it almost seemed impossible that he could also be this charming, hilarious tease.

"I've been spending too much time with Socrates. His energy is hard to avoid."

"Yes, he's quite the force of nature."

Lucien started to walk. "Bloody hell, it's cold. Monaco was quite temperate compared to this. You should've come with me."

He wished. "I couldn't. I've had the new car in the wind tunnel all week." It was the fun part of all the work he'd been doing this week. Soon, they'd have to finalise the car and get it ready for pre-season testing. Ondrej and Paulo would be in the workshop next week to do some simulation testing.

Lucien spun around and grabbed him by the shoulders. "Tell me all about it. How fast is it going to be?"

"Fuck, Lucien. Next you'll be begging me to ask Socrates to put you in for pre-season testing."

Lucien burst out laughing. "How many rumours do you want to spread?" He shook his head and breathed out, a puff of fog in the frigid air. "But seriously. Get me in that car."

"You have your own car and besides, won't you be busy actually racing that weekend?"

"Probably. Kill joy." Lucien traced his hand down Victor's spine, walking beside him with his hand resting on Victor's hip. He loved this, the easy way Lucien touched him constantly. Walking beside him in the dimming light, with the sun setting over Socrates' farm, was nice.

"You really need to come to Monaco with me. It's much warmer and the sunsets are better."

"A few days away from me and now you are a poet, Lucien?"

"Says the bloke who lets his staff call someone The Shadow!"

He huffed out a frustrated laugh at his staff, glad he'd told Lucien everything when they'd first discovered the footage a couple of days ago. "I know it's not very original, but it just stuck. You can't change a nickname once they are given."

"Seriously though. What an absolute fuckwit." The touch of anger flowing in Lucien's voice sent a whisper across Victor's neck. There was something oddly comforting about having Lucien's rage on his behalf. Yes, it was probably wrong to encourage him—definitely wrong given Lucien's history—yet it didn't change the way he felt cared for and validated by Lucien's outburst.

"Did I tell you that Skye found another piece of footage of The Shadow this morning. At Austin, it looks like someone swapping out the brake disc packages for Paulo's car as the parts were being unloaded at Austin."

"It wasn't a mechanic who put the wrong part on the car and caused the brake failure?"

"Technically, yes, the mechanic fitted the part, but only because the part was put there by The Shadow." He deepened his voice deliberately when using the nickname and Lucien squeezed his waist with a little chuckle.

"The mechanic still should've checked it properly before installing it."

He nodded. "Agreed. Paulo could've been killed." They'd already updated their procedures after the wrong part had been installed, and while this didn't absolve the mechanic of blame, it did help understand how the mistake had happened. Everyone on an S1 team worked under pressure and mistakes happened, especially during pit stops, which is why they had procedures and they practiced tyre changes. No one wanted to look like a bunch of fucking wankers by making an obvious mistake during a pit stop.

Lucien shuddered. "The risk of death is high enough without sabotage thrown in the mix."

"I thought drivers didn't care about dying."

Lucien scoffed. "It's complicated. When I'm in the car, all I'm focused on is winning, so the prospect of death isn't relevant. When I'm not in the car, and I hear about people sabotaging a car to make it more dangerous, then yes, I fucking care about the increased risk."

He slung his arm over Lucien's shoulders. "A brake failure is incredibly scary."

"It can be."

"Skye is going through the footage for the last couple of races now, checking everything we have on the logistics team. Socrates has the logistics manager, Helen, putting together a list of everyone who works for the logistics team and their connections to other teams." Victor wanted to reassure Lucien that his team were doing everything possible to find The Shadow.

"Anything?"

"Nothing yet."

The crunch of their footsteps on the gravel path punctuated the frustration Victor carried at not being to solve this problem. He still couldn't believe that someone would want to do this to a racing team. Sure, there was a ton of money involved in S1, but that only meant it was more likely that teams copied successful designs as they looked for an advantage on the track. To do something so negative didn't really make sense in their world where teams won by going faster and being more reliable, not by stopping others.

"Connections to other teams?"

He nodded. "It makes sense to check, right? I wouldn't have thought a team would do this. Everyone is too focused on their own innovation to bother with putting effort into something like this. It's more likely to be a single person with a personal grudge against one of the drivers, not a grand conspiracy. Plenty of drivers missed out when Paulo was contracted to his seat." Victor was relieved that the issues weren't something he'd done wrong, and now he had a different puzzle to solve. The sabotage had to be either aimed at the team, or Socrates, or one of the drivers. They were the public faces of the team and the people who would be hurt—physically or financially—by the engine failures.

"Weird though. I can't imagine anyone wanting to hurt Ondrej or Paulo, especially Paulo. He's a rookie; how can he have enemies?" Lucien shrugged. "I guess his father isn't the nicest person."

Victor should call Pa tonight and thank him for not being a fuckwit. "Toxic fathers everywhere in this sport."

"Ondrej's father seems nice." And many of the other drivers had supportive families who attended races when they could.

"Yes, he's lovely. I shouldn't generalise."

Lucien nudged him on the shoulder. "No. Two people doesn't make a trend. Besides, Paulo's father is toxic in a different way to mine."

"Less aggressive, more of a controlling billionaire?" Victor had met Sanchez Snr a few times when he'd first been employed in this role and the man was incredibly intimidating. "Must have been hard for Paulo to grow up with such a domineering personality."

"Maybe that's why he's shy. Although he drives with incredible confidence."

"What's that saying about watching the quiet ones?"

Lucien cackled. "Jesus, Victor. Just say you miss sex. You don't have to be all quiet in the streets, demon in the sheets about your bloody rookie driver."

His face burned with heat. "I would never."

"I know. That's why you are so good to tease." Lucien kissed him on the cheek. He swallowed. All this chatter was a great distraction from tonight's dinner. As soon as Socrates had mentioned it, a pit had formed in his stomach and now it felt like a swarm of bees were having a dance party in there. Meeting the man that he'd taken over from was a huge deal.

"What's the matter?" Lucien asked.

"Um..."

"Did I do the wrong thing by teasing you?"

"No. It's just dinner tonight with Mr Whitehall. I've never actually met him ... and I ... um ... took his job."

Lucien didn't tease, he simply nodded solemnly then pulled Victor into a hug. "Victor. S1 is a cut-throat business. Reggie knows that. We both joked about being replaced during our last season as a way to deal with the frustration of being at the back of the grid all the time. As Socrates says, Reggie is sensitive about his last few cars being slow. He must know, even if he doesn't acknowledge it, that it was more than a joke, that he was going to get sacked sooner or later."

"Thanks for the logic. It doesn't make it easier to meet him as his successor."

"I'm sure it's not that easy for him either. Imagine going to dinner and being introduced to the person whose car was miles faster and took the team off the bottom of the grid into the mid-field."

He hadn't thought of it that way. "I'm not sure that helps. I'm pretty bloody nervous."

Lucien hugged him tighter. "If anyone should be nervous, it should be him. He's meeting the upstart young engineer who is kicking goals that he couldn't."

He sighed, breathing against Lucien's neck. He'd much rather just go home and spend the night in bed with Lucien. "Are you saying that I shouldn't be nervous?"

"Yes. I wasn't nervous when I met J-P Lavigne."

"You've met him?" Almost everyone on the pit lane knew each other, and often people had friends among the other teams, but the engineers tended not to hang out with the drivers. It wasn't a formal social stratum; more that drivers found engineers boring and mechanics had their own crews to hang with. S1 was a strange blend of competition combined with the friendships that came from spending so much time together in a very small community. Friends off the track and rivals on the track.

"Of course. We drove against each other for two years. He's a World Champion and I was in a shit car. By your logic, he should be nervous to meet me."

Victor prickled. "I didn't build a shit car."

"No, Whitehall did. You are going to win a constructor's title. In this story, you are J-P."

His instinct was to argue that Whitehall had won

constructor's titles, back in the day, while Victor hadn't, but as he breathed in, the pine forest scent of Lucien's aftershave surrounded him. "Okay."

"Go home, grab everything you need for dinner, and pack a bag so you can stay the night with me afterwards. I'll make it worth your while."

"Lucien. You don't need to say that."

"Why not?"

"Being with you is enough. You don't have to do anything except be yourself." Since he'd met Lucien, all those years ago in S3, Victor had tried not to fall in love with him. There was nothing he hated more than failing, yet this was the one thing he was more than content to fail at. He'd fallen completely and utterly in love with Lucien and all his complexities, with his desperate commanding kisses that made it impossible to doubt anything, with his loyalty to their friendship and to Victor's success. He'd fallen in love with Lucien and the way he wanted to be with him. Lucien Grenville. He couldn't believe his good fortune that Lucien constantly boosted Victor's achievements.

"Hurry back. It's been too long." Lucien opened the door to Victor's car. He wasn't about to leave, so soon after Lucien had returned, without another kiss, especially not after Lucien had gone out of his way to help him understand and overcome his nerves about tonight. He wanted to believe that it was true. Whitehall ought to be nervous to meet him. He was the future of Gamble Racing. It was time to own the role, and stop worrying that he was too young for such a responsibility.

"One for the road?" He reached up and held Lucien's

chin, before leaning in for a kiss. At the touch of their lips, Victor knew with certainty that this was love. Victor tried to infuse the kiss with the riot of feeling in his chest and when Lucien moaned, creating a soft vibration on both their lips, he hoped he'd succeeded.

Lucien's phone dinged with a message, and he broke the kiss. "It's Mike. Canapes in the blue drawing room in an hour. You'd better hurry."

"Yeah." He didn't want to leave.

Lucien kissed him on the tip of his nose. "Hurry back to me." And then he walked away, leaving Victor hungry for more. As Victor slid into his car, he grinned slowly. His nerves had disappeared with that kiss, and he was going to try and hold onto this feeling for as long as he could.

CHAPTER 25

Lucien collapsed in a chair in his room and tried not to sigh like a lovesick puppy. He'd had a long shower to pass the time. He checked his watch. Again. 'Hurry back,' he'd said and now he regretted not going with Victor. Okay, he knew that if he'd gone to Victor's home, they would've fucked and then they'd probably not want to leave and then ... then Victor wouldn't get to have dinner with Reggie and Socrates. A whole week without seeing Victor had made Lucien tetchy and he'd hidden it behind teasing. Normally he loved dinners like this, hanging out with people who had the same interest in car racing as him, but after a week with his teammates and trainers talking about the upcoming season—and Victor's new car—he missed Victor and wanted to keep him to himself. Selfishly. Being selfish was familiar. Drivers did it all the time; put the car first, ignore team orders until it was apparent that they had to be obeyed with an irritated growl.

If Socrates hadn't used that damned phrase in the hanger, he would've ignored the request to attend dinner. A dinner that promised to be tense and awkward. Socrates was so fucking loyal. He closed his eyes and leaned his head on the back of the chair. There was no reason to be mean about it, not when Socrates' loyalty had also been good for him. Without it, he would've been without a seat anywhere. Socrates didn't have to offer him the Series E opportunity. Most teams would've discarded their second driver when they had a new rookie with piles of sponsorship money to fill that role.

"Hey." Victor's soft greeting had Lucien leaping to his feet. Victor wore a sharp grey three-piece suit with a burgundy silk handkerchief tucked into the jacket pocket. Small black details matched perfectly with Victor's black hair which had been slicked into a neat style. Fuck. He was so handsome. How was Lucien supposed to function when all he wanted to do was throw himself on his bed and beg Victor to fuck him while wearing that suit. He dragged in a shaky breath.

"What took you so long?" He knew. Victor would've taken ages to nervously pick exactly the right suit, then spent ages making himself look good.

"I couldn't decide what to wear. I needed to look respectful and also confident. It's a tricky balance."

Lucien held his hands out. "You look incredible."

"Really?" Victor placed his hands onto Lucien's palms.

"Stunning. Victor, you picked exactly the right suit for tonight." Lucien squeezed Victor's fingers, instinctually knowing the reassuring his boyfriend mattered more than how sexy he was. But holy fucking hell...

"Thank you."

"Come on. Before I rip that suit off you." Lucien didn't

utter his initial desire. He'd save that one up for after dinner, once Victor was relaxed. Victor nodded slowly.

"Victor?"

"I heard you. I'm just too nervous to ... Oh fuck, what if I sound like a fool?"

Lucien growled. "Then Whitehall will be a smug piece of shit with a slow car, and you'll still be the sexiest man I've ever kissed."

In the two years that he'd worked with Reggie, Lucien had never seen him lose his temper, apparently resigned to accept his slow car and the struggle that created for the whole team every race weekend. Lucien had watched him gradually become a smaller version of himself; it would've been sad if it Lucien hadn't been the one out on track in a slow car trying his best not to be fucking last in every race.

"Can you be serious? I'm freaking the fuck out here."

"I am serious." He leaned in and kissed Victor. A soft gentle closed mouthed kiss. "Come on. Let's go to dinner."

"Okay." Victor closed his eyes and blew out a long slow breath. "Yes, okay. Let's go."

Lucien kissed Victor again, then held his hand, and stepped back a bit.

"Hold on. What are you wearing?"

Lucien couldn't hold back the chuckle. "This old shirt? It's my favourite meme from my last S1 season." The shirt had a photo of his S1 car on the back of a tow with the words 'Gamble Fast Lap' at the top. He'd gone off at turn nine at Imola during FP2 thanks to an unusual blast of wind. The car had been fine and had a ride back to the pits on the back of a truck.

"You can't wear that. Socrates said not to antagonise his friend."

"Trust me, I worked with him. Reggie won't notice—" By the time they'd got to Monaco, not even half-way through their last season together, Reggie had completely checked out and was only going through the motion of his job. "The shirt is for Socrates. Besides, we are late now."

Victor's nostrils flared as he sucked in a deep breath. "Fine."

"It will be fine." He'd had dinner with Socrates and Mike and their various visitors many times, but just for Victor's sake, he grabbed a leather jacket and zipped it up to hide the shirt. Victor's single nod of relief mattered. At worst, Reggie would roll his eyes at Lucien's joke, and Socrates would—eventually—enjoy being teased by the meme.

An hour later, Lucien regretted the jacket. Socrates had the blue drawing room over-heated with several oil heaters around the room. There was also an ancient fireplace which had a nice fire in it, although it was mostly for show as it seemed to blow most of the heat up the chimney and not actually warm the room at all. Theoretically these old houses were hard to heat, or rather, they had so many draughts that it was impossible to keep the warmth in the room. Socrates' grandfather had fixed the draughts back when he'd bought the house and combined with the oil heaters, the room was baking hot. But every time he rested his hand on the zipper, Victor glared at him. The conversation was pretty boring, mostly Socrates and Reggie chatting about the past, something he could've joined in on, since he'd worked closely with Reggie for two years. He'd rather discuss the upcoming season than rehash the past.

Reggie had brought along his son, Ethan, who was a sullen faced young man, maybe the same age as Lucien—mid-twenties—who worked as a ... Actually, Lucien didn't know, and he didn't particularly care to ask. Judging by the way Ethan stood by the fireplace drinking a glass of red wine while sneering at everyone, Lucien wasn't tempted to see if Ethan was less of a dickhead than he'd been when he used to come to the occasional race with Reggie. He'd much rather stand to the side and quietly chat with Mike about Xenia's racehorse, Swap Meet, who'd won some big race in France in November and now a bunch of farms were bidding to buy him as a stud horse. The money on offer rivalled some of the top S1 driver contracts. More importantly than anything else, Victor was doing well, listening closely to Reggie and Socrates regale him with stories of their better years in S1.

Angie, the chef, walked over to Mike. "Dinner is served."

"Thank you." Mike tapped his wine glass. "Excuse me, everyone. Dinner is served. Please come through to the long dining room." Mike's announcement broke the weird tension in the room. They all followed Socrates' husband through the door into another overheated room. Usually they ate in the smaller family dining room and only used this one for when Socrates had guests. Did it make him part of Socrates' family to have dined with him, Mike, and Xenia in the more casual family room? After spending Christmas with Victor's family, he'd started to reassess his relationship with Socrates, who given him a home and family of sorts when he'd had nothing. It would've been the easiest thing for Socrates to treat him like any other driver, not welcome him in as an orphan who needed a father figure. Lucien hung back, waiting for Victor to sit, before choosing the seat opposite him. He took off his jacket and slung it over the back of his chair. Angie and some of her staff served the main course—a traditional roast lamb neatly sliced on each plate with Yorkshire puds and gravy—while the centre of the table was filled with different roasted vegetables and salads and a few baskets of fresh bread rolls. There was a selection of several different wines, something Lucien had come to associate with Socrates who was a bit of a wine aficionado.

"Lucien." Socrates warned as Lucien sat down.

"Yes?"

"What is that shirt?"

Lucien stood up and puffed out his chest. "It's one of my favourite memes from my last season in S1. S1 fans are so clever with all their memes after each race, and I always get a few of my favourite ones made into shirts."

"Is that Imola?" Reggie asked. The curiosity in his tone made Lucien smile; he knew Reggie wouldn't hate this shirt. Two years working together had given him some clues about the man, no matter what Socrates had said.

"Yes."

"I wouldn't have thought you'd want to broadcast to the world that you made such a simple mistake in FP2." Ha, nice retort. Reggie had survived decades in S1—before the last few seasons of disappointment—and it showed in that comment.

"It was the wind."

"No. You pushed too hard going into turn nine and lost the back end. One hundred percent driver error." Reggie's mouth curled up at the edges. Lucien wasn't going to concede that Reggie was probably right. He'd been so frustrated by the car's lack of pace that he'd thrown it into the corner too hard. It might've been fine if the rear wing hadn't also caught a gust of wind and spun him out onto the gravel trap.

"The fans who made this meme didn't think so." The meme was all about the car and how slow it was, but he was okay if Reggie wanted to focus on his crash, rather than the actual content of the meme. Socrates flashed a warning glance in his direction, and he gave him a quick nod to say that he understood the team order; don't upset Reggie.

"Fans have many differing opinions. I had the data." Reggie continued in the same vein, teasing Lucien and he rolled with it. Team orders, after all.

Lucien grinned. "And I had the hardest job that season."

"Respectfully—" Victor interjected, sending a flush of warmth spreading through Lucien's chest. "I'd say that Ondrej had the most difficult task that season." The way everyone's eyes focused on Victor, all of them slightly wide and intrigued.

"Why?" Reggie asked.

"Think about it. The season before he'd driven for a championship winning team, and now he was expected to take a team that had much less sponsorship money and less staff and take that team back up the grid."

"And a terrible—" Lucien cut himself off as Victor held up one hand.

"Without the funds to spend on development, there is only so much an engineer can achieve. I was incredibly lucky to arrive at Gamble Racing at the same time as a major sponsor. It's a lot easier task with good financial backing." Victor managed to find the kindest way to talk about Reggie's slow car. Lucien was so proud; he wanted to press his fist against his chest.

"Thank you." Reggie tipped his wine glass in Victor's direction. "At first, it was disappointing to be moved on, but with some reflection, I've realised my time in S1 was over. I had a long career with many highlights and I'm enjoying my retirement now."

A chair scraped on the wooden floor. Reggie's son— Ethan—had pushed back from the table and sat there with his arms crossed, glaring at Victor. A cold breeze touched the back of Lucien's neck.

"You aren't a fan of your father's retirement, Ethan?" All the hairs on his arms stood up.

"Ethan used to travel with me during his school holidays." Reggie's comment didn't seem to make any connection to Lucien's question, since Ethan never seem to enjoy the days when he turned up at the track, with pit lane access, to watch Reggie work. He'd been a contemptuous young man who didn't seem to enjoy the being there. The crews didn't really interact with him because he seemed to look down on everyone.

"Do you miss the travel?" Lucien couldn't work out what they were talking about.

Ethan sneered. "No." To be fair to Ethan, Reggie had

been a ball of stress in that last season and hadn't been pleasant to work with. It can't have been easy to be there as an observer. Retirement looked good on Reggie; it'd been a long time since Lucien had seen his old engineer banter and laugh.

"I always thought you liked coming to the races with me?" Reggie asked. "And if you don't like the travel, why did you ask me to try and get you a job with Gamble Racing?"

What the fuck? Ethan worked for Gamble? Since when? Lucien leaned forward, focused on Ethan, who didn't move.

"I'm always happy to help out an old friend and give a young person a chance," said Socrates, appearing to miss the point that was also out of Lucien's grasp. Why on earth would Ethan want to work for Gamble Racing when he had never seemed to enjoy coming to the races with Reggie? The sullen expression on Ethan's face suddenly clicked. He'd seen this expression in Monaco during his last season in S1.

"Tell me, Ethan. Are you still on Tinder?"

"What?"

"I've heard that the crews are all on the dating apps..." Lucien hadn't needed to use dating apps himself, but many of the younger single members of the crew did and they would announce their presence in whatever city they are in. Lucien had always just gone out to find the gayest night-clubs in each city and chatted to handsome men until he found someone fuckable.

"Does having a Dad who is Chief Engineer help you get laid?" Lucien recalled Ethan bitching to one of the mechanics about how women in Monaco were so picky and they weren't as easily swayed by his connections as they were in towns near other tracks.

"I don't know what you are talking about."

He'd heard that before, said in exactly the same way… "No, I'm sure you don't."

"Lucien, I'm sure Ethan doesn't need the twenty questions," Mike said. Lucien glanced at Victor, then Socrates, both of whom had the same intense curiosity written on their faces. Victor was twisting his napkin around, a mirror to the way Lucien's gut twisted too.

"Just one more. What job has Socrates got you doing for Gamble Racing?"

"Ethan works for the logistics team," Reggie said. Bells rang in Lucien's ears, clanging loudly. Fuck. It couldn't be, could it?

Ethan sneered. "Asking if I miss the travel was a stupid question. I get to travel with the team now."

"Great. That's awesome for you." Lucien spat sarcastically. "And the benefits of visiting so many cities?"

"Now that Dad isn't Chief Engineer, it's not the same." The fucking audacity from Ethan to basically confirm that he used to boast about his Dad's job to pick up sexual partners. Gross. Lucien cringed.

Victor cleared his throat. "Excuse me, Ethan. This is a bit of an odd request, but I left my reading glasses on that side table near the fireplace. Would you mind getting them for me?"

"Get them yourself."

"Please. I would really appreciate it." What was Victor doing?

"Come on son. Socrates was good enough to get you a job. The least you could do is help out." Reggie had an open expression, unlike the focused expression on both Victor and Socrates' faces.

"Thank you so much Ethan." Socrates backed up Victor, and even someone as sulky as Ethan could work out that pissing off his boss wouldn't be a great idea. As soon as Ethan pushed his chair back and started to walk across the room, everything clicked. Ethan walked exactly like The Shadow. It was an ordinary walk with a touch of contempt, as if Ethan couldn't be bothered to pick up his feet and move with any intensity. He kept his head bowed in the same way too.

"I'm so sorry, Mr Whitehall." Victor pulled out his phone and showed something to Socrates who nodded. "We believe Ethan is responsible for—"

Ethan whipped around, sneering at Victor. "Yes. I did it. You didn't need to get me to walk and get your bloody glasses to prove anything. I put a carbon fibre shard in Ondrej's tyre. I swapped out the brake discs, and I used a laser cutter to put holes in the exhausts of both cars at Abu Dhabi. I hate you for stealing my Dad's job. I did everything I could to get you sacked..."

Lucien couldn't hear anything over the roar in his ears. He barely registered what he was doing until Ethan lay on the ground at his feet, bellowing and holding his face. Rage had taken hold of him. He'd acted without thought, without control. What a fuckwit he was. Asshole. Just like his toxic father.

"Lucien. Breathe." Victor's soothing voice managed to interrupt the red mist. He shook out his sore knuckles and walked away before he could inflict more damage. As he rushed across the room, he stared at his hand. His knuckles were smeared with blood. What had he done? He shoved the door open and began to run, as if he could outrun himself and the way his lungs burned.

CHAPTER 26

Victor stared at the door. He twisted his watch around his wrist. Should he follow? He should follow Lucien to make sure he was safe. When Lucien got angry like this, he didn't care what happened to him. Not that he'd do anything awful on purpose; it was more that he didn't pay attention to potential danger.

"Leave him." Socrates sounded so certain and calm. What would he know?

"He needs me." Victor whirled around to glare at his boss. Fuck, he needed a drink of water or something to do, because this room was too hot, and his skin was chilled, and his heart felt like it was going to burst out of his chest.

"No. He needs time to work this out himself."

Victor rubbed his eyes. "He's going to get it all wrong."

"Trust him. He's one of the best drivers in the world." Socrates patted Victor on the shoulder, and Victor wanted to push him away. Saying Lucien was a good driver meant nothing right now—it was an empty platitude—illogical, too, since Lucien was still a human who'd made a choice that would have a lot of consequences. S1 drivers really were a special club of people with a strange sense of immortality, and it must be the source of confidence across every sector of Socrates' life. Not Victor, he was all too aware of everyone's mortality as he stared at the door, stressing about Lucien's safety.

Behind him, the sound of Ethan crying foul went on and on. If he wasn't so worried about Lucien, he'd march over there and tell him to shut the fuck up.

"Quiet everyone." Mike's voice sliced through the room and Victor automatically turned towards him. "I've called the police."

"Good. He assaulted me. Everyone saw that." Ethan whined.

"The police will take statements. Until then, I advise everyone to stay quiet and wait." Mike had the type of authority that was understated, and Victor hadn't ever seen him utilise it. Socrates often took up all the space when the two of them were together. Socrates was a retired S1 World Champion with a loud, charming personality—from back in the day when the safety measures were lower, and drivers died on a frequent basis—while Mike was softly spoken and calm. He'd been a bank manager before he'd married Socrates and become a part owner of Gamble Racing. Judging by the way Socrates deferred to him on financial matters, they each understood their strengths. Socrates could talk anyone into sponsoring the team, and Mike could make every dollar stretch. Why was he thinking about this now? It was a pointless distraction to the way his heart thumped erratically.

"I need to find Lucien." Surely the police would want

to talk to him. Victor really needed to know Lucien was okay. He ... He needed ... He had to find Lucien. He pulled out his phone and texted him. An erratic series of texts with no response.

"He is with Xenia." Mike and Socrates' niece lived in the big house too. She trained the racehorses that lived on the other side of the property.

"What?" Victor had only met her once and had been fascinated, and a bit intimidated, by her. Xenia was one of those older women who looked equally at home in Wellingtons and grubby jeans as she did all dressed up for the races in a designer dress and fancy hat. Mike's brother, George Patel, had married a Russian immigrant, resulting in Xenia, who had her mother's height and father's black hair and brown skin. They'd died in a car accident outside Socrates' estate decades ago, leaving Xenia orphaned, which is how Mike and Socrates had met. It was a story Victor had heard many times.

"Xenia sent me a text. Come and sit down." Mike led him back to his chair at the dining table. His half-eaten meal may as well have been a lump of sick for all that he could stomach the idea of eating anything.

"What a mess." Socrates sat beside him. "I can't believe Reggie's son would sabotage the team. Reggie's own son." He filled his wine glass and drank the whole thing in one go, then refilled it.

"Neither. I can barely believe anyone would want to do that at all." Victor needed to see Lucien, to reassure him that he had done the right thing. Seeing him leap to his feet and slam his fist into Ethan's face had been a visceral shot to the heart because it had said one thing and one thing only.

Lucien cared about Victor, and he would defend him and his reputation against all threats. It was only now as the adrenalin wore off and everything started to turn to jelly, that the thrill turned into concern. With Lucien's past, he probably assumed he'd acted in a toxic way. The shame of it washed over him, as if it were his past and his lack of control, not Lucien's. He closed his eyes.

"Is he going to be safe?" Victor breathed in. He knew Lucien would be blaming himself for losing control. Since Lucien's father had died, he'd worked so hard to stop his rage induced reactions. They'd talked about it on the drive north; how Lucien didn't want to be like his father, and how he'd been to therapy to work on unlearning the toxic behaviours his father had instilled in him. Of all the things that worried Victor, it was this that bothered him the most. He didn't want Lucien to be disappointed in himself.

"He will. Xenia will remind him that he has a championship to win."

"Racing is the last thing I care about right now."

"But it will be the thing that saves him. It always has been." Socrates pulled out his phone. "I'll text him and remind him."

Victor didn't think it would work, but right now, he'd give anything to see Lucien walk safely in that door. Socrates' order to leave Lucien alone made Victor very uncomfortable, but he deferred to Socrates since he was his boss and Lucien lived in his house. Maybe Socrates knew Lucien better? Doubt flourished in a circumstance like this. Besides, he'd already sent him several texts without response, so it was all a bit pointless. If he chased Lucien now, it was too late and he would be stumbling around in the dark unable to find him. He'd delayed too long to do anything effective.

A phone on the table dinged as Socrates pressed send on his own phone. Oh. Lucien's lack of response wasn't because he wasn't safe; it was simply because he hadn't thought to put his phone in his pocket before marching up to Ethan and punching him.

"He will be fine. Xenia has plenty of experience in patching up highly strung creatures." Mike sat down next to Socrates and gently removed his wine glass. "Socrates, darling, we need to talk strategy."

"Yes." Socrates' demeanour changed instantly. "When are the police arriving?"

"I didn't call the local police. I called a detective from Northhampton, so we have some time."

"Good."

"Do you think Reggie will cooperate?" Mike whispered.

"Two years ago, I would've said he'd put his loyalty to the team above the actions of his son. Now?"

Victor couldn't help ask. "Isn't that the whole issue?"

"Excuse me?" Mike asked.

"The son must know that his father always put his work before him." He really needed to thank his own parents for always putting him and his sisters first in their busy lives.

"Are we meant to have sympathy for someone who actively tried to harm our drivers and make our cars look unreliable?" Socrates' voice was as sharp as a shard of glass.

"No."

Mike tapped his fingers on the table. "I would rather think that the son is loyal to his father. He wanted to embarrass Victor, presumably so his father could have his old job back."

"For the benefits of the job, not for the person." Socrates made the nuance. "I rather think that will sway Reggie if we need it."

"Let's take a step back. What are we trying to achieve here?" Mike asked. Victor was glad for the conversation as it distracted him from the swirling worry about Lucien.

Mike's phone dinged and he glanced at it. "That was Xenia. She can bring Lucien here whenever we want." Relief flooded Victor's veins with a soft coolness. Lucien was obviously safe, and the fall out of how he felt about hitting Ethan could be dealt with when Lucien was ready to talk. Victor could wait.

"I'm going to call Freddy. We need to manage the story for the sake of our sponsors." Socrates walked around the table to grab his phone.

"When will the cops get here? I've been assaulted." Ethan was still bleating.

"Oh shut it." Victor was done with this. "You could've killed our drivers with your sabotage bullshit. You deserved everything Lucien gave you." He marched over to Ethan, who sat on a chair with an icepack on his face. Socrates' staff had responded rapidly to stop the bleeding on his cheek and given him first aid, not that he'd needed much more than an icepack to slow any bruising from Lucien's fist.

"I can't believe you would do something so reckless, Ethan." Reggie hovered awkwardly. Ethan made a whining noise.

"Stop." Victor had had enough of this nonsense. "Your hosts, whose business you tried to destroy, have had the decency to give you first aid and you are still making it about you. I cannot believe the fucking audacity of someone who used their father's job to hook up with strangers and then was so fucking selfish when that ended that you decided to get petty revenge. I'd bet you didn't even ask Mr Whitehall what he thought about his retirement."

There was a thump on his shoulder and he turned his head to see Socrates beside him.

"That's enough, Victor. Reggie, I'm sorry, but we are going to have to involve the police and Ethan has admitted fault. We aren't going to be able to manage a good outcome for your son," Socrates said.

"You don't need to try, Socrates. Ethan has made his own choices. He is an adult, and I do think you ought to call the S1 stewards too. It is a racing matter." That answered the question of Reggie's loyalty. "It's one thing to be disappointed in losing my job, and another entirely to put driver safety at risk deliberately."

"Thank you, Reggie. I really am sorry." Socrates pulled his friend into a hug.

"I'd happily come back on board as a consultant." Fuck. Was that a thinly veiled threat from Reggie? Victor wasn't sure he was cut out to thrive in this world. He just wanted to make fast cars, not play those sorts of games.

"Victor, can you get all of the evidence against Ethan Whitehall together?" Mike's interruption came at the perfect time. He needed to get out of this room, away from all the competing politics, and all these people trying to gain advantage from a shit situation. He needed something to do so he stopped worrying about Lucien and doing as Mike suggested would be exactly what Lucien would want him to do. Bring down that bloody wanker, Lucien would say, so Victor would take that energy and do something constructive.

"Absolutely." He straightened his suit jacket, then breathed out slowly as he tried to walk like he was in control, when all he wanted to do was run. Towards Lucien. Away from Ethan. Or simply focus on the task that needed to be done. Lucien would need time to reconcile his actions, and Victor was caught between wanting to smother Lucien in care—something Lucien would likely reject—or do his part to finalise the case against Ethan.

Once he was in the hallway, he began to write a text to his key staff.

Victor: Good news and bad. Good – we found The Shadow. Bad – I need all of you in the workshop asap as the police will be here soon to collate the evidence.

His phone started to ring. Skye. He nearly answered, then realised that everyone would be trying to reach him.

Victor: I will tell everyone the whole story at the workshop. Focus on getting here.

Before he joined them, there was one place he needed to go first. Xenia's stables. Only a coward would leave his boyfriend alone in his time of need. No more excuses. No more arguing with himself, around in illogical circles. It was time to act, to show Lucien he'd done the right thing.

For all the drama inside the big house, the night was quiet and dark as he walked along the driveway to the horse stables, using the torch on his phone to illuminate his path. Only a small light at the end of the barn shone in the darkness, and he headed there. The door was open when he arrived, and he stepped into a small room filled with horse equipment. It smelled like leather and antiseptic, and reminded him of a tool shed, but filled with alien things that he had no idea what they were called or how they were used. Lucien sat, staring at the floor, in the middle of the room on an upturned bucket with Xenia wrapping his hand in a bright pink bandage.

Lucien was okay. Thank fuck.

Victor's knees buckled and he started to reach out for Lucien. Fuck, he was light-headed and jumbled all at once and he couldn't seem to make the final step towards him and hug him. Lucien didn't look up and it formed a weird barrier that Victor couldn't force himself to cross.

"Hello," Xenia said. "Perfect timing. I've just finished icing his hand and wrapping it. I only had equine bandages, but that'll do for now."

"Lucien." Victor's voice came out all raw and he cleared his throat.

"Have the police arrived?" Lucien kept his gaze low.

"Not yet." Victor wanted to hug Lucien, hold him tight, and reassure him that he'd done the right thing in defending Victor's honour. His hands hurt with needing to touch him. "Socrates and Mike are managing the situation."

Xenia cackled. "Of course they are. My uncles are so predictable."

"I don't want to be managed." Lucien stared at Victor with eyes blazing. "I want to be arrested. I'm a monster."

"Oh darling. You are not. You never have been." Victor had a decent understanding of childhood trauma, from asking his mother about Lucien over the years without mentioning his name, but nothing prepared him for seeing Lucien so determined to believe that he was exactly like his father.

"I am."

"I have a horse that needs checking." Xenia bolted from the room. Victor wrapped Lucien in a hug. It was awkward with him standing, and Lucien sitting on a bucket, and so he slowly dropped down onto his heels, until he was crouched between Lucien's legs and waited until Lucien rested his head on Victor's shoulder. They stayed like that for so long that Victor's legs started to go numb.

"I can't do this." Lucien's voice trembled. "You deserve more than being with an out-of-control thug." For Lucien to say it aloud was worse than thinking and worrying that Lucien would take this moment and believe the worst of himself.

"You are not a thug. What on earth gave you that impression?" Victor tried not to growl and probably failed.

"I just thumped someone without even being aware I was doing it. You deserve better."

"And you think that gives you the right to decide what I deserve? Shouldn't I get to make that choice?" Victor stood up. Pins and needles in his feet made it awkward to pace over to the far side of the tiny room. It wasn't far enough. Now that he'd seen Lucien was physically fine, all the tension he'd been carrying flowed out in a rush of shaky emotion.

"Victor. I just hit someone."

"Yes." Victor spun around, still a little wobbly. "Speaking of deserving. Ethan deserved to be hit. He deliberately tried to destroy my work. Our drivers could've been killed by his actions. I think he came off lightly with just a little punch to the face." He sucked in a deep breath. "Ethan is fine, by the way. He has a small cut on his cheekbone, and he was given an icepack immediately."

"But what if I hit you one day?"

Victor held his breath. Something in Lucien's tone pulled him up short and he knew he couldn't react quickly. If Lucien truly worried about that, Victor couldn't play lightly or defensively with this one. "Have you ever hit someone you liked?"

Lucien laughed, an unhinged mean laugh. "Yes. I shoved Ondrej once after he pushed me off the track and we crashed."

"Have you ever hit someone when you weren't racing?"

"No. This is the first time."

Victor waited.

"I've never hit anyone like that."

"Like that?" Victor didn't think there was much point in asking Lucien to distinguish different situations, but he wasn't sure what else to ask. Hopefully this meant Lucien was starting to realise that this was a one-off issue, not a total disaster?

"I've been in the usual few schoolboy fights, and the odd bar fight, but never with such rage as tonight. I can't even remember doing it. I—" Lucien stood up slowly. "I scared myself tonight with how much rage I felt."

"He dishonoured me and my work. It's okay to be angry about the danger he caused. I'm fucking angry too."

Lucien waved his bright pink bandaged hand in the air. "Yeah, but you didn't punch him."

"Only because you got there first."

Lucien shook his head and stared at the ground again. "Stop making this less than it is. I've worked so hard to control my anger and it turns out that I can't. There is only one answer. We can't be together. It's for the best."

"Why is that, Lucien?"

"I have to protect you from me."

Victor shook his head. "That's bullshit."

"I can't guarantee that I won't do this again. What if I hurt you?"

Victor swallowed. Lucien was already hurting him by taking this stance. "When you find the answer, you know where I'll be." He left, unable to stop his heart breaking completely. Years ago, when he'd tried to stop himself falling in love with Lucien, it'd been the right choice, because now it was too late—he'd completely succumbed to being in love with Lucien—and now everything hurt. His whole body was too tight, aching and miserable. All he had left was his work, and he did have a pile of work to do.

Damn it, he was going to make the best case against Ethan that he could. He could put this fucking hurt fury to work.

CHAPTER 27

Lucien hadn't expected to see such devastation on Victor's face. Pushing him away was for Victor's own good; he just didn't expect being right to hurt so much. He wanted to get a knife, trace the slashes of his tattoo, and rip his own heart out, then stomp on the fucking thing. It'd hurt less than this.

"He's right, you know." Xenia leaned on the tack room door.

"About?"

"You."

"Excuse me." Lucien wanted to wipe the smug expression of her face, so he focused on his breathing until the urge went away.

"It's bullshit. You can't push someone away to protect them. You are being a coward."

"I am?" He flexed his good fist. The familiar rise of heat and the pounding in his ears grew. It was time to breathe through it and not fuck up again. Again. Every ragged breath was the reason why he couldn't be with Victor.

"Absolutely. You don't get to make that choice for someone else. If he loves you, it's his choice to decide to be with you."

"But what if I hurt him?"

"Isn't that his risk to take? What if he thinks you are worth it?"

Lucien's eyes burned white-hot and he pressed his palms against them. "I'm not."

"Do you want to be?"

"So much." The release of admitting that he wanted to be good enough for Victor and his amazing family was like standing under a hot shower and having all the muck of his life washed away.

Xenia patted him on the shoulder, slightly awkward. "Trust me on this one. I fell in love once and it scared the fuck out of me. I made all the excuses and pushed her away, and I regret it every day. Don't let being scared turn into a regret." She walked back to the door. "Turn the light off when you leave, please."

Lucien—race car driver and future Series E World Champion—stood alone, freaking the fuck out. If it wasn't the middle of the night, he'd go for a drive. Everything always made more sense when he was behind the wheel. All his worries disappeared with the thrill of speed and the focus needed to stay alive and on the limit. The problems always came back afterwards though, and this one... It was too big, too heavy, to be solved with a drive. If this was a problem on the track, he'd break it down into parts and figure out a solution. He had three competing opinions.

Xenia thought he shouldn't let being scared turn into regret. Victor thought he was capable of taking on the risk of Lucien's rage. And he ... well he thought if he could cure himself of this senseless rage inside him, then he might be worthy of being loved. But he couldn't, so he wasn't. It was better for everyone if he stayed away to keep them safe.

"Hey." Xenia ducked her head in the room again. "Mike texted me. They want you in the big house to take a statement. Sorry."

"Shit. Would you mind coming with me?"

Xenia shook her head. "Not really. I have a filly who might have colic and I don't want to wake any of the staff, since they have to be awake for track work in—" She checked her watch. "Five hours. And the vet will be here any moment."

"It's fine. I'll go. Thanks for this." Lucien waved his bandaged hand.

"Any time. You are kind of a little brother to me in a weird way."

"Okay?"

"Come on. Socrates and Mike took me in when I was orphaned, and they did the same for you. I mean, it was different for me, since I was ten, and you are a whole grown up, but they've given us a family when we needed it, so you are my little brother."

"Thanks." Lucien swayed, about to lose his balance.

"Now get in there. Give a statement and none of this I'm a monster bullshit." Xenia rushed off again, leaving Lucien too stunned to move. Eventually—fuck know how long afterwards—he turned off the light and walked out into the dark. Xenia and another woman stood on the grass in the centre of the stable block with a horse. It must be the vet, since she was holding one of those doctor things—stethoscope—against the horse's side. Xenia cradled the horse's head and the horse stomped its back legs. He stayed out of the way, quickly walking past his ... big sister? He rubbed his eyes, unable to process that right now.

"Hey, Lucien. Do you need a torch?"

"Probably."

"There's a few in the tack room."

"Okay?"

"The room you were in. It's called a tack room. On the right, by the door, there's a shelf with a box full of those torches you put on your head. Grab one of them." It was only then, that he noticed both Xenia and the vet wore one each.

"Thanks." He went back to the room and grabbed one. Well, he wasn't going to wear it on his head—too dorky—but it would work if he just carried it.

He'd almost reached the big house when he heard the helicopter overhead. Who the hell was coming here this late at night in a helicopter? As soon as he opened the door, he almost collided with Mike.

"Good. Xenia said you were on your way. Can you go and pick up Freddy from the hangar?" Mike handed him a set of keys. "The Merc."

"I'm not going to avoid telling the police what I did." He hoped Mike wasn't sending him away so they could manage him. He rolled his eyes; of course they were managing this. There was zero reason to invite Freddy unless they were in damage control mode. It had to be

Freddy Hiptonstall, one of S1's most prominent journalists, no other Freddy made sense.

"We wouldn't ask you to lie, Lucien." Mike sounded genuine.

"Okay."

"Be honest with Freddy too." Mike turned and walked away before Lucien could ask any questions. The moment he slid into the driver's seat, everything settled down. It was like clockwork. Incredible. The drive up the hill to the hangar took less than minute; nowhere near long enough to help him figure out what the hell to do. Freddy stood in the doorway of the hangar. He wore a massive black overcoat, tailored to his slender body, and managed to look like he'd stepped out of a movie. As soon as he started walking the coat caught the wind and blew out behind Freddy as if he were standing in a model's fan.

"Fucking hell. Would you just get in the car without being so dramatic?" Lucien called out.

Freddy slipped into the passenger seat. "I see they've sent their third best driver to get me. Must be a priority."

"Ha." Lucien waited until Freddy clipped his seatbelt, then spun the car around on the spot.

"Neat trick. Did you learn that from me?"

"Are you ever serious?" Lucien had had a pretty big night and he still hadn't been arrested, so he had that to look forward to still. He didn't need bloody Lord Alfred Hiptonstall, the Earl of Beautravers, former S1 driver and racing journalist, having a crack at him too.

"Seriously?"

"Socrates wants you here. I assume he wants you to break the sabotage story—"

"Sabotage?" Freddy shifted in his seat, suddenly alert. "Are you referring to the engine fires at the end of last season?"

"Yes."

"Okay. Socrates told me this would be worth getting out of bed for."

"You were in bed?" Lucien laughed. It wasn't that late. They'd been having dinner when Socrates would've called Freddy and the idea of the big talking charming journalist already being asleep so early amused Lucien. Not much about tonight was funny, so he'd take this one.

"With a very appreciative couple. We met in a club…"

"Fuck, aren't you too old for that nonsense?"

"Sex? Never."

Lucien rolled his eyes. "No. Picking up people."

Freddy chuckled. "It wasn't a night club with the masses. No, it was a very selective club for people who—"

"Like a sex club for rich people?"

"Yes, exactly like that. I often play there with this couple, who I'm not going to mention by name since their jobs require them to be seen as straight in public." Freddy could be describing hundreds of different famous couples. "You must know how hard it is to find people who share your tastes and are discreet."

Lucien swallowed. "Discretion is something I understand. It must be hard to be in the spotlight."

"You would know."

"I don't bother to hide who I am, and besides, I'm not that famous. Only racing fans know who I am. Whatever. Time to get to work, Freddy." Lucien parked the car and jumped out, leaving Freddy to sort himself out. It was time to face the consequences of his actions. He might be exactly like his father in that he couldn't control his rage, but he would always be different if he took responsibility for the aftermath. Xenia and Victor were wrong. Everyone was better off with him out of their lives. He pushed the heavy front door of the big house open. The warm blast of air welcomed him home and he needed to shed that reaction quickly. He didn't deserve to have a home when he might punch anyone in a rage without warning. Xenia had loaned him a jacket and he hung it on a peg by the front door so she could grab it next time she was here.

"Everyone is in the long dining room, third door on the left." Lucien wasn't sure if Freddy had been to Socrates' house before, although the odds were that he had visited many times over the years. Socrates loved to entertain.

"Give me the quick run down." Freddy's switch into work mode reminded Lucien of himself when he climbed into his car on race day. A familiar focus and one he could apply here too. He rolled his head on his shoulders while he tried to figure out where to start explaining this mess.

"Reggie Whitehall got the sack for making slow cars. His son, Ethan, was angry because he lost his pickup line. My Dad is an S1 engineer. Ethan got a job with Gamble Racing in the logistics department and sabotaged the cars while they were being unpacked at the tracks. Tonight he admitted that he wanted to get Victor Tsui, the new Chief Engineer, sacked so his dad could get his job back." Victor's name tasted wrong in his mouth, so he used his full title to create some distance. It didn't help. He missed Victor, would always miss the way he tugged at his hair when he was lost in thought, or how he gave Lucien little side-eyed glances when Lucien teased him. Fuck. He squared his shoulders. He had earned this pain and he didn't deserve to be Victor's boyfriend.

"Wow. And your hand?" Damn Freddy for being so observant. The reminder helped him cope and he tried to bury the yearning for Victor deep down where he wouldn't feel it anymore.

"I punched Ethan." He wasn't proud of it and the admission came out as a low whisper.

"Good. He risked driver's lives." Freddy blew out a short loud breath. "This is one hell of a story."

Lucien wanted to argue that it wasn't good to have reacted that way, but Freddy had marched off down the hallway.

In the end, there wasn't much Lucien could do but watch Freddy and a random police detective, a jaded cynical looking older woman, talk to everyone in the room. He hung back against the wall, hiding in the corner, waiting his turn to tell his part of the night. Victor, thankfully, was over in the workshop putting together information. He wasn't sure he could face Victor right now. He didn't deserve to be cared for or fussed over. It was bad enough that no one wanted to blame him for the unruly punch, except Ethan who'd said over and over that he was going to press charges.

"Let him." Lucien wanted the punishment. He probably should talk to his therapist about this. No, not should. Definitely. When was his next appointment? He patted his jeans pocket. No phone. After a moment, he recalled that he'd left it on the table, so he wandered over and grabbed it to check his calendar. A series of messages from Victor earlier in the night lit up his notifications.

VICTOR

Are you okay?

Where are you?

Please let me help you

Please be okay.

I know you won't think so, but you did
exactly what was needed. Please
be okay

Lucien slumped in his chair. By marching off, he'd scared Victor. It was just another reason why he couldn't be Victor's boyfriend. He just hurt people too much and it was better to keep his distance. The unsteady thump in his temple meant only one thing. A nasty headache was forming. Obviously no one was going to arrest him tonight, so he slunk off to his room for some paracetamol, a shower, and an attempt at sleeping.

CHAPTER 28

L ucien's phone dinged over and over with messages. He groaned and opened one eye but the morning light was too bright so he shut it again and burrowed into the blankets. This week had flown by as the team sorted out all the evidence and made statements to the lead investigator. All the team's drivers had gathered at the workshop throughout the week, and Lucien used their presence as a distraction to his own problems. He'd helped out where he could and finally, he'd managed to get a booking with his therapist. The session late yesterday evening had knocked him over—emotions were so fucking tiring—and he'd slept deeply for the first time this week.

SOCRATES

Team meeting at ten.

MIKE

Be at the workshop at 10 for a team meeting

ALEX

Are you going to that team meeting?
Shouldn't it just be for the S1 guys?

HETTIE

Where are you? You are late for today's
run.

Crap. He checked the time stamp and he'd missed the run by over an hour. He'd better call her.

"Hey, sorry about that. I had a big session yesterday and slept in."

Hettie tut-tutted. "We will do it after the team meeting today. It's a good thing you didn't sleep through that too, or Socrates would have your balls."

"Yeah."

"I hope you are dressed. The team meeting starts in ten minutes and everyone else is here."

"Fuck."

"Warm up before you sprint down here. Look after that hamstring." Hettie hung up and he leaped out of bed. He didn't want to go to a team meeting to hear the whole drama get rehashed again. What he needed was to talk to Victor about how he'd messed up. He missed his boyfriend and the therapy session had made him realise that he did deserve Victor, that he shouldn't have pushed him away, and basically, he'd been a giant fool. He needed to admit he'd been wrong and hope that Victor would understand. It was okay to trip over the same step.

The team meeting went as expected and everyone dispersed after Socrates gave a big speech about how they'd caught The Shadow, with personalised thanks to each person in the team who had contributed to finding Ethan, and now the team could all head into the new season with confidence in their cars.

Lucien waited as long as he could—tapping his toes impatiently as Socrates stoked everyone up for the new season—then he pulled a breath deep into his lungs and approached Victor.

"Victor."

"Yes?" The caution on Victor's face cut into his flesh like an actual wound.

"Walk the track with me?"

"Why?"

"Please." Lucien wasn't beyond begging at this point. Just standing next to Victor and not being able to touch him was torture. "Please."

Victor looked him up and down, then nodded once. "Okay."

Lucien followed Victor out of a small side door of the workshop, and when he vaulted the tyre wall at turn sixteen, Lucien copied him.

"Well?"

"I really fucked up."

Victor rolled his eyes. "Did you drag me out here in the freezing cold to tell me again how you shouldn't have punched my nemesis? Because I can't hear that bullshit anymore."

"No." Why hadn't he prepared for this? He shouldn't have punched anyone. "I shouldn't have pushed you away afterwards. Apparently I have a problem with ... Well, my therapist says ..." Fuck. Why was this so hard?

"Lucien. We were friends long before we were lovers. You can talk to me."

He really didn't deserve this wonderful man. Fucking hell. He rubbed the back of his neck. "Um, my therapist says that I'm pretty typical for a high-performance athlete. I am used to being good at stuff and winning and I expect to be perfect at things. I have a job where the tiniest mistakes make the difference between winning and crashing, so I judge myself harshly." He swallowed. "Yeah, so, apparently that also applies to ... Fuck. Victor. I fucked up and I miss you so much. I don't have to be perfect to deserve you."

"Say that again."

Lucien could barely breathe, his lungs screamed for air as if he'd just finished one of Hettie's awful hill runs. "I don't have to be perfect to deserve you?"

"Lucien." Victor wrapped his arms around Lucien and finally the world was okay again.

"I missed you so much. I thought I would be strong enough to push you away until I was perfect. But I don't have to be perfect."

"Lucien. It's only been a week." Victor's eyes sparkled.

"Longest week of my life. Can we go to bed now?" Lucien dropped his head onto Victor's shoulder and breathed against his skin. He missed him so much.

"Lucien."

"I even miss it when you say my name like that."

"Like?"

"Like you are telling me off for being silly but also that you are ... exasperated and admiring at once?"

"Lucien."

Lucien kissed Victor's neck. "Now you are doing it on purpose."

"Tell me more about your need to be perfect."

"Ergh. Fine. Susie, that's my therapist, she says that it's hard to unlearn all the things that came with my upbringing and it's okay if I mess up sometimes and I don't have to be perfect straight away."

Victor held him tighter. "Poor Lucien. It must be rough to discover that you are human like the rest of us. It's okay to mess up."

"I don't think you can class losing all control and thumping someone while being unaware of what I was doing because the rage had taken grip, well, let's not class that as messing up."

"Yes, it wasn't great, but also, think about your motivations. Why were you enraged?"

Lucien growled. That was easy. "Because he tried to destroy your work. You've worked so hard, and you deserve all the success and that prick tried to take it all away."

"Yes." Victor rubbed between Lucien's shoulder blades which was so nice, but then he stepped away, and Lucien almost fell over leaning towards him, chasing his touch. "So you understand why you did it?"

"He hurt you and it made me mad."

Victor paced the wrong way along the track, back towards turn fifteen, and Lucien jogged to catch up.

"What am I missing?"

"Lucien—" Not his favourite tone this time, more just annoyed. "How did you make the leap from knowing why you were enraged to the whole I'm pushing you away for your own good and I don't deserve you?"

"Right. Suzie says that's because I've worked so hard to stop the rage response and I failed." Lucien dropped down to his knees in the middle of the track. "I failed and it was all I could think about."

"You don't have to be..."

"Perfect. That's what Suzie said. She said that I was punishing myself for not being perfect at not punching people ... it's kind of absurd when you say it like that. I want to be perfect at not punching people."

"Lucien." Victor threaded his hand through Lucien's hair, and it was the sweetest fucking way anyone had ever touched him. God, his heart was going to die.

"Anyway, she says I was punishing myself for failing and the problem with that is that I ended up punishing the people who would forgive me because they see me trying to improve."

"I see you."

"Thank you. I want to deserve you."

"Lucien." There was that tone again. "You don't have to earn me."

Lucien stood up again and Victor cradled his face with his hands. The warmth of Victor's touch on his face was everything.

"Lucien. I think I fell in love with you years ago when you told me not to doubt myself. You poked me in the chest and told me I was good enough and you believed in me when I didn't quite believe in myself. Fuck, you told me that I'd be a Chief Engineer on an S1 team one day if only I could throw away the doubt."

"I was right."

Victor let out a shaky breath. "Then let me be right about this one. I believe you will never hit me in anger."

"But?"

"Let me finish. I also believe that you will defend me with everything in your heart and yes, sometimes with your fists because you learned that at your father's hand and unlearning it will be a life's journey. Lucien, I feel safe with you. I know you will protect me, not harm me."

Lucien wished he deserved this incredible man who said such wonderful things. Suzie's voice poked him in the forehead. Fine. He didn't need to deserve or not deserve him. He could just love him and let himself be loved.

"Thank you. Can I kiss you now?"

"Yes."

"Thank fuck." Lucien pounced. It'd been far too long —a whole week without kissing Victor—and it was like home. He explored Victor's mouth, his taste, loving the way Victor's tongue chased his own, with every stroke and caress. This was his forever place; being with Victor at whatever cost. He didn't need to be perfect and he could keep learning to keep his rage in check.

"Let's go home. It's too bloody cold to be kissing you on a racetrack in the middle of winter."

"Okay. My bed is closer than yours." Lucien held Victor's hand and marched towards the big house and his bedroom in the home Socrates had given him.

EPILOGUE

Pre-season testing started tomorrow, and Victor couldn't wait for Lucien to arrive in Bahrain. He had the best news for his boyfriend. He paced around their hotel room.

LUCIEN

Am pulling up now. What room number?

VICTOR

1432

LUCIEN

See you soon

VICTOR

I can't wait

Ten minutes later, there was a knock on the door and he opened it to see Lucien looking travel rumpled.

"Victor." Lucien threw himself into Victor's arms and kissed him. Victor adored the way Lucien kissed and he soaked up the sensations of finally holding his boyfriend again after a few weeks apart travelling with their respective racing teams.

"You taste so good. I missed you."

"And you taste like a podium!" Victor grinned against Lucien's cheek.

"Three of them. What a way to start the season."

"It's awesome. I'm so proud of you."

"Proud enough to show me?" Lucien winked.

Victor chuckled. "Maybe have a shower first and wash off the travel muck."

"Only if you join me." Lucien had come directly from Mexico where he'd come second in the Series E race there.

"Yes." Victor forgot his news as they walked, intertwined, towards the bathroom. He spun around in Lucien's arm and kissed him again. It was incredible to be back in Lucien's arms.

"Oh, I nearly forgot. Socrates wanted me to tell you that he is impressed with the way you've started this season."

"He should be. Pole and a win in the first race, then third in the second. Now second in Mexico to make it three podiums in three races. I'm leading the championship."

Victor knew all of that and he still loved the way Lucien owned his successes. "He wants you to drive the first session tomorrow."

"In your car?" Lucien blinked, and Victor wished he had a photo of the stunned expression. "Seriously?"

"Yes."

"Fuck. Yes." Lucien punched the air. "I've been wanting to drive a decent S1 car forever."

Victor had no idea if his car was fast, although it had tested well in the wind tunnel. Tomorrow would be the first time it'd been driven in on a racetrack. Lucien rolled on top of Victor and kissed him vigorously.

"Thank you so much. You are the best boyfriend ever."

————

If you enjoyed this book, you'll love the rest of the Gamble Racing series, beginning with DRIVEN TO DISTRACTION. The next book in this series is Jaxxon and Freddy's story, DRIVEN BY AMBITION.

Two men in the spotlight with too much chemistry...

Media personality and retired driver Freddy Hiptonstall knows one thing. Getting involved with someone in the S1 paddock only leads to disaster, so why can't he stay away from Gamble Racing's new Team Principal?

Suddenly promoted to Team Principal, Jaxxon Loharani-Jones has a lot to prove. He's always been ambitious, but now he needs to step up and run Gamble Racing as the second youngest Team Principal in S1 history. The last thing he needs is a distraction.

The chemistry between them results in kisses, but will the intimate nature of their work be too much for their burgeoning relationship with all the pressures of their jobs?

————

Want a bit more sexy romance? Socrates and Mike's story is available as an exclusive bonus when you sign up for my newsletter. www.reneedahlia.com

COMING IN 2023: Bucket List Love, as part of the Hotel d'Amore anthology. Victor's uncle Craig goes to Zac's high school reunion and meets a new lover.

ACKNOWLEDGMENTS

I pay my respects to the Wangal people of the Eora Nation, who are the traditional owners of the land on which this book was written.

My kids, who are huge S1 fans, for working out the fake race season results for my drivers in this series and helping with other technical details. If you want to see the full spreadsheet, it's an extra on my Patreon.

To my son, F, who designed the test track at Socrates Drayton's estate, designed all the driver's season results, helped me create a spreadsheet of four seasons worth of race results, and named many of the characters in this series. Thank you for being the ultimate S1 fan and an all-round amazing creative person. His track design is available on my website.

ALL BOOKS BY RENÉE DAHLIA

Thanks for reading DRIVEN BY PASSION. I hope you enjoyed it. Reviews can help readers find books, and I am grateful for all honest reviews. Thank you for taking the time to let others know what you've read, and what you thought. If you write a review for DRIVEN BY PASSION and email me (renee at reneedahlia dot com) with the link, I will send you a free copy of one of my books of your choice.

If you'd like to know more about me, my books, or to connect with me online, you can visit my webpage www.reneedahlia.com and if you sign up to my newsletter, you can grab a free book.

Twitter
https://twitter.com/dekabat
Facebook
https://www.facebook.com/reneedahliawriter/
Instagram
https://www.instagram.com/reneedahlia_author/
Patreon

https://www.patreon.com/reneedahlia
BookBub
https://www.bookbub.com/authors/renee-dahlia

You've just read a book in my Gamble Racing Series.
Contemporary Series: Gamble Racing

1. Driven to Distraction (mm)
2. Driven by Passion (mm)
3. Driven by Ambition (mm)
4. Driven to Protect (mm)

Contemporary Series: Seraph's Burlesque Club

1. Show Up (ff with bisexual heroine)
2. Show Off (ff with bisexual heroines)
3. Show Queen (ff)
4. Show Time (mm)
5. Show Dance (mm)

Contemporary Series: Kapow!

1. Out of Her League (fm with bisexual characters)
2. His Buxom Beauty (fm)
3. Craving His Spotlight (mm)
4. Her Pregnant Rival (ff)

Contemporary Series: Farrellton Foster Family

1. Betrayed (fm)

2. Forbidden (fm with bisexual characters)
3. Liability (ff)

Contemporary Series:
Margaret River TV: Boxed Set

- Homage (fm with bisexual heroine)
- Uplift (ff with bisexual heroines)

Contemporary Series:
Merindah Park

1. Merindah Park (fm)
2. Making Her Mark (fm with bisexual heroine)
3. Two Hearts Healing (fm)
4. Racetrack Royalty (fm)

Contemporary Series:
Rainbow Cove

1. His Christmas Pearl (fm)
2. His Christmas Pride (mm)

Historical Series:
Great War

1. Her Lady's Melody (ff)
2. Her Lady's Fortune (ff)
3. Her Lady's Honor (ff)
4. His Lord's Soldier (mm)

Historical Series:

　Bluestockings

Prequel: The Shipwrecked Earl's Bride (fm with bisexual hero)

1. To Charm a Bluestocking (fm with bisexual hero)
2. In Pursuit of a Bluestocking (fm)
3. The Heart of a Bluestocking (fm)

www.ingramcontent.com/pod-product-compliance
Lightning Source LLC
Chambersburg PA
CBHW070054120726
47909CB00002B/385